# THE SHATTER DEAD COLLECTION
## WRITTEN, COMPILED, ANNOTATED, AND SUFFERED BY
## SCOOTER MC CRAE

Happy Cloud Media, LLC
www.happycloudpictures.net

**ALSO FROM THE HAPPY CLOUD SCREENPLAY COLLECTION:**

**NOTLD 90: THE VERSION YOU'VE NEVER SEEN by Tom Savini**
**THE RESURRECTION GAME SCRAPBOOK – By Mike Watt**
**SPLATTER MOVIE: THE DIRECTOR'S CUT – ANNOTATED SCREENPLAY – by Amy Lynn Best**
**DEMON DIVAS AND THE LANES OF DAMNATION – ANNOTATED SCREENPLAY – By Mike Watt**

Printed in the United States of America

All photos and materials Courtesy and Copyright © 2021 Scooter McCrae except:

P. 8-9 Copyright © The Starlog Group / Fangoria Publishing, LLC. All Rights Reserved
P. 113-114 Copyright © FAB Press. All Rights Reserved.

First Printing, 2021. *The Shatter Dead Collection* © 2021 Happy Cloud Media, LLC. All rights reserved.

ISBN 978-1-951036-28-7

Happy Cloud Media, LLC
PO Box 216
Venetia, PA 15336

www.happycloudpublishing.com

# GOD HATES YOU.

SUB ROSA STUDIOS

DIRECTOR'S SPECIAL EDITION

# SHATTER DEAD

WINNER
BEST INDEPENDENT FILM USA
1995 FANTAFESTIVAL

DVD
VIDEO

SHATTER DEAD
SUB ROSA STUDIOS

## GOD HATES YOU!

When the Angel of Death impregnates a mortal woman, the dead stop dying. But these zombies aren't out to destroy the living; their only desire is to return and be back among us. And now a bloody war is breaking out between the living and the dead, bleeding the final survivors from our broken world. Amid this fetid landscape of zombie massacres rises Susan (STARK RAVEN), a lone woman desperate to get back to her boyfriend and a life of some sanity. And she's not about to let anyone, living or undead, get in her way...

New York filmmaker Scooter McCrae's (*Sixteen Tongues*) bold new take on the zombie genre won the prestigious Best U.S. Independent Feature Award at the Italian FANTAFILM Festival, which helped solidify it's status as a modern horror cult classic.

DVD FEATURES

- DIRECTOR'S FULL-LENGTH CUT
- INTERACTIVE MENUS
- 3 AUDIO COMMENTARY TRACKS
- BEHIND-THE-SCENES
- TOUR OF *SHATTER DEAD* HOUSE
- ORIGINAL AND BONUS TRAILERS

SUB ROSA STUDIOS PRESENTS SHATTER DEAD A SEEING EYE DOG PRODUCTION
STARK RAVEN, FLORA FAUNA, LARRY "SMALLS" JOHNSON, MARINA DEL REY
ROBERT WELLS AS "THE PREACHER MAN" AND CANDY COSTER AS "THE ANGEL OF DEATH"
STEPHANIE RAJKUMAR AND GEEK MESSIAH ARTHUR JOLLY AND PERICLES LEWNES
MATTHEW M. HOWE SCOOTER McCRAE

SUB ROSA STUDIOS, L.L.C. P.O. BOX 5515
SYRACUSE NY 13220 WWW.B-MOVIE.COM

APPROX RUNNING TIME:
84 MINS./COLOR/STEREO

Rated "18"
by the IDRB

DVD
VIDEO

6 74945 10223 7

4

# CONTENTS

## SCOOTER McCRAE

**director**

Scooter McCrae

**principal cast**
Stark Raven
Flora Fauna
Larry "smalls" Johnson
Marina Del Rey
Robert Wells
Candy Coster

**screenplay**
Scooter McCrae

**director of photography**
Matthew M.Howe

**special make-up effects**
Arthur Jolly
Pericles Lewnes

**music**
Stephen Rajkumar
Geek Messiah

**production company**
Seeing Eye Dog

"I had just finished reading Roger Corman's autobiography and decided that if I couldn't write a script in three weeks and then shoot it in ten days, I had probably chosen the wrong field to be working in." Scooter McCrae.

In fact, SHATTER DEAD director, Scooter McCrae came very close to his original goal - almost four weeks for the final draft and eleven shooting days spread over five non-consecutive weekends. The film was shot in Middletown, Upstate New York and financed entirely from Scooter's $250 per week wages, hence the staggering of the weekends. The final production costs were somewhere in the region of $4000.

The cast were made up of friends and friends of friends. Stark Raven who plays Susan first caught the directors eye on stage, playing a male warrior in a college production of "Thoaague." He also cast painter Robert Wells as 'The Preacher Man' and college friend and 'real' actress Flora Fauna as Mary, a part he wrote especially for her. The 'House of the Dead' at the film's centre is Scooter's apartment. There are still bloodstains on the kitchen wall.

Very much a part of the American new wave of horror film directors (others include J.R.Bookwalter, Michael DiPaulo, Kevin Lindenmuth), Scooter McCrae remains adamant that there is a future in shot on video movies, indeed shot on camcorder feature films. In his own words "...it's not the medium your working in, it's the story you're telling." SHATTER DEAD is proof of his philosophy. After winning the award for best independent feature at the prestigious Fantafestival in Rome 1995 the movie has gone on to great critical acclaim.

### FILMOGRAPHY

| | | |
|---|---|---|
| "Shatter Dead" | 1993 BetaSp feature | |
| "Original Sins" | 1994 | actor |
| "Alien Adgenda" | 1996 | actor |
| "Absolute Aggression" | 1996 | actor |

Here is a short listing of films from the extensive **visionary** catalogue.

For FREE catalogue please write to Visionary at:
PO Box 30, Lytham St. Annes, FY8 1RL, England.
Tel. 01253 712453  Fax. 01253 712362
e-mail: king@visicom.demon.co.uk
http://www.state51.co.uk/visionary/

### screen edge - feature film

| | | | | |
|---|---|---|---|---|
| Addicted To Murder | dir. Kevin Lindenmuth | 1995 | 90 mins | EDGE09 |
| Alferd Packer: The Musical | dir. Trey Parker | 1993 | 93 mins | EDGE04 |
| Bedroom The | dir. Sato Hisayasu | 1992 | 63 mins | EDGE08 |
| Criminal | dir. David Jacobson | 1994 | 90 mins | EDGE11 |
| Frontline The | dir. Paul Hills | 1993 | 70 mins | EDGE03 |
| Original Sins | dir. Howard Berger | 1994 | 100 mins | EDGE13 |
| Pope Of Utah The | dir. Bianco/Saylor | 1993 | 83 mins | EDGE01 |
| Rhythm Thief | dir. Matthew Harrison | 1994 | 84 mins | EDGE07 |
| Shatter Dead | dir. Scooter McCrae | 1993 | 82 mins | EDGE12 |
| Spare Me | dir. Matthew Harrison | 1993 | 88 mins | EDGE05 |
| Transgression | dir. Michael DiPaolo | 1994 | 78 mins | EDGE06 |
| Upstairs Neighbour The | dir. Merendino/Devlen(prod.) | 1994 | 90 mins | EDGE02 |

### classic - feature film

| | | | | |
|---|---|---|---|---|
| Big Combo The | dir. Joseph Lewis | 1955 | 88 mins | SAR2 |
| Detour | dir. Edgar G.Ulmer | 1955 | 65 mins | SAR1 |
| Freaks | dir. Tod Browning | 1934 | 64 mins | MJ020 |
| Island Of Lost Souls | dir. Erle C.Kenton | 1933 | 68 mins | MJ027 |
| Man with the Golden Arm | dir. Otto Preminger | 1955 | 120 mins | SAR3 |
| Mystery Of The Wax Museum | dir. Michael Curtiz | 1933 | 74 mins | MJ028 |
| Suddenly | dir. Edgar G.Ulmer | 1954 | 75 mins | SAR4 |
| White Zombie | dir. Victor Halperin | 1932 | 70 mins | MJ010 |

### art / experimental / documentary

| | | | |
|---|---|---|---|
| Allen Ginsberg | The Life and Times of... | 83 mins | MJ022 |
| Alice | dir. Jan Svankmajer | 1989 84 mins | MJ011 |
| Andy Warhol | Made in China | 30 mins | MJ019 |
| Angelic Conversation | dir. Derek Jarman | 1985 80 mins | MJ009 |
| Bukowski At Bellevue | Charles Bukowski reading | 1970 60 mins | MJ024 |
| Commissioner of Sewers | William Burroughs/reading etc. | 60 mins | MJ015 |
| Cyberpunk | VR/hacking/William Gibson... | 60 mins | MJ013 |
| Destroy All Rational Thought | W.S.Burroughs/Brion Gysin | 50 mins | MJ016 |
| Groupies | 1969 documentary | 86 mins | MJ026 |
| Kenneth Anger | Volume 3  Scorpio Rising | 1963.. 43 mins | MJ003 |
| Kenneth Anger | Volume 4  Lucifer Rising | 1980... 43 mins | MJ004 |
| Kerouac | A film by John Antonelli | 73 mins | 80325 |
| Lydia Lunch | The Gun Is Loaded | 38 mins | JE246 |
| Venus In Furs | dir. Seyferth/Nieuwenhuijs | 1994 70 mins | MJ021 |

### music video

| | | | |
|---|---|---|---|
| Billy Bragg | Goes to Moscow | 99 mins | UVU1 |
| Black Flag | Live | 55 mins | JE131 |
| Chameleons, The | Live at the Gallery 1982 | 55 mins | JE293 |
| Divine | Live at the Hacienda | 42 mins | JE254 |
| Exploited The | Sexual Favours | 40 mins | JE163 |
| GBH | Live in Los Angeles 1988 | 55 mins | JE288 |
| Hawkwind | Chaos Tour 1986 | 60 mins | JE287 |
| Hawkwind | Love in Space | 90 mins | JE290 |
| Johnny Cash | The Man, His World, His Music | 90 mins | MJ025 |
| King Kurt | Zulu Land | 60 mins | JE266 |
| Link Wray | The Rumble Man | 70 mins | JE300 |
| Men They Couldn't Hang | The Shooting | 50 mins | JE206 |
| Meteors The | Chainsaw Mutants | 45 mins | JE221 |
| Momus | Man Of Letters | 35 mins | JE283 |
| Nico | Heroine | 52 mins | JE258 |
| One Way System | No Return | 45 mins | JE252 |
| Paradise Lost | Live Death | 45 mins | JE204 |
| Peter & the Test Tube Babies | Cattle and Bum | 45 mins | JE230 |
| Psychic TV | Joy | 55 mins | JE190 |
| Robyn Hitchcock | Gotta Let this Hen Out | 50 mins | JE139 |
| Sham 69 | Live in Japan | 40 mins | JE236 |
| Special Beat | Shibuya On Air | 70 mins | JE233 |
| Throbbing Gristle | Mission of Dead Souls | 60 mins | TGV04 |
| Toy Dolls The | Idle Gossip | 45 mins | JE156 |

# INTRODUCTION
## By Michael Gingold

The call came in on an October day in 1993 to my desk at the FANGORIA office. It was Pericles Lewnes, a special-makeup artist and filmmaker I had met on the set of THE TOXIC AVENGER PART II and III, inviting me to a preview screening of a new movie for which he had created effects. It was, he said, a shot-on-video zombie feature.

*Hmmmm*, I thought, *another grassroots auteur remaking NIGHT OF THE LIVING DEAD in their backyard.* It didn't sound promising. I'll admit that at the time, I didn't have a very high opinion of the SOV trend, which by that point was nearly a decade old. The examples I'd seen, from BOARDINGHOUSE (which had managed to achieve theatrical release) to a dreadful monster comedy called FRANKY AND HIS PALS, had by and large struck me as pretty amateurish stuff, rife with tacky gore and painfully nonpro performances. There was little of the artistry one could find in even the lowest-budget horror productions lensed on film.

I must have expressed some kind of misgivings about this latest example, because I recall Peri convincing me that this one would be different, that it was an atypical take on the livingdead form. He had himself contributed to the SOV ghoul ranks as director of the Troma-released REDNECK ZOMBIES, so I took him at his word, and on the evening of October 20, I headed down to the Ward-Nasse Gallery in SoHo for a showing of SHATTER DEAD.

Right from the opening scene—a lesbian sexual encounter in which one of the participants turns out to be an angel—it was evident this was indeed going to be something unusual. As SHATTER DEAD introduced its heroine Susan (Stark Raven) in a world depleted of life, the tone was distinct and melancholy, and its zombies were not mindless, flesh-hungry revenants but sentient, tragic beings. Some even had a rueful humor about them, like an undead panhandler with a sign identifying him as an unemployed crash-test dummy. Within the first 10 minutes, I knew I had never seen a SOV horror movie like this before.

It could even be described as an art film, albeit one done on a tiny budget. That might have been, I initially surmised, why some of the zombies eschewed the usual rotting/mangled makeup and looked just like us, but then these walking dead were far more human than the cinematicnorm, waxing philosophical and offering varying points of view on their condition. They weren't even the bad guys—the real villains were living people like the Preacher Man (embodying thereligious themes also running through the story) and the gun-toting radicals who murderously invaded Grandma's house.

That latter setpiece in particular showcased some pretty nasty bloodshed; the de-emphasis on disfigured visages didn't mean Peri and fellow effects artist Arthur Jolly had little to do. The "shotgun abortion" was a particularly squirm-inducing bit of business, and by the time the movie got to its (literal) climax and the unusual use of a firearm, I was convinced that the creator of SHATTER DEAD was both some kind of DIY cinema genius and one sick puppy.

Once I met and got to know Scooter McCrae, I discovered that both were true, and more. He was passionate, knowledgeable and opinionated about film and a diehard fan of boundarypushing genre fare, and had a sense of humor that was geeky and profane in equal, great measure. We became fast friends, and soon I was visiting him on the set of another SOV fright flick, ORIGINAL SINS, where he played a cranky demon for writer/directors Matthew Howe (SHATTER DEAD's cinematographer) and Howard S. Berger. A few years later, I traveled with Scooter and a group of friends and movie folks to the wilds of Ohio to play parts (Scooter's fairly substantial, mine mercifully brief) in BLOODLETTING for director Matthew Jason Walsh and producer J.R. Bookwalter.

In between, I wrote an article for Fango called "The Video Dead," covering the SOV likes of SHATTER DEAD, SINS and Bookwalter's OZONE (as well as Leif Jonker's shot-on-Super-8 DARKNESS). I had discovered that not all homegrown horror projects were necessarily hapless affairs, and that there was ambition and talent to be found on the camcorder production scene. That appreciation began with SHATTER DEAD, an exemplar of the idea that a lack of funds need not mean that imagination—both dramatic and perverse—be constrained. Nearly 30 years (wow...) after that SoHo screening, SHATTER DEAD, which recently saw its Blu-ray debut via Saturn's Core and Vinegar Syndrome, remains an intriguing, unsettling and engrossing note from the underground. This book is a celebration of its creation, and a peek into the uniquely twisted mind of its creator.

**SPECIAL REPORT:** Horrors that Hollywood won't film!

K47909
DGS
U.K.
£2.95

# FANGORIA

**#132** MAY

The #1 Horror Magazine
—Now in our 15th year!

VIDEO GAME NIGHTMARE

Stephen King's
THE STAND
Smile! The world is ending

## CRONOS
Mexican
bloodsucker

## THE HILLS HAVE EYES
Making
Craven's classic

## John Waters'
## SERIAL MOM
Every home
should have one!

## UNBORN II
Baby bites back!

## NO ESCAPE
From an island hell

$4.95 U.S./$6.25 CANADA

0 71896 47909 6    05

# BRAINSCAN
Say hello to Trickster—
and goodbye to reality

8

# VIDEO DEAD

"When I was first writing the script, it was a much more traditional blood-and-guts zombie film," he continues. "And I felt it was avoiding the biggest issue of all, which is death itself. The horror of being eaten alive is secondary to the dread people have of being dead someday. That's a fear everyone has, it's so primal. Suddenly I was writing from that perspective, and it came out pretty easily." This cerebral approach doesn't preclude numerous outbursts of shocking violence, though; it just means that much of it is committed upon the talking, thinking, feeling undead. (The FX were created by Pericles Lewnes, who helped launch the video gore genre with 1987's *Redneck Zombies*.)

Explicit bloodshed is, in fact, a common thread uniting most of this breed of indies, and perhaps none is redder than *Darkness*, a gruesome vampire film written, produced and directed by Wichita, Kansas filmmaker Leif Jonker. "It's definitely a gorehound's movie," he says. "It culminates with probably the biggest meltdown sequence in a vampire movie ever, with I believe a world record for exploding heads. We had 50 extras, and used about 150 gallons of blood for that scene alone."

Jonker shot his epic, about a nomadic vampire named Liven who transforms practically the entire population of a small town into bloodsuckers, on Super-8 film and transferred it to tape. He claims that shooting on video was never a consideration. "I felt that I had to do it on film," he says. "It's really the best way to start. Whether it's Super-8 or

16mm, you have to cut your teeth on the real thing."

That's how Akron, Ohio's J.R. Bookwalter made his own leap into the splatter field. His zombie shocker *The Dead Next Door* was shot on Super-8 and, like *Darkness*, took nearly four years to complete. On the strength of *Dead*, Bookwalter was hired by David DeCoteau to produce

No good-looking young actress is safe on the world of low-budget horror. (Lotte V. Anne in Pericles Lewnes makeup for *Shatter Dead*)

and direct movies for his Cinema Home Video line, which led to a pair of 16mm productions, *Robot Ninja* and *Skinned Alive*, a slew of shot-on-video titles and the formation of Bookwalter's own Tempe Video company. His latest creation is *Ozone*, in which a detective on the trail of the title drug winds up injected with it and, in Bookwalter's words,

"starts to see the world a little differently and goes through bizarre transformations."

Not only is *Ozone* the biggest of Bookwalter's post-*Dead Next Door* video movies, it's the first he's happy with. "Everything from *Robot Ninja* on down was something that somebody was paying me to work on or make for them," he explains. "They were being made to fill a niche, not because I wanted them to exist. On this one I took the approach that I started with on *Dead Next Door*, where I set off on my own, and did it myself for whatever funds I had available."

The self-financing route can certainly pose its share of technical challenges, but it also results in complete creative freedom, which allows the filmmakers to be as extreme and occasionally perverse as they want. This holds particularly true for *Shatter Dead*, which opens with a young woman having sex with a female angel and features what McCrae describes as "a shotgun abortion," and even moreso for *Original Sins*, a project McCrae is acting in that, like *Shatter Dead*, is being shot on professional-level video. As McCrae is put into makeup for his role as the demon Kaps, writer/directors Matthew Howe (*Shatter Dead*'s director of photography) and Howard Berger ("not the makeup artist") take a break on the Staten Island set to discuss their venture into down-and-dirty horror.

"It's about three Catholic girls who are immaculately violated by a presence they believe is Jesus Christ," Howe begins. "Every time they come out of their delirium they feel more religiously inspired, but

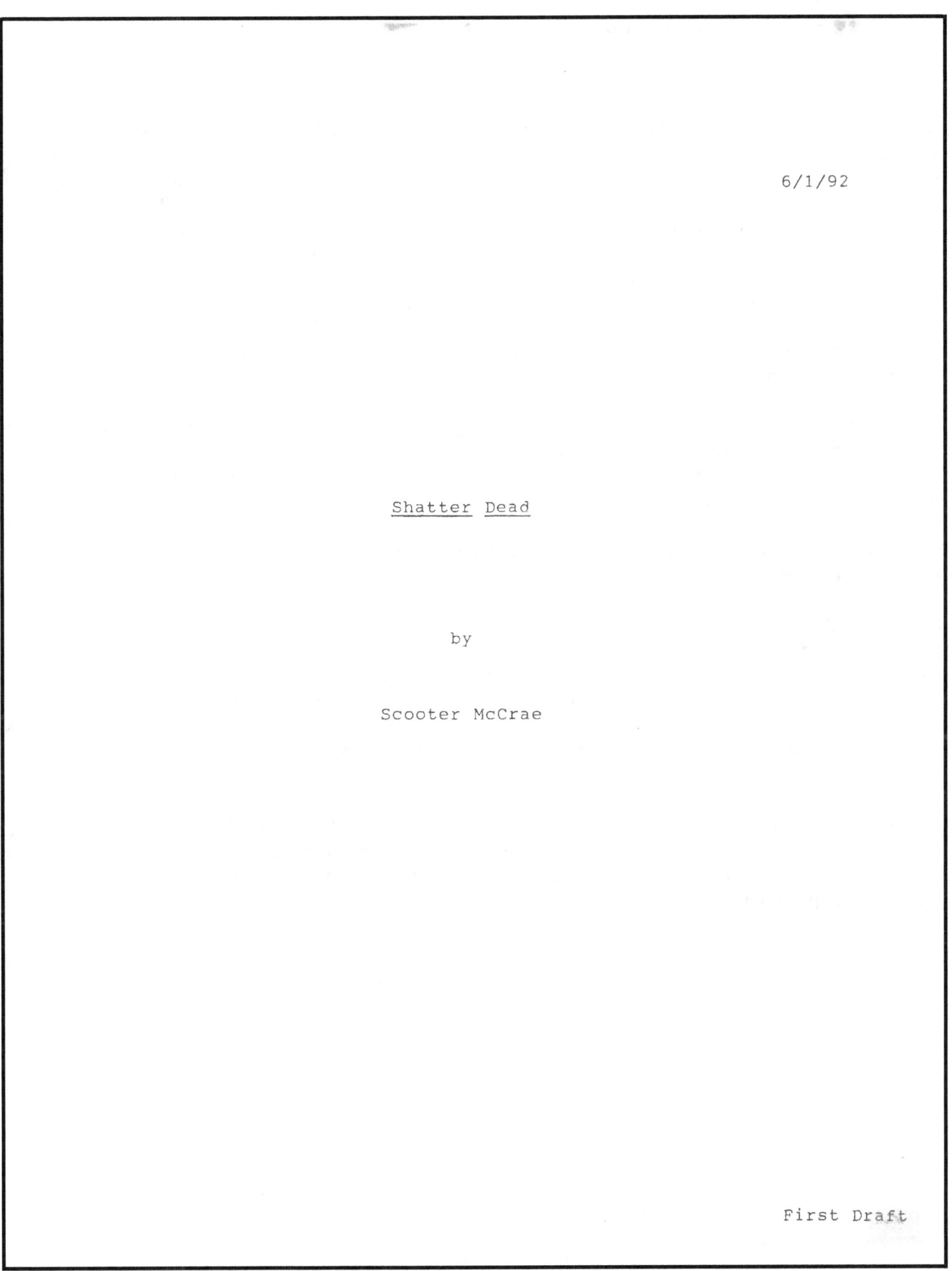

6/1/92

Shatter Dead

by

Scooter McCrae

First Draft

## SHATTER DEAD Screenplay Annotations

**Page 1:**

I think the first thing that anyone who has watched SHATTER DEAD will notice here is the fact that the screenplay does NOT open with The Angel of Death "raping" a woman in her bedroom. So where did this scene come from? SHATTER DEAD was a living document while it was in-production, so while the screenplay was the blueprint for what we would shoot, many scenes were still in flux due to budgetary concerns (especially makeup EFX and stunts), locations that we could get and actor availability. In this case, the idea for the Angels came along during production because not only was it an affordable get and an arresting image, it was also something to help spruce up the running time of a movie that was woefully short of its goal to achieve a feature-length of 75 minutes or more.

(The original running time of SHATTER DEAD before it's 2021 retooling was 82 minutes and has since been tightened to my preferred length of 76 minutes)

The opening Angel scene was suggested by a comment actress Marina Del Rey made after seeing a Butthole Surfers concert while we were still in-production. She said it was a fantastic show and comparable to being "raped by Angels". My jaw dropped, I laughed and realized that I now had a better opening for my little movie – and could even afford to shoot it once I found another willing actress and someone who could make the wings (that would be, respectively, Barbara 'Candy' Coster – a knowing nod to Jess Franco's beloved Muse and mine, Lina Romay – and Krista Essler made those lovely wings that also ended up appearing in Matt Howe's and Howard Berger's ORIGINAL SINS).

What about the other Angel footage? We'll get to that when the time comes....

You'll also note on this page that I've written the city footage with some kind of control of the location in mind, when of course we had absolutely none whatsoever. Heck, we were lucky to get the footage we got quick enough to get out of the area before we were harassed by police or locals, so waiting for traffic lights to change and walking over dead bodies strewn along the street as the sound of gunfire fills the soundtrack was not in the cards for this hit-and-run production.

Also note that from page 1, I was already starting to winnow down Susan's dialogue as I thought her character would be more interesting and imposing with less wiseass yapping. My most recent re-edit of the movie removed a few more lines that I think benefit both the character and the performance. Also, she's nastier on the page than in the movie.

Ext. City Street - Day

The streets are deserted, save for the occasional vagrant
running across the frame from one shadowy doorway to another.

Enter Susan, a 26 year old woman with long black hair, carrying
a well filled bag of groceries. For a woman with a huge shotgun slung across her back and another gun in a belt holster, she
walks with an airy gait.

She reaches the corner to cross the street, but the "Don't Walk"
sign stops her in her tracks even though there are no cars coming.

She turns and a vagrant sitting against the wall behind her
catches her eye. He has only one arm, and is covered with dirt
and some unbelievably huge gashes that are unclotted with rich
red blood. Next to him is a cup and a sign; "Help. Dead. Sold
my arm for medical experiments. What next?"

Susan is unimpressed. The light changes and she crosses the street.

Susan walks another block. There is the sound of gunfire in
the air, but she ignores it. She steps over one or two dead
bodies that beg for help and than rounds the corner.

Here she bumps into an especially hideous and forward dead person
with a tin can for a cup. He blocks Susan's path.

Finally, she stops trying to pass through him, standing in place
and assuming a listening position.

                    Dead Person
          Help a dead fella', sister?

                    Susan
          Yeah. Get a life.

                    Dead Person
          Gimme' a break, lady. Look at me.
          I took a job as a crash test dummy
          to feed my kids, and now I'm too
          damn ugly to go home. That's gotta'
          be worth some loose change to you.

Susan sighs and fishes around in her pants pocket. She
finds a quarter and tosses it in his can.

                    Susan
          Here.

                    Dead Person
          Thanks, lady. God bless you.

## SHATTER DEAD Screenplay Annotations

**Page 2:**
In case the condition of the pages before you hasn't made it obvious, the materials that have been scanned in for this book are derived from the last surviving printed script I could find some nearly 30 years after the shoot. This is the one that accompanied me on-set and in the editing room, so in addition to me scratching out scenes as we shot them, there are various notes to myself to get certain shots that I'll need at a later date.

"Need trunk insert" would seem like an obvious get when you're out shooting the scene on the streets of Middletown, New York, right? Well, since we had a trunk full of various weapons, we in fact got that insert shot as FAR AWAY AS POSSIBLE from anywhere that people might walk by and see those contents. So that insert shot was taken somewhere else at another time entirely. And when you're in the heat of production as writer, director, producer and microphone holding guy, these really are the kinds of silly notes you make to remind yourself of something so obvious.

Going back to a note I made on page 1, we did shoot the scene where Susan takes back the change she put in the cup, but I wasn't happy with the footage as it was shot in such a rush and we didn't get the coverage we needed. Also, it made her character seem more like an asshole and less worthy of the audience sympathy we'll be looking to elicit later in the screenplay. And let's face it; we have enough crazy stuff going on with her character arc that there's only so far I can push a viewer before having to make some choices that make her eventually redeemable. So even though running time was an issue, I still had to take into account what made for the best characterizations and also the quality of the footage we had to work with. So shooting footage with Angels in a controlled environment trumped trying to make use of location stuff that was shot under duress and not up to snuff – and if you've seen the movie, just try to imagine the stuff that *wasn't* good enough to use....!

Susan laughs unpleasantly and continues walking.

Ext. Susan's Car - Day

Susan pops open her car trunk and inserts her groceries. She slams the trunk closed and looks around.

*Need Trunk insert*

Across the street is an available payphone which catches her eye. Susan looks both ways and crosses the street.

Ext. Payphone - Day

Susan searches through her pockets for spare change, but she finds none.

                    Susan
          Fucking corpse.

Ext. Street - Day

Susan walks up to from behind the Dead Person she gave a quarter to. She grabs him by a clean spot on his shoulder and spins him around. They are face to face.

She grabs the tin cup from his hand and rummages through it, finding at last her quarter. She pulls it out and places the cup back in his hand.

                    Susan
          Sorry.  God bless you.

Susan walks away.

The Dead Person sighs and hangs his head low; he sits down and buries his face in his hands.

From out of a dark doorway, the One-Armed Dead Person steps out and into the light with a gas can and a tube - and watches.

Ext. Payphone - Day

Susan slams her quarter into the slot and dials a number. Pause. She gets a busy signal.

Susan leans against the phone and looks across the street at her car. She sees something odd. She squints and lowers to her haunches for a better look.

At this lower angle, from her P.O.V., we see a pair of legs by the rear tires, and a gas can.

## SHATTER DEAD Screenplay Annotations

**Page 3:**

Having grown up in Middletown, I was intimately aware of the layout of the area I knew we'd be shooting in, which is why I specifically wrote in that the chase would end up in a children's park. I also knew that there was no way we'd be shooting our explosion in the middle of – or anywhere near – North Street, which is where we shot the rest of our city footage.

The park they ended up running into was actually about six or seven full blocks away from everything else we shot. The magic of movie editing!

Why would I have even written a body burn stunt into a script with nearly zero budget? One of the key people involved in the production was Arthur Jolly, whom I had met, worked with and befriended in my senior year of college, and he was intimately involved in all of the make-up and stunt EFX as I was writing the screenplay. In addition to everything else this production was envisioned for concerning my potential career, it was also meant to be a calling card for Arthur as a stuntperson and make-up artist.

So Arthur asked me to write in a full body burn and as much gory mayhem as possible for him to work on, and without his involvement, SHATTER DEAD would have been a very different movie, and not for the better.

Once we established our One Armed Person and Susan in the park in Middletown, the explosion and burn was shot in the backyard of Steve Rajkumar (who composed and created some of the music for the production) out on Staten Island. Thankfully, there were no problems and if you've never spent the day lighting a guy on fire without hurting them for your movie shoot, add that to your bucket list. It's a fucking blast. Literally.

I also need to point out that for some odd reason, I scratched out Susan's line, "my last gallon", proving that I had no idea what the fuck I was thinking as that line usually gets a good laugh at every screening I've attended. She probably talked me back into it on-set and good for her for doing so and I'm glad we shot it this way. For me, a screenplay is always a living document that can be changed as often as it needs to be on-set as circumstances or performances demand. Thankfully this bad choice was corrected on-camera

On the other hand, removing the line and even the bit where she gets back into the car after the zombie fireball was the right thing to do and saved us the set-up time and lousy dialogue that I'm sure I would have lost in the editing room. The hard cut to her driving that jumps to the top of page 4 instead is what ended up in the movie and that works perfectly.

16

Susan unslings the shotgun from her shoulder, loads it's chambers, and stalks off to her car.

Ext. Car - Day

The dead person hears a loud click and looks over the hood of the car; he sees Susan coming towards him with her shotgun at the ready.

The dead person quickly slides the tube out of the gas tank and nervously tightens a cap onto the can.

Susan reaches the car just as the dead person finishes up; he rises sharply and runs away.

                              Susan
                    Now what the hell..?

Susan tightens herself like a bolt and chases after him.  They run around the corner and into a large children's park.

Ext. Park - Day

The park is completely deserted.  The one-armed dead person runs through the swings and past the see-saws with Susan in hot but distant pursuit.

The dead person gets his foot caught and trips, landing on top of the gas can.  Susan stops and takes aim.

The dead person struggles to rise.  Susan fires, and the dead person is engulfed in a huge fireball.

                              Susan
                    Shit!  ~~My last gallon~~!

Ext. Car - Day

Susan opens the backdoor of her car and tosses the smoking shot-gun in, onto the floor.  She walks around to the driver's side, gets in, and turns on the car.  Almost.  The car grinds and the gas guage needle tickles the "E".

                              Susan
                    Great.  I can't get more till next week.

Susan plays with the key until the car finally starts.  Looking around nervously, she begins to drive.

# SHATTER DEAD Screenplay Annotations

**Page 4:**
Note mention of hitchhikers along the road that we didn't shoot – time, money and actors once again getting in the way of any lofty ideals I might have had had about the nature of loneliness and mankind's inhumanity towards fellow mankind. Maybe next time….

I also wrote myself a note about mentioning how martial law is now in effect, which I suspect was less of a tribute to the films of George Romero and more to do with having shot the scene between Susan and the Security Guard earlier and then wanting to plant the seeds for that in advance of that scene for eagle-eared listeners. Sometimes world building in a movie is as cheap as adding stuff to radio voice overs.

And speaking of voice overs, the voice artists in this scene were the aforementioned Arthur Jolly (as the Scientist) and Stephen Rajkumar (as the Announcer), who both did excellent work and helped sell a shitload of exposition as entertainment. For many years prior to this project, they were part of a five-person comedy group called The Lunatic Fringe who were inspired by Monty Python and any number of other great British comedy troupes. In fact, they made a a feature-length movie that never got released entitled THE END OF THE WORLD that I was the director of photography on that was shot on Super 16mm (anyone remember that format?). And while it was pretty funny and strange, it was a bit too esoteric for mainstream consumption, but was also charming in a very low-budget backyard kind of way, as it was made dirt cheap and the biggest expense was film stock. I had almost forgotten about this venture entirely until sitting down to make these notes, so it was a nice memory to have pop back into my tired old brain.

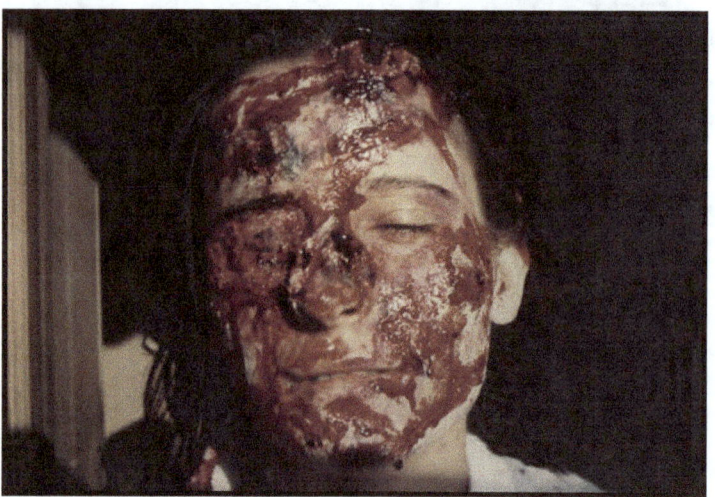

Int. Car - Day

Susan is driving down a country road with nothing but trees and fields on either side of her.  Occasionally she passes a desperate looking hitchhiker; she pays them no mind.

Susan turns on the radio; a talk show is in progress.

                    Annoucer (V.O.)
          Yes, I'd heard something about that.

                    Scientist (V.O.)
          Sociologically, we consider this to
          be a model town for this phenomenon.
          Here was a small town where the pop-
          ulace finds there graveyards being dug
          up and bodies being stolen.  At the
          same time, fresh bodies are disappear-
          ing from the local morgue and hospitals.
          An investigation begins, and a cult
          group is immediately brought to blame.
          A cult group that doesn't even exist.

                    Announcer (V.O.)
          Frankly, that seems like a logical
          mistake to me, based on what we
          know now and could not even imagine
          at that time.

                    Scientist (V.O.)
          Well, you can imagine their surprise
          when it was discovered that the freshly
          dead - embarassed, frightened - unsure
          of what to do or even what to make of
          their own situation, congregate where
          they know they're supposed to be; a
          graveyard.  Here, these people would
          later describe that they heard the
          voices of long dead friends and relatives
          calling to them from their graves.

                    Announcer (V.O.)
          Right.  And it doesn't take a genius
          to know that trying to push 6 feet of
          dirt out of your way isn't going to
          happen without some outside help.  So
          they dig them up.

                    Scientist (V.O.)
          Exactly.  Suddenly, dead people are
          missing; graveyards are being desecrated.
          Conclusions are reached.

**Page 5:**
"That fucker took my last gallon"? Really, this late in the game that line is nowhere near as funny as "Shit, my last gallon!" two pages earlier when it was still relevant to the scene. And I almost cut *that* damn line! Welcome to Comedy 101 class, students.

Reading this again today, I'm kind of sorry I didn't shoot her rolling up the windows and locking the doors, as that's all just taken for granted in the final edit. It would have added a little bit more tension to a scene that – onscreen, with our limited budget – is nowhere near as tense as I wanted it to be based on what was written on the page.

You don't have to be the most eagle-eyed viewer to note that most of the zombies attacking the car are many of the same people who were visible on the streets of Middletown in the earlier scenes. We found our extras via free listings in the local supermarket newsprint handouts a month or two before shooting as we needed to keep costs down by using locals. The response was enthusiastic from those who did reply, but the numbers left something to be desired. Everyone was great and I was so happy to have them, but it would have been nice to have twice as many people to work with. I'll trade enthusiasm over quantity any day of the week, so my enteral gratitude to those who showed up and put in a lot of hard work on a long day in two different locations that were not very close to each other.

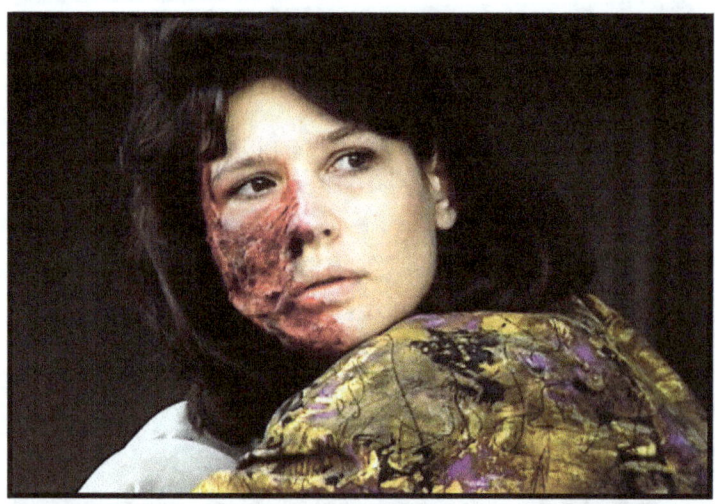

> **Announcer (V.O.)**
> The first phone call is always the
> hardest.  I've been hearing rumors
> lately about the possibilites of
> unionization and labor talks.

> **Scientist (V.O.)**
> Right, in the underground circles;
> I've heard that, too.  That's not
> my area of concern, however, so I'm
> not prepared to make a public opinion
> either way.

> **Announcer (V.O.)**
> So your concerns right now are mostly
> the scientific angle?

> **Scientist (V.O.)**
> What?  I guess so.  To be blunt, I'm
> not really sure what science means
> anymore...

Disgusted, Susan turns off the radio.

The engine of her car is making a strange sound so she slows
down.  Finally the car rolls to a stop.  Susan tries to re-
start the car, but the engine just grinds.

> **Susan**
> That fucker took my last gallon.

Susan slams the wheel and curses.  She sits back and takes a
deep breath.

Through the windows, Susan sees dead people angrily coming
towards her.  She rolls up her windows and locks her doors.

She checks the status and the safety catches on her weapons,
and reaches under the passenger-side seat to pull out a huge
Rambo knife.

The dead people hoot and holler to one another, more of them
than before approaching her car from up and down the road,
from out of the woods, etc.  They have sticks, and rocks, and
bricks; and a leader.

An angry looking man dressed in black with a big hat to match
makes his way through the ruckus.  He is the Preacher Man.

# SHATTER DEAD Screenplay Annotations

**Page 6:**
Somehow, this page mostly accurately describes what we ended up shooting, which makes is a blessed anomaly at this point in the proceedings. Halleluyah!!!!

There are now about 20 dead people surrounding the car. Susan struggles to reach the floor of her backseat to re- trieve her shotgun.

The Preacher Man steps out of the crowd onto the car's hood and ascends to the center of it's roof.  He stands there, tall and proud, his hands clasped behind his back.

Susan is back in her seat.  She hears someone on the roof, but she cannot see him.  She does not look frightened, but really pissed off.

> Preacher Man
> I claim this vehicle for my people
> in the name of the lord.

Susan bangs on the roof of her car.

> Susan
> Fuck you!

> Preacher Man
> Let's explain this to her.

The Preacher Man steps off the roof, onto the trunk, and jumps off the rear bumper, avoiding Susan's line of sight.

Once he is off the car, the dead people start banging on the windows and shaking the car in general, throwing Susan from one side to the other.

> Preacher Man
> Okay.  That's enough.

Everyone stops what they are doing and looks inside at Susan. She picks herself back up on her seat and shoots an angry look at them.

She displays her guns and knife to the dead people, and her delight at the thought of being able to use them.

She takes aim at a particularly ugly dead person just outside her window.  He gives her a look and backs off.

Other dead people, sensing a very real threat, start to back away from the vehicle.

The Preacher Man is disappointed by his followers lack of bold initiative.

**Page 7:**
Susan's initial line about the food being in the trunk was redundant and dropped. The audience knows this already and she says almost the same thing towards the bottom of the page.

Have you noticed my very complicated system by now? The stuff we shot gets the wavy line, and the stuff I'm cutting gets the straight line covering up the words to near oblivion. Not sure where I learned this technique, but I'm sure at the time I imagined it was something Hitchcock might have done.

Note that Susan was more aggressive here than what we ended up shooting. Again, I believe this was changed to make her more acted upon than acting against others. That passivity, I thought, would make her more sympathetic to viewers.

Of course, there were also the shooting logistics that also added to this decision.

You see, the day we shot with all of these zombie extras was at a different time than when Preacher Man actor Robert Welles was available, so we had to shoot all of this footage around his absence. In fact, I doubled for Robert this particular day, as I was the one who walked up the front and then down the back of the car amidst our tiny crowd of extras.

So while it would have been nice to see The Preacher Man escort the zombie who puts the gas back into the tank of Susan's car (played by our director of photography Matthew Howe, by the way), shooting logistics took care of that possibility.

                    Preacher Man
          Give her some room, people.  She's
          frightened.  Let's not get her
          uneccessarily violent.  Give her
          some room.

More dead people back away from the driver's side door, opening
up a part in the crowd.

Susan quickly gathers up as much of her stuff as she can.

                       Susan
          ~~Shit!  The food's in the trunk.~~

~~Susan pounds the dashboard with anger.  Everything that she can
attach to her person, she has.  With a gun leading her path, she
cracks open her door.~~

                    Preacher Man
          Nobody touch her!  The car is ours.
          Forget about her for now; she'll
          join us later.  Only by choice -
          that is our strength!

~~Susan walks nervously through the crowd to the other side of the
road; all eyes are on her.~~

~~The dead people move to the passenger side of the car along
the road, while Susan is given the other side of the road to
walk on.~~

                              *Need C.U. Susan - P.O.V. crowd*

The Preacher Man puts his arm around a dead man in the crowd
who is holding a gas can, and walks him to the car.  He drops
him off at the car's rear.

The Preacher Man continues around the car to the driver's seat;
he sits down in it.  He flips a switch and the gas tank door
flips open.  The dead man pours the gasoline into the tank.

Susan shakes her head angrily.

                       Susan
          Bastard.  What about my food in
          the trunk?  You guys don't even eat.
          Let me have it.

The Preacher Man closes the car door, starts the engine, and
drives off as the adoring crowd of dead people cheer him on.

The dead people quiet down when he is out of their range and
turn their attentions back to Susan.  Things are getting ugly.

## SHATTER DEAD Screenplay Annotations

**Page 10:**
Okay, so even the most casual reader must have noticed that we unceremoniously jumped from page 7 to page 10. What happened here exactly and what are we missing? It's an excellent question.

Going back to my earlier mention of Arthur Jolly and this movie being as much of a showcase for my writing and directing talents (hah!) as his stunt work and make-up talents, I left a blank space in the script for where zombie killing mayhem could ensue.

But due to budgetary and shooting schedule reasons, this mayhem did not come to pass.

Note that at the top of the page, Susan is "covered with the blood of others and completely exhausted". Well, I could afford exhaustion in spades and we happily shot that big time, but unfortunately the production did not have the time nor the financial wherewithal to shoot a big zombie takedown as originally planned.

In retrospect, I have ZERO regrets about it as this kind of blood soaked hijinks was never what the movie was about anyway, and while it would have been fun – and let's face it, grueling to shoot – it also would not have added anything to the subtext. And in fact, it would have ended up distracting from what the movie was really all about in the first place.

So in the end, the lack of time and money in this particular situation, helped us out.

As for Susan not firing off her gun to stop the car, as we were accosted by the police along that road earlier in the day while shooting, it seemed like a bad idea to be brandishing live weapons whilst we were under the microscope, which is why she stops the vehicle by standing in the middle of the road instead. There are only so many laws you can get away with breaking while shooting a low-budget movies, and we weren't about the to tempt the gods of cinema any further on a particularly grueling day of shooting as – yes – this scene was shot the same day as all the zombies attacking the car.

Ext. Country Road - Day

Susan, covered with the blood of others and completely exhausted,
walks down the road in a series of dissolves.

From Susan's dreamy P.O.V. we see her pass by a series of dead
people who stare at her in her pathetic looking state.  Their
looks betray their anger - they know what she's been up to.
She's covered with blood but she's still alive; the dead recognize the suffering of their own kind.

Susan just looks back at them; sometimes confused, sometimes
angry - but never with compassion.

Susan stops walking.  She is so tired she can barely stand.
She closes her eyes and lets her head fall back against her
neck and her hair blow in the wind.

In the distance behind her, a car comes speeding down the road.

Susan hears the engine approaching and snaps her head back straight
and into full conciousness.  She storms into the middle of the
road and raises her shotgun towards the distant car which grows
less distant with each passing moment.

The car is close now.  Susan fires a warning shot to slow the
driver down.  The sound of the car's brakes quickly engaging
fill the soundtrack and the vehicle stops a few feet in front
of Susan, her weapon still raised.

The driver of the car turns off the engine and just sits there.
Susan lowers her shotgun and goes over.  The driver rolls down
his window.

                    Driver
          Howdy!  Need a lift?

Susan doesn't say a word.  She just observes him closely and
looks into the backseat for anything unusual.

                    Driver
          Oh Man.  You're not gonna' steal my car,
          are you?  They got that scam goin' on a
          couple of miles down the road.  They
          steal the juice out of all the cars in
          town, wait a couple of miles down the
          road and wham!  The bastards drive off
          in your car with the gas they stole
          from you in the first place!

# SHATTER DEAD Screenplay Annotations

**Page 11:**
Cinematographer Matt Howe is the one who suggested we shoot this in a long single take for two good reasons. The first one was as a tribute to Joseph Lewis' GUN CRAZY – which, if you've seen it, you'll immediately know what I'm referring to, and if you haven't, well then just put down this book and go find it and watch it as it's one fucking amazing movie and totally worth your time.

The second reason is that we were short on time and needed get this shot and done as quickly as possible so we could move on to the next set-up, which was the more important reason. But Matt's first reason made the second one more palatable at the time.

On top of everything else, we had run out of performers to choose from, so at the last moment I took the part of the Driver. Not my best performance but also probably not my worst, it was fun but terrifying to have to play the part in a long take since I had almost all of the dialogue – and surprisingly, in retrospect, I'm impressed with myself at having hewed so close to the written word, especially on such short notice.

You'll note that I removed both my and Susan's capper lines, so we never even shot them. And nobody has ever missed them. Another good on-set decision about which I have no regrets.

Susan shivers from exhaustion.  She really wants to believe
this guy, but something feels wrong to her.

                    Driver
               Lady, you look exhausted in the
               worst way.  Are you alright?  Is
               that what happened to you?

Susan is upset at the remembrance.

                    Susan
               Yeah.

                    Driver
               Come on.  Let me give you a lift.

Susan digs into her coat pocket and pulls out a small mirror
with one hand, while with her other hand she grabs a small
gun out of her pants holster.  She lurches forward, pushing
the mirror under the driver's nose and the gun to the side of
his head.

A look of blind terror crosses the driver's face.

                    Driver
               Holy shit.  Fuck it.  You win.

                    Susan
               Shut up and hold still.

The driver is so frightened he is hyperventilating, but no
breath appears on the mirror.  Susan's eyes widen with anger.

                    Susan
               Get your dead ass out of that car
               right now.

The driver opens the door and gets out of the car with his hands
high in the air.

                    Driver
               Listen, lady.  I'm just tryin' to
               make a living - no pun intended.
               I mean, what do you do to get by?

Susan kicks the driver down to the ground and then kicks him
again for good measure.  She gets into the car and drives off.
She checks the gas guage, and finds it bobbing on the "E".

                    Susan
               Shit.  Nightfall.  I give up.

**SHATTER DEAD Screenplay Annotations**

**Page 12:**
It's at this point in reminiscing that I'm probably as flummoxed as you are, dear reader: why are there five page twelves? What the heck is the story behind that?

I really wish I had an answer to this question, because I am sincerely as curious as you are to know what the heck happened here. But I've got nothing.

Also, surprisingly, these five page twelves – with the exception of the bottom of page 12D – are almost a letter perfect rendition of what we shot, which makes this a rare section of the screenplay, indeed.

Why is Grandma named "Grandma"? She's the same age as everybody else as far as we can see, and she's even pregnant – which indicates youth and virility. I don't really have an answer, although it felt right at the time and we did give Marina Del Rey a faux strand of grey hair to indicate that she was a little bit older than she looked compared to the people around her, although I do remember toying with the idea in my mind that the ribbon of grey hair was a byproduct of the shock she felt at being 'raped' by an Angel.

My biggest regret reading over this section is that we didn't shoot the Preacher Man dialogue at the bottom of page 12D. it sets up the fireside scene nicely and also is indicative of the fanaticism the character represents and trades in on, and I'm honestly not sure why I cut it. In retrospect, it was a mistake and I'm sorry I made it.

Ext. City Street - Night

Susan pulls the car over to the curb, parks next to a fire hydrant, and turns off the engine.  She sits there in the dark for a moment, looking up and down the street from her seat.

Int. Car - Night

Susan opens the glove compartment and finds a small flashlight and some photos.  She looks at the items for a moment and then tosses them back inside.

Susan yawns deeply and pushes her seat back; she lies down and squirms into a more comfortable position.  She closes her eyes and starts to fall asleep.

There is a loud knock on the window.  Susan snaps awake and sits up to find a Patrolman with an uzi tapping his gun's nozzle against the glass.  Her eyes pop wide open.

                    Patrolman
          Excuse me.

                    Susan
          Hello?

                    Patrolman
          It's past curfew.  Please step out
          of your car.  Now.

                    Susan
          Curfew?

The Patrolman steps back, giving Susan enough room to open the door; she steps out of the car.

                    Patrolman
          Just went into effect this evening.
          Everyone off the streets by night-
          fall.  I don't care where you go, but
          this is my street and I'm not fucking
          around out here.

                    Susan
          You don't look like a suit.

                    Patrolman
          Neighborhood patrol.  Problem?

> Susan
>
> Yeah.  Where the hell am I supposed
> to go?

> Patrolman
>
> I'll show you.  Come on.

Susan slams the car door shut and stands there looking at him
really pissed off.  He takes a deep breath and softens his
tone a little.

> Patrolman
>
> You're not gonna' leave all that
> stuff in your car, are you?

> Susan
>
> What?  Oh.  No.

Susan turns around to open up the car again, but stops.  She
speaks to him tentatively.

> Susan
>
> There's a shotgun and some other
> things like that, you know?

> Patrolman
>
> Right.  And?

> Susan
>
> And?  And I just have the feeling
> that you're not in the mood for
> any surprises.

> Patrolman
>
> I wish everyone around here was as
> smart as that.  It saves me bullets.
> Go ahead, you're shaking too hard
> to be dead.

> Susan
>
> Thanks.

Susan opens the door and snatches up her weapons and her bag
of personal belongings.

Int. House Entranceway - Night

There is a knock at the door; through it's tiny windows we can
see Susan and the Patrolman.  A young woman of about 27 years old
answers the door tersely; she is called "Grandma".

                    Grandma
          Hello?

                    Patrolman
        . Hello.  Open the door please.

                    Grandma
          Who is that?

                    Patrolman
          Neighborhood patrol.  Open up now.

Grandma opens up the door; he steps half-way into the doorway
to keep the door open.

                    Grandma
          So what'll it be tonight?

                    Patrolman
          I got a vagrant here, Grandma, with
          no place to go, and no reservations.

                    Grandma
          Oh come on; I don't have any more
          room here.  I've got enought people
          in here already between...

                    Patrolman
          It's martial law now, lady.  No
          private residency.  Now shut-up
          and put-up, or I'll arrest the
          whole bunch of you.

                    Grandma
          Fine.  Fuck all this shit.  Send her in.

                    Patrolman
          You'll thank me later, Grandma.
          She's a real live one.

The Patrolman and Grandma stare at each other for a moment
without blinking.  She nods, and he steps back out of the
doorway, allowing Susan to pass by him and into the house.

Int. Apartment Hallway

Grandma closes the door and locks it.  She turns and faces
Susan who is just standing there looking mighty forlorn.

>                    Grandma
>           You look exhausted.  Come on into
>           the kitchen and I'll give you
>           something to drink.

>                    Susan
>           Thank you.

They start walking down the hall towards the kitchen.

>                    Grandma
>           Everyone's in the kitchen.

Int. Kitchen

There are four or five people hanging out in the kitchen
around the table; the three at the table facing Susan as
she enters the room just stare at her.  The fourth keeps
his head down in his hands, his back to her.  One woman is
standing near the sink; she turns to Susan.

>                    Melody
>           Would you like some tea?

>                    Susan
>           Yes, please.

Melody looks visibly surprised.

>                    Melody
>           Really?

An uncomfortable silence fills the room.

>                    Melody
>           Have a seat in the living room.
>           I'll cook you up some water.

Grandma takes Susan by the arm and directs her to the living
room entrance.

Int. Living Room

The room is dark except that the television is on.  The light
from the television illuminates a room filled with staring,
blank faces.  On the TV itself, a graphic autopsy is in progress.

Susan is horrified, but struggles to remain in control.

>                    Susan
>           Never mind the tea.  Where am I
>           gonna' be sleeping?

                    Grandma
          Upstairs.


                    Susan
          Please, just take me up there.
          Okay?  I'm very tired.


                    Grandma
          Sure thing.


                    Melody
          Hey, wait a minute.  Jack?

The person at the table with his head in his hands moans loudly.


                    Jack
          Yeah?


                    Melody
          Why don't you show the lady to
          her room, Jack?

Jack lifts his head from off of the table and turns to look at
Susan.  He looks her over, up and down, and sighs.


                    Jack
          You got it.

Jack rises and walks right up to Susan's face.  She steps back
from him, and he smiles.


                    Jack
          Turn around.  It's right back the
          way you came from.

Susan turns and walks down the hall.  Jack follows her closely.

From out of the darkness of the entrance to the Living Room,
a familiar dark shape emerges; it is the Preacher Man.


                    Preacher Man
          So that'll be in the usual spot out
          in the back, in one half an hour.  I
          have an unusually powerful revelation
          I will need to discuss with all of you.
          Be prepared to be changed.  Our purpose
          is clearer to me now than it has ever
          been before.

**Page 13:**
The recently revised cut of SHATTER DEAD sheds Susan's "save it for someone who cares" line, and I'm glad to finally lose it all these years later. The tone was as wrong as the line itself, and I saw firsthand from audience reaction over the years that elicited a laugh where none was intended. I'm glad to have gotten a second chance to remove this mistake that made it to the screen and am thankful for the second chance.

<u>Int.</u> <u>Stairwell and Hallway</u> <u>Night</u>

Susan walks down the hallway with     Jack          close behind
her,                        .  Their conversation is slightly more
casual.

                    Jack
          The farther upstate you go, the worse
          it gets, is what I've been hearing.
          Cities are used to overcrowding and
          rioting.  Balance is more delicate
          around these parts.


                    Susan
          Running out of places to run.

                    Jack
          So what's your story?  Everyone around
          here has a good one.


                    Susan
          Sorry.  Just another tragedy.

                    Jack
          Tell me about it.  Four years of
          college for this.



<u>Int. Hallway</u>


    Jack pulls a mirror out of his pocket and turns to Susan.

                    Jack
          Sorry.  Standard procedure here.

He puts the mirror under her nose and vapor forms quickly.  He
nods knowingly and puts the mirror away.

                    Susan
                         No surprises.

                    Jack
          Glad to hear that.  I hate making
          passes at corpses; you're good looking.

                    Susan
          Thanks.  Save it for someone who
          cares.  I came here to sleep.

**Page 14:**
Once again, simply ran out of performers so this scene was greatly simplified to focus on Susan and Mary. And while I'm sorry to have lost the young couple in this scene in terms of world building, the scene itself doesn't suffer in any way from their loss. Although the lack of extraneous personages does help the audience focus more on the main characters overall, which is probably a good thing in a movie with such a short running time.

Still, I liked the idea that in an emergency situation like the one depicted in SHATTER DEAD, people are still finding ways to hustle for funds, and renting out rooms so travelers have a place to stay for a little while rang true to me and felt depression era desperate. Twenty something years later and Air BnB is a way for anybody to generate extra income at home, at least until the COVID pandemic shut that down (although I'm sure the industry will recover).

Losing Mary's "I'm homeless and alone" at the bottom of the page was a blessing. She gives a wonderful performance and didn't need to be bogged down by amateurishly simplistic dialogue like that. Her acting did a far better job of conveying her desperation.

Int.    _Bed_Room Night

Susan enters the room which is already occupied by three other
people scattered around the room; a male and femal couple of
about thirty years old, and a blonde  woman about Susan's age
with a round face named Mary.  No one is talking - everyone looks
exhausted.

The couple are busy packing up their bags.  Mary is sitting down
on the floor cross-legged.  Mary looks towards Susan and smiles
warmly.  Susan responds with a vague look and approaches the couple.

                    Susan
          It's pretty bad out there right now.

                    Man
          No worse than it was before.  Just darker.

Pause.  The young couple look at each other, pick up the rest of
their belongings and head for the door.  They exit without looking
back.

Susan and Mary are alone in the room now.

                    Mary
          Howdy!

                    Susan
          Hi.

Pause.  They just stare at each other for a moment.

                    Susan
          Is there a working telephone in here?

                    Mary
          Sure.  Right next to the _Bed_ ..

Without acknowledgeing Mary, she turns and goes towards the _Bed_ .
She picks up the phone and punches in the same number she is always
trying to call.  Pause.  She gets a busy signal, sighs, and slams
down the telephone.

                    Mary
          Travelling alone?

                    Susan
          Trying to get home; got friends there.

                    Mary
          Wow.  Your're lucky; I'm homeless.
          And alone.

**SHATTER DEAD Screenplay Annotations**

**Page 15:**
Mary's line about having paid for two nights was meant to reinforce the transient nature of the people who had come to Grandma's for shelter (as if the couple on the previous page leaving the room wasn't evidence enough).

Here begins the shower scene, which is in fact the very first scene I wrote for SHATTER DEAD. I started here, wrote all the way through to the end and then went back and wrote the first third of the movie. The shower scene also happens to be the first scene we shot on the first day of shooting.

I've told this story before, so forgive me for repeating myself. Basically we shot this scene first because I wanted to make sure nobody was going to 'chicken out' about taking their clothes off in front of the camera. Thinking about it in retrospect, I have no idea what I would have done if my two wonderful actresses had balked at the idea on-set, as it's not like I could just go out and find new performers. I sure didn't have anybody on stand-by. I guess I figured the worst case scenario is we would have simply shut down production on day one and we'd be over and done with at a minimal financial loss (ie: the weekend video equipment rental fee).

And let's face it – my life would have been a lot easier for a long time if we hadn't gone ahead with the shoot, so there might have been some subconscious appeal for it to not happen.

But go figure. Two fearless and talented performers in Stark and Flaura and a great and tireless cameraperson in Matt. In working with people like this, I had set myself up for the failure of successfully seeing this shoot through to the very end. And I have no regrets about that.

The bathroom was so tiny and the day was so fucking hot and humid when we shot this that the actresses were more than happy to be naked in the shower for the duration. All Matt and I could do while shooting was look at them with envy as they were far more comfortable than we were.

The rationale for writing this scene (that I gave myself) was that every horror movie made in the 1980's has a shower scene, but they were always just a gratuitous moment and never did anything to move the plot forward or build character, etc. It was always just a momentary excuse to ogle the performer getting naked before they (usually) got killed.

I wanted to try to come up with something unique, so this shower scene meant a lot to me and I figured that – as a writer – if I couldn't crack the code and come up with something different and special, there was no need to continue writing anything else for the project; and that was the other main reason that this, for me, was where the whole thing began.

Susan is deeply unaffected by Mary's statement.  Mary senses
this and her happy tone flattens out.

                    Susan
          Is there anyone in the shower?

                    Mary
          Nope.  Over there.

Mary points to the bathroom.  Susan grabs up what little of her
belongings she has and follows the direction.

                    Mary
          Listen - I paid for two nights, so you'll
          be sharing the place. OK?
                                    room
                    Susan
          Sure.                              Cut

Susan enters the bathroom and closes the door.

Mary lifts up her arms and smells her own armpits.  The smell makes
her wince.  She rises and also moves towards the bathroom.

Int. Bathroom - Night

Susan carefully places her gear and undresses.  Underneath her
clothes she wears a shoulder holster with a small gun strapped
tight against her breast.

She turns on the shower and tests the water.  She enters the water
with her gun still on, and a bar of soap.

The bathroom door opens again.  Mary enters the room quietly, but not
quietly enough to not be heard by Susan.

Susan stops lathering up and watches Mary approach her through the
diaphonous shower curtain.

                    Mary
          Um...excuse me?

Susan does not mask the annoyance in her voice.

                    Susan
          Problem?

                    Mary
          Listen...My name's Mary.  I don't even
          know your name.  What is it?

                    Susan
          (Terse)  Susan.

# SHATTER DEAD Screenplay Annotations

**Page 16:**

The first written scene, and it's already obvious that I was trying to give Susan as little dialogue as possible (using Clint Eastwood in a Sergio Leone western as a model) and also make her character more acted upon than acting. I wanted her to be submissive to what was going on around her, not out of weakness but as a way of letting things happen until the moment came where she might need to assert herself.

Susan is as close to nurturing in this and the following scene as she'll ever be in this story. She gives Mary the space to tell her story and her philosophy, and Susan listens and responds with questions and genuine curiosity.

Until it becomes time to destroy Mary's face, of course – but that's still a few pages away (and technically not really Susan's fault as the act is unintentional at first).

People still make fun of me for the lousy bar of soap prop we used for this scene, where I just put silver spray paint onto the Ivory Soap packaging. I was going for something that looked like a utilitarian ARMY issued soap ration that she might have picked up along the way, but it just looks cheap and stupid. In the recent re-edit of SHATTER DEAD, I shortened the shot of the damn thing as much as I could.

According to the internet, "naked as a jaybird" is slang that originates from sometime in the 1920's and 1930's in the United States. "J-bird" was what you called a 'jailbird' for short, and when a prisoner was brought into the facility, they were forced to walk along naked to the showers as they carried their folded uniforms with them – not to be worn until they were clean. Aren't you glad you're reading these notes now?

                              Mary
              Wow.  Howdy Susan.  Listen...I heard
              you open up a bar of soap and, well,
              I don't have any.  Haven't had any for
              for days.  So I smell really bad, you know?

Susan just stares and listens as Mary comes closer.

                              Mary
              I know how weird this sounds,  We don't
              even know each other.  But we're both girls,
              you know what I mean?  I'm just really afraid
              to be left alone.  Now you're here.  Every-
              thing's so weird lately.  People have to stick
              together if we're gonna' make it through all this.

Mary reaches the shower curtain with no verbal response from Susan.

Susan reaches up and unlatches the leather safety strap of her
holster.

Mary slowly places her hand on the curtains edge and parts it
just enough to reveal her face; a tear is running down her cheek.

                              Mary
              I don't mean to scare you, but I'm
              really scared.

Susan pulls the gun from it's holster and aims it at Mary.
Mary sighs with diappointment and shakes her head.

                              Mary
              No one trusts anyone anymore.  Do you
              think I have some kind of advantage
              over you?  I'll show you.

Mary turns and goes to the center of the room.  Through the shower
curtain Susan watches her undress and re-approach.

Mary slowly re-opens the curtain.

                              Mary
              You see?  Now we're both naked as Jay birds.
              And you've got the gun.  And the soap.  Listen-
              I'll do your back if you want.  I'm good at it.

Susan lowers her gun and the firm look on her face softens
a little.  Mary steps into the shower and they face each other.
Susan hands her bar of soap to Mary.

                              Susan
              Here.  You wash first.

**SHATTER DEAD Screenplay Annotations**

**Page 17:**
In case it's hard to read the crossed-out lines, they are:

"The blood just kind of pools up in one place from the gravity."

"Mouthwash, not chewing gum, for fresh breath – you need saliva to chew."

I removed the gravity bit as it was starting to sound less conversational and more scientific at that point. The mouthwash bit is interesting, but in the context of everything else she's talking about, it's an unrelated as opposed to a personal anecdote.

Also, starting to throw a lot of pseudo-scientific babble into a script like this gives the audience too much potential stuff to chew on while watching the movie. I'm trying to promote the willing suspension of disbelief in a situation that is a very tough sell to the audience to begin with, and dwelling on such niceties is not a good idea. Yes, a few touches of semi-science mumbo-jumbo as an accent here and there, but with our budget and resources it's a better idea to sell the characters and situations instead. Also, thankfully, GOD HATES YOU is a damned good umbrella to have everything taking place underneath during the most ludicrous moments; faith is the band-aid that lets the story get away with lots of things that would otherwise be inexcusable. Just like the Bible.

                    Mary
          Thanks.  I can't even begin to tell
          you how much I appreciate this...

Mary starts to lather up and immediately drops the soap.  She
smiles embarassedly and turns around, bending over to pick up
the soap.

Susan looks down at Mary and sees large purple blotches on
Mary's ass and her upper thighs.  Susan gasps loudly.

Mary hears Susan's surprise - she has almost forgotten herself
that she is dead.  Mary rises slowly, afraid of startling Susan.

Susan's eyes narrow to tiny slits, and her body tightens like a
wound-up coil.


                    Mary
          I don't want to hurt you or anyone else.
          Please, just let me go on.  I just want
          to be left as I am.

Mary pauses a moment to draw the strength to continue speaking.

                    Mary
          That's what happens when I sit in one
          position for too long now.  The blood
          just kind of pools up in one place ~~from~~
          ~~the gravity~~.  It feels kinda' gross and
          and it sounds just terrible when it start
          draining down to my feet again.  When I
          know I'm gonna' be around people I make
          sure to stand on my head for a while to
          get the color back into my cheeks.  ~~Mouth-~~
          ~~wash, not chewing gum, for fresh breath~~
          ~~you need saliva to chew~~.  You use the mirror
          trick to find us?

                    Susan
          Yes.

                    Mary
          Well I know a way using heated mineral
          spirits to fool it.  I'll give you every-
          thing I own or can get my hands on for
          this bar of soap.  I need it to move freely.
          Help me.  I am not alone.  There are more
          of us like me, than you think...

                    Susan
          What do you mean by, "like me"?

## SHATTER DEAD Screenplay Annotations

**PAGE 18:**

Susan has six words of dialogue on this page that's bursting with verbiage – most of which belongs to Mary. Again, a very deliberate choice. Susan has almost nothing but questions now that she's getting to spend some time – probably her first time – with a dead person who she isn't actively trying to get away from or kill. I like writing about people who have a healthy curiosity about things they haven't experienced. Susan's continuing quest for knowledge marks her as someone who still has a vibrant hunger to continue being alive.

And kudos to Flaura yet again for pretty much nailing on-camera what's written on the page. When you're shooting on a tight schedule, a performer who has memorized their lines and can deliver the goods take after take is the kind of production value that no amount of money can buy.

This brief near-monologue by Mary was a separate element at some point in the writing process as Flaura had asked me if I could write her an odd and memorable audition piece for when she was trying to get gigs. I asked her if I could write her a zombie monologue, as that might be the kind of thing that producers didn't get to hear very often. I'm not sure if she ever actually ended up using this piece for auditions or not, but if she did it obviously didn't work and I'm sorry she didn't get a lot more gigs as she's a very fine actress, easy on the eyes and an absolutely wonderful person to work with.

Int. Bedroom - Night

Susan and Mary are in various states of dresses and drying their
hair with plush hotel towels.

Susan is sitting on the edge of the bed while Mary stands and
paces around the room, pausing occasionally for dramatic effect.

                    Mary
          Sometimes it's a real drag.  Got to keep
          on moving or everything settles - you know,
          gets flat.  Blood...organs.  I don't even
          want to or need to sleep anymore.

                    Susan
          What about taste?

                    Mary
          No.  I don't need to eat anymore.  So far.
          Oh wait.  You mean taste like flavor?
          Nope.  Nothing.

                    Susan
          And you're happy?

                    Mary
          Listen; what are you gonna' do?  You're
          gonna live your life without a home, with-
          out a job - grow old and decrepit and die.
          But you won't die, because nobody dies any-
          more.  And you'll spend the rest of eternity
          wandering the earth in your pathetic state
          wishing you could die and rest already like
          people used to in the good old days.  But
          you can't.  Not anymore.

Silence.  Mary pulls up a chair next to Susan and sits on it,
facing her.  Susan stops what she is doing and gives Mary the
attention she so obviously wants.

                    Mary
          Look at me, Susan.  I'm beautiful.  And
          I will be forever.  And young, and strong,
          and healthy.  Today is the beginning of
          the rest of my life; for real.  And I'm no
          burden on society - I don't comsume or
          waste anything.  What's wrong with the choice
          I've made - can you honestly look at me in
          the eye and tell me what I've done wrong?

Susan looks at her coldly, thinking long and hard.

# SHATTER DEAD Screenplay Annotations

**Page 19:**

I am pleased to say that, some nearly 30 years later, I know how to spell 'Beethoven' correctly. It was a long, hard journey and I'm very proud of myself.

Another verbiage besotted page where Susan has 11 words and Mary an avalanche of locution. Overall, these couple of pages are probably some of my favorite writing in the entire screenplay. It was nice to have a character express themselves and their point of view in a way that was, at the time, unique. It's hard for me to remember offhand if I had ever seen a zombie talk about how they came to be up until this point. Vampires were chatty creatures, but the zombies I few up with were almost always silent. I remember thinking at the time that I was writing this that — if I wasn't breaking new ground — I was at the very least walking along a path not very often trodden upon in the horror movies I recalled and referenced. I think RETURN OF THE LIVING DEAD 3 was the first time I saw a sympathetic, articulate and even sexy zombie character; although even in that movie, they still needed to eat brains for some kind of relief.

I dispensed with the need for feeding on humans entirely because I wanted to see if there was some new and interesting angle I could take the zombie cliché' into.

Part of trying to discover this new path was also at least partially a budgetary aspect, because when it came to funds for elaborate make-up EFX, I had next to none.

So the old oldest cliché' of all still holds true, even in storytelling: necessity if the mother of invention.

And thankfully, when I'm writing, morality is not the mother of prevention — because if she was, at least half of this screenplay would not exist at all.

                    Susan
          I don't know.  Yet.


                    Mary
          Well?  So what are you waiting for?

Susan feels her lack of curiousity getting the better of her.
She becomes curious.

                    Susan
          How did you do it?

Mary holds up her arms and models them, twisting her wrists
around and waving her fingers.  She is grinning from ear to ear.

                    Mary
          No visible scars whatsoever - very
          professional piece of work, don't
          you think?

Seizing the drama of the moment, Mary leans forward and whispers
slowly into Susan's face.

                    Mary
          Sleeping pills, a plastic grocery bag,
          and a piece of string around my neck
          to hold the bag in place.  A little
          Beehtoven to set the mood.  And there
          you have the secret of my success.

Mary loses her focus on Susan and finds herself talking inward.

                    Mary
          It was exhilirating - it was a
          giddy experience to have all those
          poisons trapped inside my body with
          no way out and just going to sleep
          and knowing that I would wake up
          immortal, forever young and beautiful.

                    Susan
          But dead.

                    Mary
          This isn't death.

Mary sits up straight in her chair and points to her head.

                    Mary
          I still think and feel.
          Dead people are the ones who give
          up hope.  Like you.

## SHATTER DEAD Screenplay Annotations

**Page 20:**
Lost almost all of Susan's dialogue on this page as it just wasn't necessary and, again, trying to reduce her word count to increase her Eastwood 'Man With No Name' vibe. She rolls over and goes to sleep much more abruptly in the version we shot.

It's interesting that I added in the harmonium as a handwritten afterthought. The harmonium was mine and it was already in the room I knew we'd be shooting in, but I guess when I was typing this up it hadn't occurred to me to incorporate it into the story.

Once the harmonium was brought into play, I knew immediately that I would want use the Bach piece from Andrei Tarkovsky's SOLARIS as the source music. I remember when directing Flaura during the scene that I talked her through the hand movements and the speed of her playing as I knew the piece well enough in my mind and we didn't have the facility to do a live playback for the piece on a tight shooting schedule. 'Get the shot and move on' was all we had time for.

Flaura did a great job selling the music performance overall and I love showing her feet playing the organ pump as most people don't know what a harmonium is in the first place and it helps show how it functions. Also, her playing the background music for the Preacher Man as he preaches is a great way to tie these two bits of business together and helps connect the narrative flow as we go off onto tangentially into Susan's dream.

Mary stands up and flips her chair around, placing it on the other side of the room.  She walks around in a small circle, explosive with energy.  She stretches her legs and massages her flatened ass back into shape while she walks.  Her attitude towards Susan continues to be playful.

                    Mary
          Don't want to stay in any one position
          for too long now...But in your case
          I'll make an exception.

 Susan is starting to look dead herself.

                    Susan
          I'm going to sleep now.

                    Mary
          I'll get the lights.

Mary leaps to the lightswitch playfully and flips it off.

Susan sits in the dark a moment, wondering.

                    Susan
          And what are you going to do?          *plays the harmonium*

                    Mary
          Watch over you.

Susan lies back in bed slowly, pulling the covers up to her neck protectively.  Mary moves over and tucks Susan's sheets into the bed's corners.  Susan watches this quietly.

                    Mary
          Listen; I don't mean to be annoying.
          Thanks for putting up with me.

                    Susan
          Just keep it down, okay?

                    Mary
          Sure thing.  Goodnight, Susan.

                    Susan
          Goodnight.

Susan rolls over in bed to face away from Mary.

Mary tiptoes through the room and goes over to the window.  She parts the curtains and lets the pale moonlight fall across her face. Outside, we hear the voice of the Preacher Man in Voice Over, yelping to god for blood and vengeance.

**Page 21:**
The Preacher Man's voice-over at the top of the page is a lost bit of audio that exists in the original release of SHATTER DEAD but has since been trimmed from the recent re-edit. This was because the original audio elements have been lost and trying to use the recording from the initial release had such awful sound quality that I preferred to drop it entirely instead of suffer with sub-standard audio. In retrospect, I don't miss this bit and think that it flows better without the distraction that was meant to make the audience feel like they were arriving in the middle of a sermon already in progress. It works just fine starting at the middle of the page instead. Sometimes just getting to the damned point is better.

                    Preacher Man (V.O.)
          "Help me, Preacher Man.  Help me,
          Preacher Man!"  And those were her
          last words.  She'ld be here with us
          today, except that death claimed her
          body in the form of a flame.  But
          when the wind blows, I hear her whispering
          soul calling...And it's the most beautiful
          thing you could ever imagine.

Ext. Campfire - Night

The Preacher Man is holding a captive audience around the campfire.  All we see is him and his excessive weaponry from behind,
silhouetted by the open flame.  The crowd of groupies yell
questions to him, which he answers with great aplomb.

                    Groupie #1
          Why, Preacher Man, why?

                    Preacher Man
          Why?  Did you ever expect that you would
          live to see the last generation of humans
          as we've known them for the last five
          thousand years?  Look over there, man.

The Preacher Man points to a nearby tree.

                    Preacher Man
          Look at that tree.  That tree is the
          end.  That's how clear it is to me;
          the end.  Does that scare you?  Do you
          see what I'm seeing?

                    Groupie #1
          Yes, Preacher Man; I see!  I'm
          scared too, Preacher Man!

                    Preacher Man
          Wrong!  Of what I'm seeing right now,
          you see nothing!  Well, what are you
          afraid of, man?  You see the end of
          the world?  This is god's world, man.
          It's never gonna' end!  Sure, god's
          gone and opened up a really big can of
          theological worms this time - but he's
          testing us.  We are at the beginning of
          a better way for this world.  And all
          we're really seeing is the end of these
          things as we know them.  Something beautiful
          is beginning.

**SHATTER DEAD Screenplay Annotations**

**Page 22:**
As written here, I had originally intended to show the reaction of the followers to The Preacher Man's speech, but fate and budgetary restrictions chose another path for the way we shot this scene. We had no extras available to us the evening we shot this, and we needed to shoot that particular evening no matter what since we were on location in Middletown (it's my parents backyard, no less!). Matt suggested we shoot it the way we did and it was an excellent idea. Thankfully, Robert Wells was a good enough performer that just keeping the camera pointed at his face was enough to hold visual interest. Not everyone is that cool looking and charming oncamera, so luck was on our side or something (I know what you're thinking...).

(With sincere apologies to Duran Duran)

Also note that this character was supposed to be 35 years old with wild hair and huge blue eyes, as the part was written for another actor entirely – my friend David Bower, who receives on-screen credit as "Spiritual Advisor" for the project. And while I love Dave and think he would have done a great job, I think having a more mature actor like Robert was better for the part and his look and age brought a bit more gravitas to the proceedings than another relatively young actor would have. That age difference brought some variety and more than a little bit of spice to the production.

The Preacher Man throws his arms up into the air and spins
around, giving us our first good look at him.  He is 35 years
old with wild hair and huge blue eyes; he is lovely and intense.

                    Preacher Man
          Man, we're so close to the fireworks
          they're going on behind us!  Join me!
          Turn around!!

                    Groupie #2
          I'm not afraid, Preacher Man!
          Tell us what we have to do!

The Preacher Man spins around to face his breathless audience.
He gets a look on his face that demands silence.  .

                    Preacher Man
          Now that's the kind of talk I
          want to hear man.  But are you
          really ready to know?  To know -
          what I know?  Are you ready to
          have your eyes opened - to be struck
          blind so that you can see with your
          other senses?  Are you ready to know
          the why?

Everyone around the campfire is in a frenzy of excitement, yelling
"yes Preacher Man", and "Show me, Preacher Man!"  He raises his
hands and begs for silence.

                    Preacher Man
          Please!  There are people trying to
          sleep here!  And who are we to dis-
          turb the world as it slumbers peacefully?

                    Groupie #3
          Fuck the world!!

                    Preacher Man
          You watch your language, man!

The Preacher Man laughs loudly; challengingly.

                    Preacher Man
          I mean, look at us.  Who are we,man?
          Who are we to change the world?  We
          are the homeless, the jobless, the
          forgotten; and we smell really bad.
          So who are we?

**Page 23:**
"Interior Hotel Room – Night" is the last remnant in the script that the entire scene at Grandma's house was originally written to be either a hotel or a trailer park as I had originally envisioned it in the handwritten first draft of the screenplay. Once budget became an issue to the reality of shooting, that expense was dropped and the location became the house I was living in at the time in Brooklyn.

And while we're on the subject, yes; I used to do all my first draft script writing in long hand in the pages of a spiral notebook, and then type that up and consider the typewritten version the true 'first draft' of whatever I was working on.

It's a way of working that I miss, but as I've gotten older it is more difficult for me to write legibly or comfortably for long periods of time, so with the advent of computer software I now do almost all of my writing that way instead – although I do occasionally jot down notes on napkins to myself to be typed up at another time.

## 23

> Groupie #4
> Then who was Jesus, Preacher Man?

> Preacher Man
> Indeed; who was he, if not one of
> us?  A downtrodden wanderer who
> spoke the truth at all costs, who
> liberated us with that truth, and
> continues to do so.

The Preacher Man scans the crowd; they are his now more than ever.

> Preacher Man
> The redemption of all mankind is 100
> years away from this breath that I am
> now breathing.  In the end, everyone
> who has died will live again; the
> resurrection is coming.  In 100 years
> when everyone and everything on this
> planet is dead, we will all join hands-
> generation after generation after gener-
> ation will be united in the spirit and
> the flesh.  The big book says it all,
> man; we're all gonna' be shaken hands
> with the almighty himself.

Pause.  The audience is quiet - looking to him and into the flame
for answers.  Nobody seems too sure of anything.

> Preacher Man
> But people - now I have an important
> question for you to think about: are
> you ready to sit back and wait 100 years
> for everybody to die?!  The lord is wait-
> ing for your answer.  And he is a very
> busy man.

Int. Hotel Room - Night

Mary, still standing by the window listening to the Preacher Man,
closes the curtains and sighs.  She just stands there and turns
to look towards Susan - she is sleeping restlessly and thrashing
about in bed.

Susan is in the midst of a horrifying nightmare.

Dream Sequence:

The screen whites out, and the image returns to clouds in the sky
as the camera tilts down to reveal a graveyard.

# SHATTER DEAD Screenplay Annotations

**Page 24:**
Not quite the dream sequence we ended up with, is it?

Thankfully, I think the dream scene we shot and edited mutated into something much better than what was originally suggested by the screenplay. Intellectually, there's something very interesting about hearing those trapped, tortured voices screaming for release from beyond the grave. But let's face it; more than likely, it would not have worked and just turned out laughable, which would have been disastrous.

As a scene in a novel, it would have been much more effective, but as something on-screen in a low-budget production like this there was just no way to do it right.

As it is, I think we took the best of what's here – Susan walking around with her gun, screaming and then fellating the weapon – and then added our other lovely Angel to accompany Susan through her dream (nightmare?) like Virgil guided Dante in The Divine Comedy.

Although obviously, that was not the way this was originally written. So what happened?

In the midst of production, my friend (credited in the movie as Kamal DuPree) was very sad that I wasn't able to find a role for her in the movie as she really wanted to be part of the camaraderie of the production. I, in turn, felt bad leaving her out of project, but it was so late in the game that we had already shot almost everything we needed at that point.

And that's when it occurred to me that maybe what I could do was add another Angel into the mix. After all, if you're going to do something like that once in your movie, why not twice? Heck, thrice even by the time the climactic sex scene rolls around (but more on that later).

When I offered her the part she was intrigued, but she insisted on not doing full-frontal nudity for reasons I never quite understood, but I was fine with it. In the end, it didn't matter as it was easier to shoot the scene from the waist up as I was the cameraperson and crew for this shoot and working with the wings was never easy. In fact, her footage was shot with a Hi-8mm video camcorder, a crappy little format that was notorious for having dropouts as the tape it got recorded on was so damn thin. You can see a few dropouts in the movie as there was no way I could edit my way out of them in some shots.

## 24

Ext. Graveyard - Day

The camera pans from one grave to another, each with it's own
voice - the long dead occupants struggling to get out.

Screams, cries of help, and prayers of forgiveness flood the
soundtrack.

From out of nowhere, Susan appears with a gun in her hand, walking
through the rows of graves.  She stops and listens.

Susan covers her ears and screams to stop the noise, but it does
not go away.

Susan opens fire in all directions with an infinite supply of
bullets.  The voices grow louder, encouraging her; begging for
her help.

She falls to her knees, her spirit broken, and places the gun in
her mouth.  Slowly, longingly, she fellates the gun - her finger
tight on the trigger.

There is the sound of a gunshot on the soundtrack.

Int. Bedroom Night

Mary turns her attention away from Susan and back towards the
window.

                    Mary
          What the hell was that?

There is the sound of another gunshot.  And another.  Screams and
commotion and more gunfire are heard on the soundtrack.

Mary walks over to where Susan is struggling in her sleep.

                    Mary
          Susan...wake up.

Susan groans and rolls over, revealing a sweat stained pillow and
the extent of her pained nightmare.

Mary reaches out to Susan, touching her shoulder to wake her.

Susan awakens with a screech and tears the gun out of her breast
holster, jamming it into Mary's face.

Susan, still not fully awake, pulls the trigger three times,
spraying Mary's face all over the room.

Susan finally wakes up and realizes what she has done.  Mary is
lying on the floor panting through what is left of her head.

**SHATTER DEAD Screenplay Annotations**

**Page 25:**

If you know the movie well enough, you'll notice that what is conspicuous by its absence on this page are the cutaways to the home invaders who come crashing into the apartment and start firing away at all the characters we met when Susan first arrived. Also, the loud declarations of Dale Customer, Lord of the New World Order, are also missing – which makes this whole page feel quite rushed for the amount of stuff that is happening.

As with my friend Kamal, I had a few other acquaintances I wanted to work into the movie just to keep things entertaining, so I added Dale's monologue into the mix as it also gave us some make-up and pyrotechnic effects to keep Arthur happy. In fact, the version of the Manifesto of The New World Order that he reads on-screen in the scene is the handwritten screed I came up with the night before shooting, so I never had a chance to type it up. He reads it out loud, tosses it to the floor and I no longer have a reference copy of it in the archives. Ahhh, the ephemeral nature of low-budget moviemaking.

I'd also like to mention that the issuing of "eternal handicaps" as a phrase in that Manifesto was a winking reference to a great Kurt Vonnegut short story entitled Harrison Bergeron and available in his collection of short stories, Welcome to the Monkey House. It's well-worth the read if you're not familiar with it.

Cutting back and forth between these two violent scenes makes for probably the most exciting section of the movie (if anything in the movie can be said to be 'exciting'), and I'm especially pleased with how it has all come together in the most recent re-edit. It is so much tighter in the cutting than what I was able to achieve nearly 30 years ago with analog editing techniques that were not frame accurate due to the system I was working on.

                         Susan
               Jeezus fucking Christ...

Mary is sobbing loudly through what is left of her mouth.

                          Mary
               Oh no...Oh no...

                         Susan
               I'm sorry.

Susan reloads her gun and closes her shirt as the sounds of a
skirmish continue outside.  She rolls out of the bed and onto
the floor next to Mary.

                         Susan
               What the hell is going on out there?

                          Mary
               I must be dreaming.  Please, tell me
               this is a dream...

Susan snaps her fingers in Mary's "face".

                         Susan
               Hello?  Hello?

                          Mary
               What's gonna' happen to me?  This
               is just the beginning of forever.

                         Susan
               Fucking useless.

Susan begins to rise, but Mary rolls over and grabs her.

                          Mary
               Oh no!  And where do you think you're
               going, Susan?

They struggle on the ground, rolling all over each other.

Susan ends up on top of Mary and bashes her in the head repeatedly
mashing her face and brains into a chunky puree'.

Mary continues to writhe, although less enthusiastically.

                          Mary
               Sorry, but I'm not up there.  It's
               not the brain, but the soul.  How do
               you kill the soul?

**Page 26:**

You can see that by the time we reach the bottom of this page, we're about to go down a rabbit hole of numerous changes that were made for budgetary and performer availability reasons – many of which, in the end, were for the better and overall make the movie leaner and meaner this late in the game.

As the screenplay clearly shows, the person on the other side of the door yelling wasn't the character Jack, but once we saw how strapped we were for actors this late in the game, it made sense to use him here. Plus, John Weiner was a great performer and a blast to work with (no pun intended).

I admit that the one thing I miss not shooting here is Susan kicking the door open that leads into a bit of physical comedy meant to lighten things up a little bit, but it really wasn't necessary once we introduced the home invaders – who brought with them their own unique and very dark brand of humor.

Still, I do miss the dialogue exchange at the top of the next page...

## 26

There is a loud knock at the door, and the sound of the door-knob being forced.

> V.O.
> Hey!  What the hell's going on in
> there?  Are you alright?

Susan rolls Mary over onto her face and sits on her to hold her still.  She pulls a shirt off the bed and uses it to tie Mary's hands behind her back.  Mary realizes what is happening and begins to fight back more fiercely.

> Mary
> I'll get you for this.  God, the ways
> that I'll find to make you suffer.

> Susan
> Shut up!  I'm trying to think.

From behind the door comes the booming voice of the man trying to force the door open.

> V.O.
> Open up in there, damn it!

> Mary
> Yeah!  Help!  She's gone mad!!

Susan grabs Mary by her hair and slams her face into the floor a few times.  Mary becomes very quiet.

> Susan
> Don't fuck with me, dead bitch.

A scream pierces the air.  It comes from the male voice on the other side of the door.

A shotgun blast tears through the door, spraying blood everywhere.

Silence.  Susan and Mary freeze in mid exchange.

Susan jumps off Mary and scrunches herself into a corner, her gun pointed at the door of the bedroom.  She fires a warning shot at the door and hears the sound of voices and footsteps scattering.

Susan rises cautiously and moves towards the door - she kicks it open, smashing it into the face of the person on the other side who got shot.  The door bounces back off of his head.

**SHATTER DEAD Screenplay Annotations**

**Page 27:**
This entire bit was removed once we had a home invasion going on to fill in the violent blank that this sequence once provided; it worked better the way we ended up doing it instead. Susan beating up this guy with a pipe would have squelched any sympathy she might have built up from the audience at this point, and for the final third of this movie I need the viewer to emotionally connect with her no matter how crazy things get (and they do get a little bit crazy, don't they?).

Also, this was a needlessly complicated set-up that I'm sure was written to give Arthur some more stunt work and make-up footage for his reel. I think at this point, he had more than enough to work with as our backyard movie budget was already stretched way beyond where it was supposed to end up.

Finally, this bit doesn't feel like an organic part of the Susan character that has already been established. Feels more like some kind of outtake from a $1.98 James Bond rip-off. At this point in the story, we don't need distractions like these.

Very much worth noting here is the absence of the scene of Grandma giving birth to her technically unborn baby. It's a scene I'm very happy with, but it came about after the first-draft writing process was complete. I find it hard to believe that it wasn't part of the story initially, but as this script was written so quickly everything was in a state of flux from the original inception until the time we got on-set to do the shooting. I wish I could remember where the baby birth idea originated. Just a drunken inspiration one lonely evening or something that came up as a plot point in discussion with my collaborators? Whatever the source of origin, it was through everybody's tireless efforts and talents that it came to fruition at all, and it's a testament to team spirit that such things can happen at any moment in a production when everybody is committed to helping out on a project.

## 27

> **Dead Person**
> Ouch!  Dammit that's enough already!

Susan is startled and aims her gun at what is left of his face.

> **Dead Person**
> Whaddya', kidding?

Susan steps over him and turns to walk the hallway to the living room, the front door, and freedom.

Int. Hallway - Night

Susan cautiously slow steps her way down the hallway, her gun raised and pointing into the camera, the trigger cocked.

As she walks away from him, the Dead Person yells his free advice to her in broken, arhytmic sentences to throw her off balance.

> **Dead Person**
> Don't be an idiot, just get out of
> here.  They ran away, you fool.  Now
> hurry up and get out of here.  You
> know, all that dramatic bullshit and
> bravado is gonna' get you killed.

Susan is about to round the corner to the living room when a lead pipe comes flying out of nowhere and misses her - she rolls across the floor, spins around and fires.

She hits her potential attacker squarely in the chest, throwing him back over the couch.

Int. Living Room - Night

Susan, not one to waste bullets, grabs the pipe off the floor and swipes the wounded attacker into submission with it

Susan turns and faces the Dead Person at the other end of the hall, her face filled with betrayal and rage.

> **Dead Person**
> Damn.  Lousy fucking bitch.

Susan suddenly realizes the full trap that was being set for her. She raises her gun, aims, and fires - hitting the Dead Person in the head.

The Dead Person is thrown back flat on the floor; lying there, he laughs to himself.

Susan, horrified beyond words, exits.

## SHATTER DEAD Screenplay Annotations

**Page 28:**

Now the script indicates we're at a motel. Hotel? Motel? Trailer park? My apartment? Who the fuck knows anymore? Looking back on details like these, I kind of admire the fact that I didn't waste any time going back to fix inconsequential details like these with Wite Out or even retyping whole pages to unify these errors. Once the shoot was in motion, we just went with it and took things as they came. If this were a real production or if I thought I had to submit the screenplay to someone else to produce, all of this would have been taken care of. I certainly never thought anyone besides those few of us working on the movie would ever see this shooting draft of the script, so here you have it, warts and all.

That all being said, here is one instance where I feel that the script is superior to the final product. I much prefer that Susan would have bumped into The Preacher Man amidst all sorts of violent turmoil right outside the House of the Dead she had been staying in. The way it is now in the movie – with Susan approaching The Preacher Man on a swing set and then getting attacked by one of his messed-up minions is a poor substitute for what was originally written. Also, the chase through the woods nonsense in the movie is the height of we-need-to-shoot-something-NOW desperation that hit us once or twice during production. I'm sorry things did not turn out as planned on page 28.

Yes, the chase through the woods does appear on page 29, but in hindsight the two scenes could have easily been combined into a single, far more effective scene taking place during the orgy of violence. I guess that's something I can work out for the hundred-million dollar remake (hah!).

## 28

Ext. Motel Grounds - Day

Susan runs through a montage of turmoil and violent "death";
people being shot and stabbed and mutilated in the most horrifying ways as their attackers cry out to god with pleasure.

Susan rounds a corner and comes face to face with the violence of
the Preacher Man.  She is stunned and recognizes him immediately
as the leader of the group of Dead People that stole her car.

She steadies her gun sights on him.

                    Susan
          Where's my car?


                    Preacher Man
          Hey, who's side are you on?

Susan cocks the trigger of her gun and fires a "no bullshit" look.


                    Susan
          I'm packin' enough ballistics here to
          make you look airy as a fly swatter,
          holy man.  Now where the fuck is my car?

                    Preacher Man
          That's not fair!

                    Susan
          Life's not fair.

                    Preacher Man
          Neither is death.

                    Susan
          Sorry to hear that.

Susan pulls the trigger and slams a bullet through one of the
Preacher Man's upraised hands.  The Preacher Man just looks
stunned at the remains of his hand.

From out of nowhere, a crazed Groupie jumps on Susan from behind
and knocks her to the ground.

The Preacher Man turns to speak to them as they struggle on the
ground for control of the gun.

                    Preacher Man
          Welcome to the last days of the old
          generation, cunt.  Welcome to the
          beginning of the redemption.

# SHATTER DEAD Screenplay Annotations

**Page 29:**

I miss the gun play that gives The Preacher Man one Helluva' good reason to run away as fast as he can. I'm sure once on location we realized that firing weapons and also having to do the squib effects on a children's playground without permission was probably a bad idea. Plus both of those things cost money in addition to having the time to do it properly. Time and money are equal enemies in the low-budget arena.

I also miss The Preacher Man fumbling with the keys in the car door. When we shot the confrontation between him and Susan we were running late in the day and losing the last remnants of sunlight, so if we didn't get the absolute bare minimum of usable footage in a very short amount of time we were fucked, as there was no way that I could afford to bring people back to Middletown again for another day of shooting. This might well have been one of the most rushed scenes I've ever had to shoot.

It's surprising how we nailed almost all of the dialogue the last couple of pages. Robert has most of it in his role, but in this instance we didn't cut any of Stark's lines. At this point, it seemed like a good idea to keep the antagonism between them alive with words, especially as The Preacher Man is as close as we come to having a full-blown villain in the piece. I mean, besides god.

## 29

The Groupie is on top os Susan now, and almost has her pinned down on the ground.

> ### Preacher Man
> Tell me; what did you have in your past that was so special that you feel the need to hold onto it this tightly?  Relax for just a moment and awaken.  Join us.

The Preacher Man turns and walks away as Susan and the Groupie continue their struggle.

> ### Preacher Man
> I have important work to do, and many more souls to shave...

Susan steadies her leg firmly and kicks the Groupie off of herself. She rises quickly and kicks him back down to the ground.

Susan picks up her gun off the ground and quickly re-loads it. She fires a shot into each of the Groupie's legs to slow him down.

Susan turns and chases down the path where the Preacher Man had just fled.

Int. Woods - Day

The Preacher Man hears a loud noise and spins around to look; he sees Susan charging towards him, weaponry flying.

The Preacher Man smiles and starts running.

Chase Montage:

Susan pursues the Preacher Man through various thickets and goat paths until finally they reach a hedge fence; they both jump over it, and find themselves in the middle of the -

Parking Lot - Day

The lot is deserted except for a few scattered cars - one of which is Susan's.

The Preacher Man reaches her car first and struggles with the key in the door.  Susan reaches him just as he gets the door open; she places the gun next to his head and he freezes.

> ### Preacher Man
> That's a little redundant in this day and age, don't you think?  I mean really; the times they are a
>
> changin'!

**Page 30:**
As if it wasn't obvious enough already, at the bottom of the page I spell it all out by giving Susan a wooden-nickel version of a Clint Eastwood speech. Can you believe the shit I was trying to pull? Thankfully, we didn't even try shooting this bit of dialogue, because nobody on Earth with even a thousand years of thespian training would have been able to make anything worthwhile out of it. Thank goodness for small things every now and then.

There are a few other little trims along the way here, of course, but nothing I'm sorry to see missing. Well, except for The Preacher Man's half-hand raised in the air. I wish we had been able to afford to do that as it would have been funny.

## 30

>                    Susan
>          I'd hate to ruin my last clean shirt
>          with the back of your head.

>                    Preacher Man
>          What's your name, lady?

>                    Susan
>          Susan.

>                    Preacher Man
>          Don't try to stop me, Susan.  It's
>          god's decision that I do what I'm
>          doing.  No earthly force - not you,
>          not anyone, has the right to stop me.

Susan's eyes narrow to demanding slits - with one hand waving
the gun in the Preacher Man's face, she reaches the other hand
into her pocket and pulls out her tiny mirror; she raises it up
to under the Preacher Man's nose.

>                    Preacher Man
>          What on god's good earth are you doing,
>          Susan?  Fixing your make-up?

Susan looks at herself in the mirror, making faces.

>                    Susan
>          Fixing my ethics.  My morality.

>                    Preacher Man
>          How very strange.  I think I'm startin
>          to like you, Susan.

As the Preacher Man speaks, he leaves no vapor on the mirror.

>                    Susan
>          Wow.  No breath.  Jeezus, you're good.

>                    Preacher Man
>          Good?  Jesus was the best!

>                    Susan
>          It's a question that's been bothering me
>          for a while - you stole my car, and now
>          you continue to keep me from taking back
>          what is rightfully mine.  And I'w wonder-
>          ing now; would I be killing someone who's
>          still alive, or just slowing you down?

The Preacher Man smiles and raises his 1 1/2 hands slowly into
the thick air.

## SHATTER DEAD Screenplay Annotations

**Page 31:**

Ahhh, yes; good old page 31. How I do not miss this brief monologue one damn bit.

And yes, we did shoot it, but under such rushed conditions that it was unusable. Not that it would have been usable under even the best of circumstances.

This is the only bit of dialogue that I technically did not write. Arthur had come up with this gag and presented it to me and asked me to put it into the script, and as Arthur was being so helpful with all of the other amazing stuff he was doing for zero money, I did my best to have this in here for his sake.

In addition to the make-up and stunt work, Arthur was also an excellent writer and a very funny comedic performer. He belonged to a writing and performing quintet called The Lunatic Fringe (along with one of our music composers, Steve Rajkumar) that was a modern multi-media iteration inspired by folks like Monty Python, Spike Jones, etc., and they were legit funny.

At the time, I was fine with this piece and felt bad that we were not able to shoot it to satisfaction and use it. I felt a bit like I had let Arthur down on this. But thankfully he had so much other input into the movie that in the end, I think he was okay with this bit being excised, especially in the context of what this scene eventually evolved into.

All these years later, looking back upon this particular page, in retrospect I am so happy this did not make the final cut, but I'm happy to see it preserved here nonetheless. Such is the siren call of Nostalgia that draws us smilingly towards the sharpest rocks in a raging storm.

                    Preacher Man
          You wanna' know how I died?

                       Susan
          Suicide, right?

                    Preacher Man
          Of course not, Susan.  That's illegal.
          I died in the electric chair.  In
          prison, of course.  Everything you've
          heard about the food is true, by the
          way.

                       Susan
          What for?

                    Preacher Man
          It was a case of mistaken identity,
          actually.  The judge and a jury of
          12 of my peers mistook me for a man
          who had killed his lovely wife; with
          a shovel, and then dragged her limp
          body into the bathtub and then care-
          fully dismembered her with a hacksaw
          into pieces so small that the very
          deed could be hidden from the eyes of
          god and man.  But they were wrong.

                       Susan
          You didn't do it?

                    Preacher Man
          Oh yeah, I did all that - but I wasn't
          trying to hide anything.  I was trying
          to make soup.  You know you look just
          like her...

The Preacher Man chuckles and licks the back of Susan's out-
stretched mirror hand.

Susan pulls the trigger of the gun she has been holding in her
other hand, shattering the mirror she has been holding all this
time under the Preacher Man's nose.

The remains of the Preacher Man and the mirror fall to the ground
as Susan's car roars out of the parking lot.

Driving Montage - Daytime

Down country roads to city streets, finally parking in front of
a tall apartment building.  Susan pops open her trunk and retrieves
her valuable grocery items.

## SHATTER DEAD Screenplay Annotations

**Page 32:**

Not sure what prompted me to hand write and circle the word "Exhausted!!" at the top of this particular page. Was that an acting note to Stark or was it me berating myself during a particularly exhausting day of shooting? Well if I don't remember, nobody else will.

The building we ended up shooting in did not have an elevator, so we nixed that bit at the top of the page. Isn't it obvious from the difference in my scratch-out code? X's and straight lines for the stuff we shot and obscuring wiggly lines for the stuff that was completely cut out. I believe that's still the standard taught in film schools around the world to this day, right?

I would have loved to have the stairs we did shoot on covered with supine bodies watching Susan step over them, if nothing else as a kind of visual tribute to some of the nightmarishly overpopulated imagery in Richard Fleischer's classic, SOYLENT GREEN (which is what I'm pretty sure I was referencing when I wrote this bit — the movie, coincidentally, takes place in 2022...!).

Once again, Susan's brief nonsense dialogue got snipped. Who really says shit like "are you okay, dear?" out loud? "Oh god no..." comes in as a close second to lousy writing like that.

## 32

Exhausted!!

Cut

Int. Apartment Building - Hallway

Susan presses for the elevator, waits, and nothing happens. She puts her ear to the elevator door and hears nothing. She sighs and walks towards the stairs.

Int. Stairwell

It is dark, but bodies are visible sleeping all over the place. Susan carefully steps over everyone as she goes up the stairs; she is not shocked by this procedure - she is used to it.

Int. Hallway

Susan steps over the bodies in the hallway until she reaches her own apartment door.

She puts down the grocery bag and searches her pockets for her keys when she suddenly realizes that the door is slightly ajar-she just pushes it and it opens.

Int. Studio Apartment

Susan enters the apartment slowly, her anxiety increasing with each step.

Inside, there is evidence of a struggle occuring - furniture overturned, some broken dishware, etc. The phone is lying on the floor, the reciever off the hook. Artwork sits undisturbed on various easels and drawing tables.

On the floor is a bloody knife.

                    Susan
          Dan.  Dan.  Are you okay, dear?

There is no answer. She moves in a daze through the center of the apartment to the bathroom.

Int. Bathroom

The door is closed and the light is off. Susan creeps the door open and turns on the light.

The bathtub is half-filled with blood.

Susan wilts back aghast and makes her way towards the bedroom.

                    Susan
          Oh god, no...

## SHATTER DEAD Screenplay Annotations

**Page 33:**
Daniel did a great job remembering his lines to the letter on these pages, and I certainly gave him a mouthful of Greek salad to memorize with this shit.

"Oh please ,no" – again, who says shit like this out loud? Thank goodness I didn't get my writer's card revoked after trying to cram garbage like that into some poor actor's mouth. Thank goodness I knew to cut out that kind of crap by the time we were on-set. I think I cried out on-set more than once that whoever wrote this shit should be fired. If nothing else, I vowed to never again work with anyone who wrote dialogue that bad. Unfortunately, further collaborations ensued.

We shot this scene in Dan's actual bedroom and all of the other scenes that were supposed to be their shared apartment was in fact his apartment at the time. There is no better way to secure a performer than to shoot them where they live. They will hate you, but you will get the footage that you need and time forgives most sins. The sins that count, anyway.

## 33

Int. Bedroom

Susan enters and finds Dan sitting on the edge of the bed in
his bathrobe, his back to her and his head in his hands.  There
are blood stained bandages wrapped around his wrists and his
lower arms.


                    Susan
          Dan...?


                    Dan
          Don't look at me, Susan.  Something
          bad happened here while you were
          away.  I'm sorry.  I'm so sorry.


                    Susan
          Oh please, no.  What happened?


                    Dan
          You've been to the bathroom.  You
          know.  That's me in the bathtub.
          It was me.


                    Susan
          How?


                    Dan
          Why don't you sit down.


Susan sits in the place where she has been standing; in the
bedroom doorway.


                    Susan
          Who did this to you?


                    Dan
          The phone just wouldn't stop ringing,
          you know?  When my mom died of cancer
          all those years ago, I thought that
          was it; I was rid of that bitch for
          good.  Ring!  Ring!  Hello son.  Hi mom.


                    Susan
          Dan, that's impossible.  You're mother
          was cremated.  What're you saying?


                    Dan
          My youngest sister was killed in a car
          accident.  Her child safety seat broke
          free of the seatbelt when we got rear
          ended by a silver Cadillac.  Ring!  Ring!
          Where the hell did she ever learn to use
          the damn phone?  That's insane.

# SHATTER DEAD Screenplay Annotations

**Page 34:**
Judging from the time code numbers I scribbled next to the shot of Susan at the top of the page, this must be the copy of the script I had with me in the editing room while I was putting the assembly together. I remember having a copy next to during the process as I would use it as the only guide I had to make everything fit into place.

Post-production was kind of nutty for this project. It was shot on Betacam-SP, which was at the time a very high-end analog format that network TV news was using. That footage was transferred over to Hi-8mm videotapes with a visible time code window burned into it, so once I had an edit put together from that consumer format I would be able to go back to the original Betacam tapes and match the code numbers to reassemble the edit from the lower format into the professional format.

(For viewing purposes before even beginning any editing at all, I transferred those Hi-8mm tapes to VHS so I could watch everything and make notes on my home VHS deck)

Now here's where it gets tricky and interesting. After making extensive notes based on my VHS viewings, I sat down with a two-in-one deck Hi-8mm editing system that I rented and banged out the entire edit over the course of two or three weekends as that's all I could afford. And when I tell you I was editing all weekend on those days, I'm talking about doing 18 hour days in order to make sure I didn't have to rent that machine for a fourth weekend that I could not afford.

That Hi-8mm system was frame accurate when it came to editing, so whatever I saw was what I was getting, which was pretty damn sweet. It took me back to film school days where, with film, whatever edit you made WAS the edit. Frame accurate video editing systems outside of the big professional level outside of high-end production studios were not the norm back in the early 1990's.

Once I had my frame accurate Hi-8mm edit, I wrote down every single cut – in point, out point, actual duration in seconds and frames, and a brief description of the shot – into a notebook, and that became my editing bible for the finished Betacam edit.

One tiny catch, though. The Betacam editing system, unlike the Hi-8mm one, was not frame accurate.

Why not? It's just the way things were back then and it's all I could afford to work with – which was still a pretty damn high-end editing system and not to be scoffed at. But the Betacam edits had a plus-or-minus of about four frames of accuracy in either direction (give or take; sometimes only two frames and sometimes as much as six frames, so it was never consistent).

I am not complaining, as I was lucky to have access at all to any of this equipment, especially at the reduced prices at which I was renting everything (thanks again, Mr. Lui!). These are simply the facts of the matter, and at the time I had to work around these technical limitations.

Susan nods her head to herself in agreement. 07:05:12

                          Dan
               And it just kept ringing - everytime
               I answer a newly forgotten friend, a
               relative I've never even met or heard
               of.  So I take the phone off the hook-
               but it still kept on ringing.  I mean,
               what the hell is that?!  What was I
               supposed to do?  And where were you?

Susan just sits there quietly, looking paler with each word he
speaks.

Dan gets up from the bed and steps towards her while at the
same time keeping his face out of her line of sight.  He steps
over her and out the door, heading towards the kitchen.

Susan is totally apathetic - she turns her head stiffly and
watches him.

Int. Kitchen

                          Dan
               I'm sorry about the mess.  I got
               really upset.

                          Susan
               Is there something wrong with your face?

Dan laughs lightly without turning.  He opens up the refridgerator
and grabs a half-empty container of milk from it.

                          Dan
               I saved the rest of this for you.

                          Susan
               Thanks.

Dan puts the container down on the counter top and pulls a clean
glass out of the dish drainer.

                          Dan
               Nothing, actually.  There's nothing
               wrong with my face.  Or is there?

They both chuckle with various degrees of comfort.

                          Susan
               It's always been fine by me.  Very fine.

## 34

# SHATTER DEAD Screenplay Annotations

**Page 35:**

There's a single line of dialogue scratched out at the bottom of the page and for the life of me I have no recollection of what it was and no matter how I hold the page up to the light I cannot figure out what it is. Jeezus, whatever that line was I cannot imagine how much I must have really hated it to obliterate it so entirely from existence.

Surprisingly, I did not write in a stage direction for the snap-zoom into Dan's face that we shot for this scene. I love snap-zooms. I guess it's possible we came up with the shot on-set as it's no crazier than some of the other stuff we made up on the spot during this production.

Also, funny to see how I had to handwrite in the word "Bedroom" as I was probably typing this up with such ferocity that I somehow lost track of keeping up with locations while in the midst of the writing process. I can get that way when I'm in the moment and plunging forward during a 'creative' session.

                              Dan
                    You're as sweet as ever, lover.

As Dan is talking to her, we see Dan's hands in close-up opening up some capsules and emptying them into her glass as quietly
and as carefully as possible.  He finishes up and slowly turns
around to face Susan.

                              Dan
                    There.  You see?  No scars to hide.
                    Only shame.

He picks up the glass off the counter and starts walking towards
her.
          Between

Dan crouches down before Susan, dangling the glass of milk from
his fingers invitingly.  She just looks at him blankly.  Dan
smiles back at her warmly.

                              Dan
                    Here, sweet.  Drink up.

Susan takes the glass from his hand.

                              Susan
                    When I look at you, I can tell.
                    You're dead.

Dan turns his head away self-conciously.

                              Dan
                    It's in the eyes, isn't it?  My face
                    feels like it's floating a foot in
                    front of my head and the space in-between
                    is filled with wet concrete.  Making a
                    face is like placing a long-distance tele-
                    phone call.

Susan touches the bandages around his wrists, examining them
tenderly.

                              Dan
                    The wounds aren't healing.  I have
                    two slits that flap open everytime
                    I make a fist.  Like angry mouths
                    screaming in pain.

                              Susan
                    Does it hurt?

                              Dan
                    It hurts inside, but not outside.  Not
                    for real.

# SHATTER DEAD Screenplay Annotations

**Page 36:**
Once again I had to indicate a failed location marker at the top of the page, which indicates to me that I probably wrote this batch of pages in some kind of 'automatic writing' typing frenzy.

Susan's "The milk went bad..." line eventually became "This milk tastes sour" on the day of shooting. I can tell that my very literal original line here was meant to be some kind of placeholder until something better could be thought up. I write things like that on occasion in order to keep the creative flow going without interruption if I hit a speed bump along the way while typing furiously.

Lemme see.... Anything else on this page worth commenting about before moving on.....?

Oh, right. The gun fuck.

Yep, this is the red letter page that has caused the most censorship troubles for my little movie.

As you can see, it's written in a relatively genteel manner considering what is being described. In fact, except for Susan's deleted line at the bottom of the page (we never shot it), the word 'fuck' is nowhere in sight in the descriptive text.

Well look at me, trying to keep things classy on the page.

I distinctly remember writing this scene. I was sitting on the floor in the living room (I always prefer sitting on the floor while doing creative work whenever possible) with my electric Smith-Corona typewriter chug-chug-chugging away (it was pretty loud). As usual, I had music on in the background as I always work with music and it was helpful to drown out the considerable typewriter noise.

Stark was in the next room (the kitchen) pouring herself something to drink. We were living together at the time.

I believe I had just finished writing Susan's line, "We'll find a way", and stopped to think for a moment. I wasn't 100% sure what exactly was going to happen next.

I called out to Stark: "Hey hon, would you be okay with fucking a gun in the movie?"

A few moments later, Stark appeared in the doorway between the two rooms, cradling her drink in the palms of her hands contemplatively. I could see she was giving the question serious thought.

"is it important to the story?", she asked.

Now it was my turn to consider a good question, but it didn't take me long to reply.

"If I didn't think it was important, I wouldn't ask."

Stark took a sip of her drink.

"Okay", she replied, and then went back into the kitchen.

I went back to animatedly typing almost instantly. Sometimes we worked really well together.

## 36

I.A. Bedroom

Dan pauses and chews tensely at his lower lip.

                    Dan
          Jeezus, you look beautiful.  Drink up.

Susan sighs and drains the glass of milk.  A strange look passes
over her face.  She puts down the glass and coughs.

                    Susan
          The milk went bad.  Yuck.

Dan leans into Susan, nuzzling at her neck and ear.  Susan
responds, embracing him and pulling him into herself.

They kiss passionately.  Dan hesitates a moment.  They stop.

                    Susan
          What's the matter?  I miss you.

                    Dan
          I can't.  I can't do it.  No blood.
          Can't get hard without blood.

                    Susan
          But I love you.  We'll find a way.

Susan undoes the belt that holds Dan's robe closed, exposing
his naked body beneath.  Susan bunches up the belt and slides
a gun from out of her belt holster.  She motions to Dan to
stand up.

Dan stands up and Susan rubs her nose against his inner thigh;
there is no response from his penis.

Susan threads the rope through the gun's trigger hole and ties
the apparatus around Dan's waist.  Next to his own limp penis
now hangs a cold, hard gun.

Susan now rises.  She kisses Dan and rubs against him.  She
gentley leads him by the hand into the bedroom.

Next to the bed, Susan slowly undresses for Dan's pleasure.
She is naked now, and pulls Dan towards her eager body.

She kisses him deeply and carresses the gun between his legs.
She pulls Dan and the gun closer to her, rubbing the gun's tip
against her moist pubic region.  Closer still, until the gun
enters her quivering frame.

                    Susan
          Fuck me.  Make me come.

**SHATTER DEAD Screenplay Annotations**

**Page 37:**
Another key character moment in the movie that does not exist in the screenplay is Susan's brief flashback to her blowing Mary's face off with her gun as she sees her blood-stained shirt in her bag and remembers how it got that way. I'm so glad I added that brief bit as it's a nice touch for her after the sex scene (that gun is good for both big deaths and 'little deaths', if you'll pardon my French) and that brief touch of violence is a reminder of what guns are usually used for in movies and – sadly – in real life.

No mention of our Angel during the written sex scene, either. I had fallen in love with the idea of our Angels being Old Testament ones that bring bad ideas and instruments of destruction to those they touch, so it just seemed natural to re-use the footage here and turn the gun fuck into a threesome. As if we weren't already cooking with enough spice with gun powder alone, the Angel always seems to show up with a gun that leads Susan to a passionate response.

I also changed Dan's killing method from sleeping pills to poison in the dialogue. Honestly not sure why, unless I thought sleeping pills would take longer than necessary for the scene to play out. Although where the heck did he find poison on such short notice? These are exactly the kind of things a writer tosses in and hopes goes by the audience as quickly as possible while the next thing happens so nobody stops and thinks about it for too long.

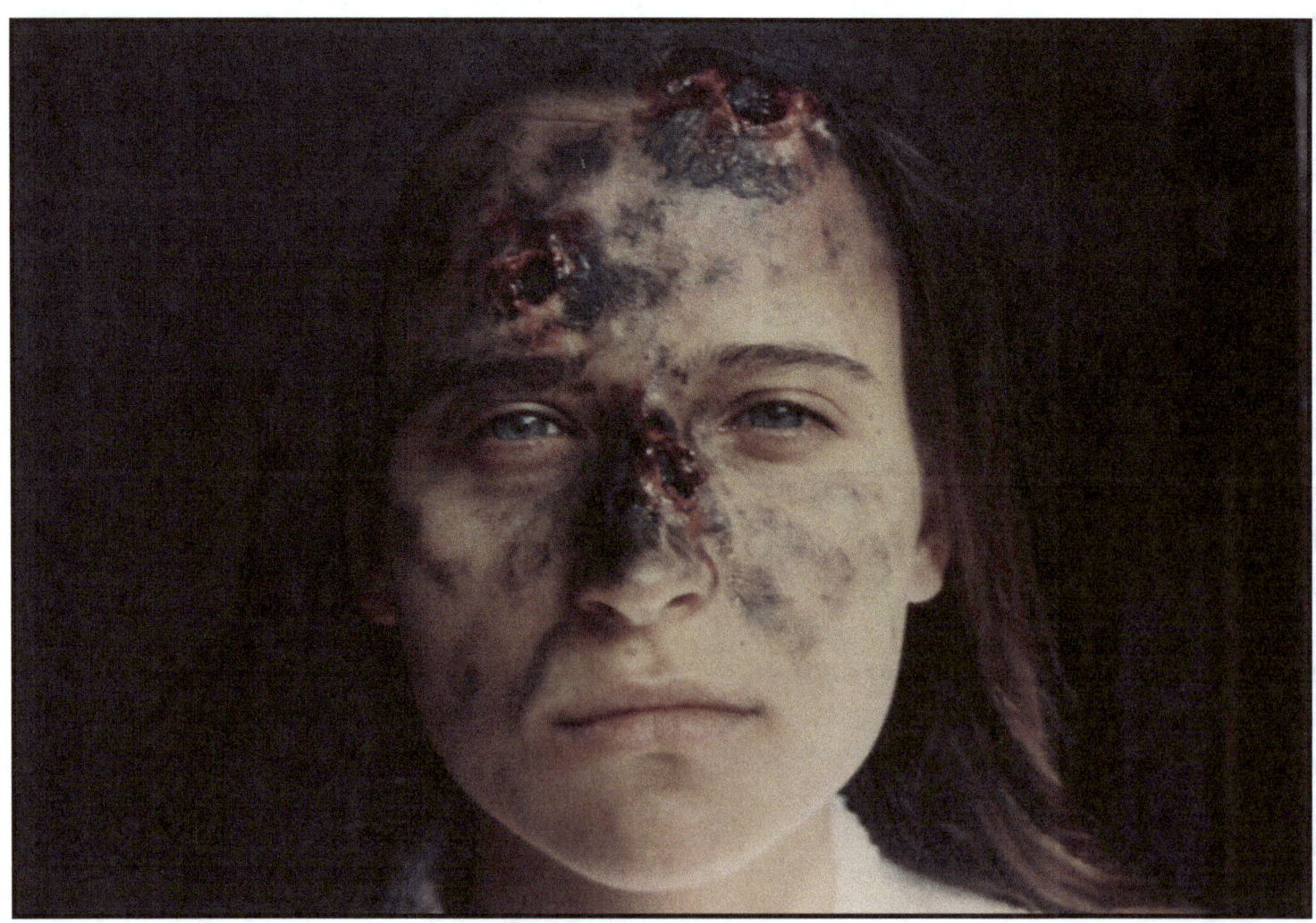

## 37

Susan's body is tight and dark with pleasure.  Dan's eyes are
wide with terror and a strange delight.

Susan brings a leg up behind Dan to start him pumping.  Dan
overcomes the strangeness of the moment and starts kneading
her ass and chewing at her neck.  They moan with delight.

Fade to black.

Int. Kitchen - Day

Dan is standing by the kitchen table watching Susan get dressed
in the bedroom.

                    Dan
          I'm sorry.  I feel like such an idiot.
          Sometimes you get really carried away
          with your emotions and make rash
          decisions.  Look at me.  What an ass-
          hole!  Look what I did to myself
          in a sane moment to escape from this
          insanity.

Susan wobbily enters the kitchen, rubbing at her stomach.

Dan displays his torn wrists to her.

                    Dan
          What an idiot!  My sin quite literally
          on my sleeve for eternity.  I mean,
          what was I thinking?  Things would be
          different for me?  That I've just been
          going, thank god, mad all this time and
          that this would end the madness?

Susan coughs loudly, painfully.

                    Susan
          I feel sick.

                    Dan
          Do you want to lie down?

                    Susan
          Not now, I want to hear you talk.

                    Dan
          Crazy.  Forever young, forever dumb.
          Why didn't I have the good sense to
          think of sleeping pills for myself?    Poison
          I guess I love you that much more
          than myself.

## SHATTER DEAD Screenplay Annotations

**Page 38:**

"Susan's head clunks against the bedroom door jamb" – what the fuck logistical error was that while I was writing this? Go figure. When we finally ended up blocking this scene for the shoot, we didn't have enough time to start figuring out new set-ups, so we just kept Susan in her seat until she bolted upright to run for the bathroom. These are the kind of simple things you don't think about while staining the page, but they are essential to figure out on-set once you're working under the tyranny of the ticking clock.

This long after the fact, I regret that we couldn't work in the two of them laughing together at the poison reveal. It was an odd detail, but I liked that they somehow found the whole thing funny from very different points of view. I'm always intrigued by dramatic situations in which two people want the same thing but for very different reasons, and that certainly applied here.

In the most recent re-edit of SHATTER DEAD, I lost Susan's "for who?" after she says "Poison". The line never quite worked and the loss of those two words makes the moment work better and improves the on-screen performance.

Note that, like The Preacher Man on page 28, Susan exclaims "that's not fair!" Having two very different characters say the exact same thing as they find themselves betrayed by the situation they find themselves in is exactly the kind of writerly conceit that people concoct scholarly essays on when talking about cinema. Apparently even I'm not immune to this kind of cheap attempt to impress people looking for this sort of thing. Please consider me guilty as charged.

## 38

Susan's head clunks against the bedroom door jamb.  A drunken
smile crosses her face.  She coughs and doubles over with pain;
clutching at her stomach, she sits down on the floor.

Suddenly she realizes what Dan has said; she is dreamy with pain.

                    Susan
          Poison
          Sleeping pills for who?


                    Dan
          For the woman I love.

Susan laughs.  Dan laughs.


                    Susan
          But that's not fair!


                    Dan
          I know.  But you'll thank me later.


                    Susan
          For killing me?


                    Dan
          I'm not killing you; you can't die.
          Death; what a silly word.  It doesn't
          mean anything anymore.  And now we're
          all equal because of it.  What I am
          isn't "dead" - what you're becoming now
          isn't "dead".  You're imagining an
          eternity of sleep, but what does that
          mean?  I've gone beyond living and
          I'm standing here talking to you.  I
          haven't died; I'm just folded a little
          differently.  And soon, so will you.


Susan reaches into her shirt with difficulty and extracts her
smallest gun.  She rises uncertainly, and waves her gun dizzily
at Dan.


                    Susan
          You're out of your fucking mind.

                    Dan
          Why?  You can't tell me you're ready
          to grow old and die and watch me stay
          young and healthy.  Who would be hurting
          who more in that situation?  Think I'll
          wanna' stick around and feed you through
          a straw and wipe away your shit?  Now we
          can be together as equals.

**Page 39:**
These exchanges between the two of them are probably Susan's most substantial amount of dialogue in the entire script. So of course, unbeknownst to us while shooting, there was a microphone malfunction and we recorded none of her dialogue during this scene. All of her lines needed to be dubbed later in my makeshift attempt at homemade ADR (Automatic Dialogue Replacement, which is what they used to call 'dubbing'), which also gave me the opportunity to re-record my own voice to be used in place of the Crash Test Dummy Zombie on page 1. In that case, it needed to be done because the sounds of the city traffic were too loud and the actor was no longer around to dub themselves by the time it needed to happen. It's never the best way to work, but once again, time and money, etc.

## 39

Susan is struggling to stand with the help of anything within reach as she makes her way towards Dan, her gun floating before herself like a guide.

                    Dan
          Come on.  I know you're not going
          to shoot me.  What's it gonna' do?
          You'll just end up messing me up.
          Can you live with that?  Are you
          really ready to take care of me
          forever?  I don't think so.

                    Susan
          You're right.

Susan makes her way past him and towards the bathroom.

Int. Bathroom

Susan kicks the door open and slaps on the lightswitch.  She falls to the floor and forces herself to vomit in the bathtub thick with Dan's blood.

Susan finishes vomiting and sits against the bathtub, facing the bathroom doorway.

Dan appears in the doorway, solemn.

                    Dan
          You will fall asleep eventually and
          fold, you know?

Susan smiles wanly and raises her gun.  She points it at Dan. He just shakes his head with disappointment.

                    Susan
          Doesn't bother you a bit, does it?

She slowly turns the gun and points it at her own head.  She watches an expression of horror creep across Dan's face.

                    Susan
          That's what I thought.  Not ready
          to spend eternity kissing a squashed
          tomato, are we?  You vain, frightened
          son of a bitch.

                    Dan
          Please, Susan.  Don't even think it...

                    Susan
          Get out of my sight now!

**SHATTER DEAD Screenplay Annotations**

**Page 40:**
Here is the only overt attempt at a suspense scene in the entire movie, and frankly it's a little bit ridiculous, isn't it? Basically we're watching a guy fill up a glass of water and move it along from the sink to Susan at the table. I'm sure when I was writing this, in my mind I was imagining Cary Grant bringing the glowing glass of milk up the stairs to poison Joan Fontaine in Alfred Hitchcock's classic SUSPICION. I'm certainly no Hitchcock, but I certainly did my best to 'milk' (hah!) as much tension as I could by prolonging this particular moment.

                         Dan
              Yes, Susan.  Whatever you say.

Dan quickly backs away into the kitchen.

Susan grabs the edge of the bathtub and rises.

Int. Kitchen

Susan floats into the room with her gun to her head.  She sits
down at the kitchen table and Dan watches nervously.

                         Dan
              Careful, babe.

                        Susan
              I can still feel it in my system.
              Pour me a glass of water so I can
              puke it out.  From the sink. I
              wanna' see that glass at all times.

Dan complies to her wishes as slowly as possible.

                        Susan
              Come on!  Hurry!

Dan's pace does not change.  He slowly walks the glass over to
her, not spilling a single drop.

                        Susan
              Okay.  Put it down on the table.

Dan puts it down on the table.

                        Susan
              Now step back.

Dan moves away from her as slow as possible.

Susan can't wait.  She grabs the glass and begins to wildly
chug it all down.

As she kicks her head back for the final precious drops, Dan leaps
at her and knocks the gun out of her hand.

Dan wrestles her to the ground and pins her down with his body.

                         Dan
              Come on, baby.  Please go to sleep.

## SHATTER DEAD Screenplay Annotations

**Page 41:**

The compromise made on this page is that we jettisoned the whole big fight scene and simply had Susan shoot Dan in the head so he would fall out the window from that. There were a few reasons for that change.

First and foremost: we didn't want to fuck up Dan's apartment. Slamming against walls, rolling around on the floor and then faux fighting next to an open window with a considerable fall below it seemed like a bad idea.

And yet once again, we were competing with time and had to try and get as much footage as possible in the shortest amount of time. Trying to choreograph a full-scale fight scene between two people were not specifically trained to do stunts is a time killer and trying to do it halfassed is just dangerous.

Besides, as is well known in the dramatic arts, when you introduce a gun in act one, you need to use it in act three – although we certainly have made enough use of guns for every conceivable thing up until now, haven't we?

So there you have it. We saved time in the end and got one last chance to fire off some blanks, which is always a lot of fun.

Note that as written, unlike in the movie, Susan does not collapse to the floor after shooting Dan in the head. In fact, in this version Susan stands at the window and watches the approach of the broken Preacher Man and all that transpires between him, his minions and their resurrection of Dan.

Dan's line while lying on the ground is completely different in the movie. The one we ended up using was an adlib that he came up with on-set that made all of us laugh so hard we couldn't not use it ("I should have shot her when I had the chance…"). His line was much funnier than the generic "… let me die…" that I wrote and it provides a much-needed laugh before we descend into the dark night of the soul that climaxes this story.

## 41

Susan's breathing is labored — she is too tired to fight back.
She begins to relax.  Dan leans close to her and sings a
lullaby softly in her ear.

                    Dan
          Now I lay me down to sleep, I pray
          the lord my soul to keep.  But if
          I should fold before I wake, I pray
          the lord my soul to take,  Please?

Susan's breathing has almost stopped.  She emits a low feral
growl and with a sudden burst of energy kicks Dan off of herself.  They both roll clumsily and rise.

                    Dan
          You were almost here, babe.

Susan lashes out and punches Dan in the face.

                    Dan
          Careful, don't hurt yourself.

She turns and charges towards the bathroom.

Dan leaps after her and grabs her from behind, trying to pin
her down.  They struggle.

Susan uses her back to slam Dan against a wall.  Twice.  He lets
go of her.  She turns and punches him again, throwing him off
balance.

Dan spins out of control and falls out an open window.

Susan stops dead in place, just standing there for a long moment,
staring in desbelief.  Like a zombie, she moves towards the
window and looks down.

Ext. Street - Day

Dan is lying face up on the street, practically flattened out
and splattered all over the place.  He speaks in a hoarse whisper.

                    Dan
          Please...let me die...please.

Dan repeats this over and over again as his body quivers uncon-
trollably.

*The Preacher Man*
*approaches and gives*
*last rites.*

# SHATTER DEAD Screenplay Annotations

**Page 41A:**
Why is this page 41A instead of 42? Heck, why are the last two pages of this script completely different looking than the rest of the pages? I've got nothing. Suffice to say, I'm sure I was as happy to have reached the end of the script as a writer as you probably are right now as a reader.

I wrote a far more ambitious dressing-up of Dan's character by The Preacher Man and his crew, but as we only had three people as extras for this day (two of whom were recycled from the previous shoots), we had to make do with what we had. Thankfully, we had enough to work with so the point gets made and we're able to establish that they are repairing him.

I wrote a far more ambitious dressing-up of Dan's character by The Preacher Man and his crew, but since we only had three people as extras for this day (two of whom were recycled from the previous shoots), we had to make do with what we had.

I wish we could have done more with making The Preacher Man a total mess, but Robert is great here and his "Typical, I understand," line lands perfectly with his one-of-a-kind delivery.

Down the street appears the broken form of the Preacher Man with half a face, being supported in each step by a small group of faithful followers.

                    Preacher Man
          Look!  There's another one.

The small crowd moves towards Dan's broken body.  Dan shakes and gurgles because it's all that he can do.

                    Preacher Man
          Put me down.  He needs help to.

                         Dan
          Help me...

They sit the Preacher Man down next to Dan's body.  People begin searching the ground and their pockets for bandages and sticks and strings.

Montage:  Dan's fingers, hands, arms and legs are carefully but tightly wrapped up in whatever is to be found lying around as an attempt is made to keep what is left of him in one piece.  Boards are placed around his chest and ropes are tightened to create a human barrell.

                    Preacher Man
          And how did you come to find yourself
          in this sorry state, my friend?

The Preacher Man wipes the hair from Dan's face and helps him to sit up.  Dan looks at the Preacher Man and then looks up at the sky.

                         Dan
          I fell.

                    Preacher Man
          Typical.  I understand.

                         Dan
          Please take me home.  My lover is
          waiting for me.

                    Preacher Man
          Certainly, my friend.  We will help
          you.

**SHATTER DEAD Screenplay Annotations**

**Page 42:**

Susan's swoon at the top of the page happens earlier in the movie edit and is also presented far more gently on-screen than the violent collapse that is described herein. Not quite sure why we made the change, but I have no regrets. At this point in the storytelling, the gentle lead in to dying works better in my opinion, but I'm often wrong about many things.

Somehow in my initial video edit of the movie I had forgotten we shot this footage and I ended my assembly on the close-up of Dan walking toward the camera on his way back to their apartment – at which point it would cut to black and the end credits would roll.

Which might explain why these two pages are a different color. The originals may have gotten lost after the shoot, and I didn't add these back in until either during or even after the editing process, because if I had these pages with me while editing I would not have made the mistake of ending the cut too early.

But this is all just conjecture.

What it all comes down to is that as I rewound the source videotapes, I suddenly saw the footage we had shot of Susan applying the water droplets as tears to her eyes and I gasped, hit the STOP button and jumped right back into editing and finished up the assembly with the correct edit.

I'm glad to see I got it right the first time on the page.

Int. Apartment - Kitchen

Susan falls to her knees and lets her head spin around freely
on her neck with her mouth open.

She sits back on her haunches and eventually collapses face-up
onto the floor.  She struggles for a moment, and finally closes
her eyes.

Fade to black.

Int. Apartment - Kitchen

Susan is lying on the floor, curled up in the fetal position.
She slowly awakens and helps herself to get up.

Susan shakes the dust from her body and heads for the bathroom.

Int. Bathroom

Susan enters the bathroom.  She unstops the bathtub and lets the
blood and vomit drain out.

Susan goes to the mirror and examines herself for sighns of
visible damage; her eyes, her mouth, etc.  Shs is convinced
that she is reasonably fine and looks relieved.

She pauses a moment and a new fear wipes across her face:  She
touches the mirror and realizes that she is leaving no vapor
on it.

Susan turns on the water and runs a finger under the faucet.
She brings her finger up to one eye and places a drop of water
next to it and lets it run like a tear.  She repeats the procedure with her other eye.

She reaches out and touches her own reflection in the mirror, and
a look unlike any other registers on her face as she realizes,
unspeakably, that she is dead.

On the soundtrack can be heard the voices of the Preacher Man and
Dan talking and knocking at the door of the apartment; they are
calling to Susan, begging her to come open the door.

Fade to Black.

# FURY AS CENSORS BLOODIEST VIDEO PASS EVER!

By EMMA JAY

A SHOCKING film which features sickening scenes of a girl having a shotgun ABORTION has sparked new fury.

The movie, so gruesome that it was seized by Customs as being obscene, is to go on sale as Prime Minister John Major launched a crackdown on video nasties.

And last night one of his MPs insisted that the bloodthirsty *Shatter Dead* should not even have been MADE, let alone been given its 18-Certificate.

Censors demanded that one scene in which a naked woman uses a handgun as a PENIS be cut. But they allowed a sequence showing a zombie woman being blasted with a shotgun, sending her intestines flying in all directions.

She is forced to ABORT her child through the grisly shotgun hole in her belly.

Nigel Evans, Tory MP for Ribble Valley, said last night: "How anyone can watch films like this is beyond me."

## SHOCK NEWS EXCLUSIVE

# YOU THE JURY

## Is there too much violence on our screens?

PRIME Minister John Major this week launched a new initiative over video "nasties." Ministers condemned the decision to give 18 certificates to chilling movies like Natural Born Killers and documentaries such as Executions. They have also ordered censors to explain how they plan to cut down on video violence. But, in the week when the BLOODIEST and most HORRIFIC film yet goes on OPEN SALE in Britain we ask IS there too much violence on our screens? We've brought in two experts to give their views, but the final vote is down to YOU.

**YES** says Nigel Evans, Tory MP for Ribble Valley.

**NO** says Allan Bryce, editor of Video World.

I WELCOME all moves from the Government to clamp down on gratuitous scenes of sex and violence on our screens and I believe there should be even more research into the link between violent movies and real-life crimes.

IN a society where there is a growing level of social problems, I find it amazing the Government can point the finger of blame on films and video which contain scenes of violence and sex.

They seem to think that if they dictate what we can and cannot watch on films and videos then the

"A disturbing, gutsy and very different horror film!"
- Frank Henenlotter, Basket Case & Frankenhooker
"The most original zombie film since Romero raised the dead..."
- Michael Gingold, FANGORIA
NOW THERE'S NO MORE ROOM IN HEAVEN, EITHER.
SHATTER DEAD
GOD HATES YOU.

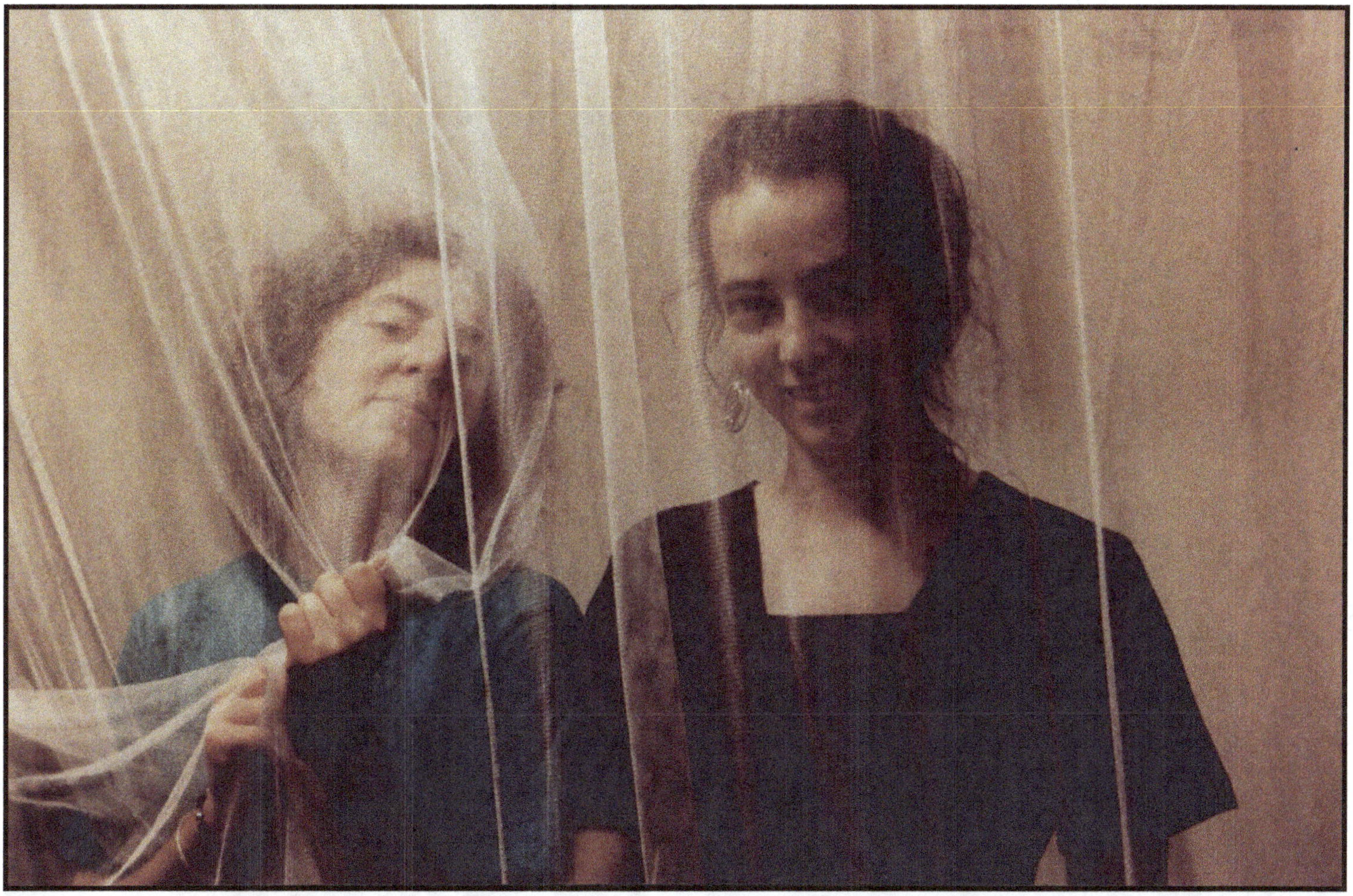

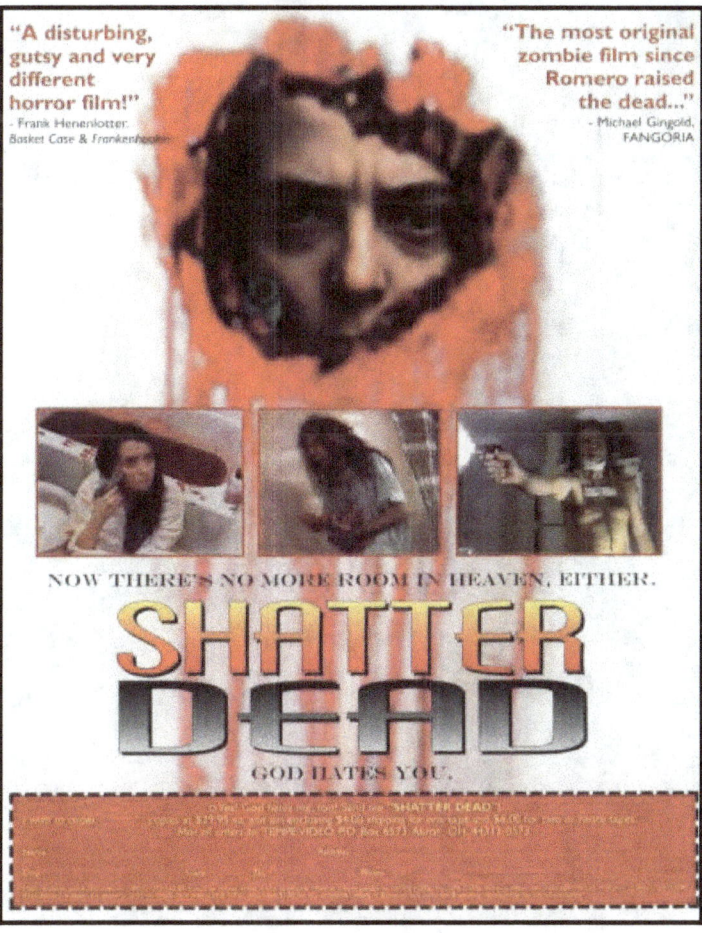

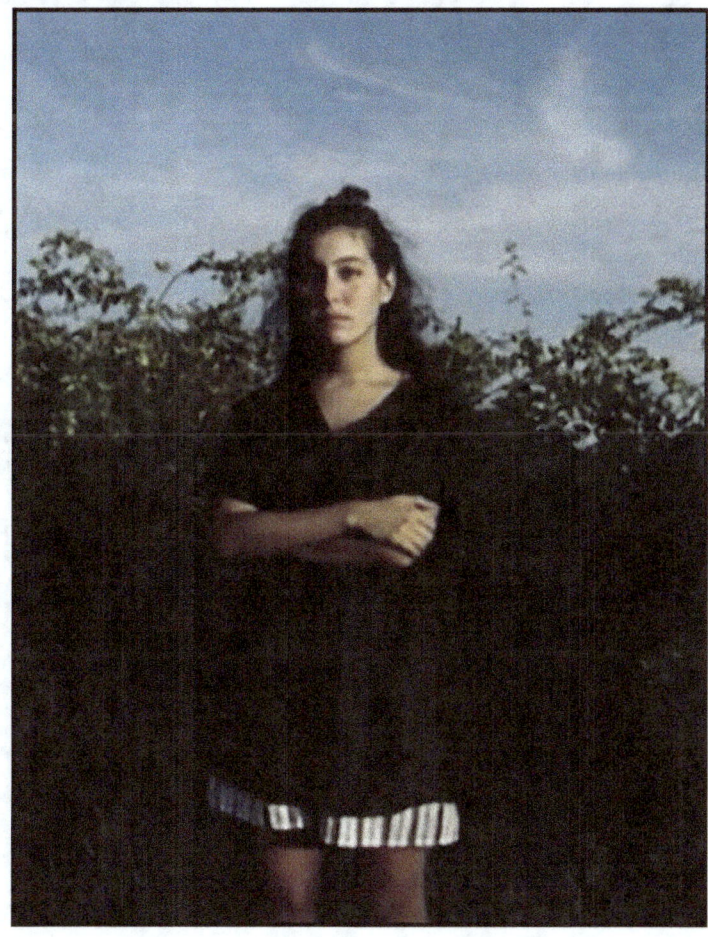

**MANIC ENTERTAINMENT**

Regisseur Scooter McCrae schuf mit SHATTER DEAD einen Zombiefilm, der, wie mit einem gezielten Kopfschuß, sämtliche Grenzen und Konventionen des Genres wegsprengt! In einer Welt, die fast ausschließlich nur noch von lebenden Toten bewohnt wird, ist auch den letzten Lebenden die Aussicht auf ein erlösendes Sterben genommen. Mit jedem neuen Tag ihres Daseins wird ihnen eine Tatsache immer bewußter: GOD HATES YOU!

...S/PAL,
ca. 82 Minuten
Originalfassung

# SHATTER DEAD:
# THE WRATH OF GOD

A Treatment for a
Feature-Length Screenplay
by

Scooter McCrae

# SHATTER DEAD

It is a starless night in Haiti as two young men with flashlights stumble through the wind in a misty graveyard with their flashlights pointed low to the ground. They find a fresh, shallow grave and dig up the mildly decomposing body within. One of the boys keeps watch while the other sits on the corpse and removes all the jewelry from it's stiff fingers while maggots swirl around in open wounds. The wind increases, swirling the mist and tossing loose dirt as a storm approaches. The boy on the corpse hurries his way up to it's mouth with a pair of pliers, searching the dead teeth for any gold filled cavities. The eyes of the dead body suddenly open just as the young man's flashlight batteries die out; he calls out to his friend to hurry over with his flashlight. As the jagged beams of light cut through the angry night wind, we see the corpse grabbing the screaming young man on top of him by the arms and yelling at him while they struggle; choking with dust and trying in vain to cry, the corpse is thanking the young man.

The screen cuts to black. The title card "17 Months Later" fades-up from black and fades back down again.

In a police state supermarket, customers file through the grimly stocked shelves as military men armed to the teeth keep watch over them and the food. Susan, a frail-looking young woman, moves through the slow check-out line impatiently whilst clasping at the few food items she can afford. She watches as, after each customer pays their bill, they are made to take a very official-looking breathalizer-type test. Susan's turn finally comes after paying for her goods; "She's alive," the doctor at the apparatus declares, and the soldiers let her pass through their gauntlet unharmed.

Once outside, walking through crowds of filthy street panderers and halfdressed people nursing at unhealing bruises, Susan looks for a working payphone. The deeper we move through this mass of struggling people, we eventually come to the realization that these are not just ordinary "street people." As the military men and equipment come moving in around them and mercilessly beating them out of the way, the true nature of the situation is revealed; these are all dead people. Begging for change, protesting for equal rights, demanding to be noticed - we are now in the middle of a world where something has gone horribly wrong. A world where nobody dies anymore.

Avoiding the masses of "zombies" surrounding her as they try to avoid being beaten, Susan finds a payphone; her effort is rewarded with a busy signal from the other end of the line. In the mass panic and confusion, she sees a derelict tampering with the gas tank of her car in the distance. Grabbing the shotgun from her back, she charges through the crowd towards the siphoner, who rises and runs. Bang! Susan blows him away with a double-barrelled blast that destroys the "zombie" as the canister of gasoline he is toting explodes. Susan curses, realizing that her last gallon of rationed gasoline has just been wasted, literally, in a puff of smoke.

In the midst of all this havoc, a renegade band of soldiers comes roaring down the street and opens fire on anyone, living or undead, that gets in their way. This band of troops is led by a crazed warrior of conviction known simply as "The General." The men under his command follow his every last order without question; maiming and destroying at will with guns, grenades, bazookas and cannons. Susan hops into her car and narrowly escapes the onslaught.

Driving on the empty back-roads of some nameless Upstate New York town, Susan's car finally sputters and slows to a halt. Moments later, from the surrounding woods, what seems like an endless supply of angry dead people comes spilling out onto the road. They attack Susan's car, but they do not damage it. Pushing, slapping, and shaking the vehicle, they try to scare the furious occupant from it. Grabbing up all her scattered weaponry from the floor, Susan prepares to do battle with the numerous undead forces.

Suddenly the undead attack ceases. The crowd of angry "zombies" before her filthy windshield begins to fold open in an improvised choreography like an ever widening funnel. At the farthest end of this tunnel of corpses, a mysterious man dressed in black appears and walks with a dignified sense of drama towards Susan's vehicle; he is the Preacher Man. The Preacher Man steps onto the hood of her car and ascends to the roof; he claims this vehicle in the Name of the Lord. The undead masses cheer and raise their arms in triumph. Chilled to the marrow, Susan exits her car with a defensive posture, keeping all who surround her at bay. The Preacher Man hops into the car, has an assistant pour some stolen gasoline into its tank, and wildly drives off into the horizon as Susan yells obscenities behind him.

The assembled masses of undead move back towards each other, closing up the hole in the road they have created for the Preacher Man and the car. Susan's path is now also effectively blocked; she has nowhere to go but back the way she came from. Angry Susan fires her weapon randomly into the crowd, but to no avail; the undead continue to stand their ground. Frustrated, she turns and marches down the road in the other direction.

Hours later, walking in the middle of the road, Susan blocks the path of the first car to come zipping by. Pulling her gun on the driver, she slips a little pocket mirror under his nose and looks for condensation to form on the glass; none appears. She opens the car door, rips the driver from his seat and kicks the shit out of him; she now knows how the "zombie" driver obtained this vehicle. She gets into the car and drives back the way from which she came - back after the Preacher Man and her car.

Dusk falls and Susan, exhausted from the activities of the day, pulls her stolen car off the road into a motel parking lot and takes a nap. She is rudely awoken by the loud rap of a hand against her windshield; it is a neighborhood patrolman making his rounds. He informs her that a street curfew is in effect, and he must clear her from her car immediately now that it is night. She grabs her few personal belongings from the back seat (ie: weapons), and is escorted to the motel lobby.

In the lobby, people are milling about looking refreshed and vigorous as they are escorted into overcrowded rooms and given rations of spoiling fruit and cans of warm soda. The overwhelming military presence helps keep everyone under control. Susan is taken to her room; a small, single occupancy closet with two other people already milling about inside. Susan immediately tries the telephone, but she can't seem to reach anybody on it. Mary, one of the women already in this room when Susan arrives, introduces herself and makes an effort towards friendship with Susan. The other woman is Grandma; she is Susan's age and quietly self contained, very pregnant and with a long streak of white strands staining her dark hair. Susan is too preoccupied with her own concerns to give a shit; she just wants to take a hot shower and unwind.

Entering the tiny bathroom, Susan gets undressed and unwraps a bar of emergency soap she carries in her survival kit purse. While Susan scrubs off the grunge of the day in the shower, Mary enters the bathroom and begs to borrow the bar of soap. Surprised but ready for anything, Susan slides the gun from her wet holster and keeps Mary at a safe distance. Mary undresses and, starting to gain Susan's trust, enters the shower with her. In her enthusiasm to get cleaned up, Mary accidentally drops the bar of soap. When she bends to pick it up, Susan is shocked to see the purple blotches that have formed on Mary's ass where blood has settled from sitting in one position for too long; Mary is a "zombie".

Outside, beneath the full moon in a quiet corner of the motel, Mary explains to the curious Susan what it is like to be dead, and how it came to be that she herself is dead yet looks perfectly alive. Suicide by sleeping pills is becoming a new craze that is sweeping the nation for those who want to die while their bodies are still strong and beautiful. Why grow old and wait to die? By then, one's body will be worn and unable to withstand the pressures of eternity. Small problems arise, however, if one wishes to move undetected through the world of the living; like needing to shower with soap as often as possible to prevent bacteria growth and foul smells.

Susan has heard enough of this crap; she just wants to go to bed. Mary walks Susan back to their room and then goes out to the back of the motel where a large gathering is forming in the darkness around the Preacher Man and his bright camp fire. Mary takes her seat at a small organ and plays somber music for the Preacher Man as he works the crowd into a frenzy. "This is the will of God!", he declares to the eager listeners. "This is the resurrection! Are you ready to wait a hundred years for everyone to die, or are you ready to help the Lord by taking the problem into your own hands?!"

The music, the cheering, and the booming voice of the Preacher Man rise up through the air and into the room where Susan is fitfully sleeping. Her dark dreams are shattered by nightmarish images of the dead clawing from their graves as an Angel tries to calm these angry risers back to sleep. The Angel shows Susan visions; how to use her gun to pleasure herself, the Angel of Death impregnating Grandma, etc. Susan's restlessness awakens Grandma; she sits up in bed and rubs at her full belly while watching Susan gracelessly sleep.

Bang! Through the front gate of the motel parking lot, a band of renegade undead comes crashing into this makeshift compound and opens fire on anyone and everyone with their weapons. Unlike the beautiful, "normal" looking people in the hotel, these undead minions are covered with scars and braces that they have acquired in their travels. They are the Liberators; their leader reads aloud from the Manifesto of the New World Order while his soldiers go about mutilating and harming all the motel residents. "We cannot have a new caste system of young, good looking dead people vs. older, crippled dead people! We must have equality! Everyone must be issued an eternal handicap so that everyone suffers equally!!"

Grandma rises and gets the hell out of her room to see what is going on outside. Moments later, Mary comes charging into the room to wake Susan and get her out to safety. Awoken from her terrifying nightmare, Susan pulls out her gun and opens fire on Mary in the darkness. When the smoke of her violent discharge clears, Susan is left with Mary's ripped open face staring at her in wide-eyed hatred as gunfire and screams struggle in the background. Mary throws Susan to the floor as the violence continues around them, angrily wrestling until Mary is finally subdued by Susan. Grandma rounds a corner in the hallway and is spotted by the leader of the New World Order; he grabs a shotgun from a co-conspirator and blows a huge hole into her pregnant belly. Their mission accomplished, these undead thugs vacate the buildings as quickly as possible, running right past Grandma and her open, flowing wound.

Amongst the wet tiles of the bathroom, Grandma unfolds the flesh of her unpleasant wound and pulls out the child tangled in her knotty organs. She turns on the shower and washes off the bloody "child" she has snatched from her steaming innards, clutching at it and feeding it from her painfully swollen breasts.

Stepping over the writhing bodies of those who have been "crippled" by the minions of The New World Order, Susan stumbles into the bathroom containing Grandma and her newborn child. She watches as Grandma wipes the blood and gore off of her miraculous infant, repulsed and intrigued by the events she has witnessed.

Outside, Susan discovers the Preacher Man absently swinging back-and-forth on a ride in the children's playground amongst a carpet of freshly-dead bodies writhing on the ground all around him. In the background, at the far end of the parking lot, she sees her car. Administering a breathing test on the Preacher Man with her tiny pocket mirror reveals that he is still alive. His masquerading as a dead person to gain power in this topsy-turvy world makes her twice as angry at him; she brutally shoots him in the face and fishes her car key out of his wet pockets while he complains about the now-missing one-third of his head.

Susan drives home and unpacks the valuable groceries from the car's trunk. She enters her apartment and finds it mysteriously empty, with much of the furniture tossed over or broken. In the bathroom, she finds the bathtub filled with still-warm blood. She walks down the hallway and into the bedroom, finding her boyfriend, Daniel, sitting on the edge of their bed with his red wrists wrapped in makeshift fabric bandages. He explains that the blood in the bathtub is his; he has killed himself by slashing his wrists so he will stay young and healthy forever.

Shocked and horrified, Susan sits down and Daniel goes to get her a drink which, from outside her range of sight, he secretly poisons with some pills from the kitchen. After quickly finishing the glass of milk, the two of them settle down and become intimate, finding ways to move around the obstacles that death has provided to their lovemaking. Afterwards, Susan awakens from a well-deserved sleep and feels some kind of sickness weakening her body. When she tells Daniel about this, he freely admits that she is probably experiencing the poison that he has given her to drink. He just wants her to go back to sleep and die in peace so they can experience eternity together as equals, but Susan is furious at having been so thoroughly taken advantage of while placing all her trust in him.

Susan threatens to disfigure herself and destroy the happiness of their being forever together, making Daniel nervous and helpfully obedient. Holding a gun to her head, she orders him to bring her a glass of water so she can try to vomit the poison out from her system. As she drinks deeply from the glass, Daniel suddenly leaps at her, knocking the gun from her hand and wrestling her to the floor. As he holds her tightly down, she slowly fades away and dies in his firm arms. Re-opening her now dead eyes, she regains her strength and kicks Daniel off of her and out through the nearby window.

Daniel tumbles three-stories and flattens against the pavement which shatters every bone in his flailing body. From around the corner of the street comes a small parade of dead people being led by the remains of the Preacher Man. They surround Daniel and put him back together again using the loose boards and pipes from the nearby garbage cans to create an exoskeleton structure held in place with loose wire and strings. Daniel rises and goes back into the building he has just fallen from, followed by the Preacher Man and his small army of the undead.

Susan rises with great effort and examines herself in front of the bathroom mirror; she looks the same as she always has. A sickening grimace distorts her face as she breathes on the mirror and looks for the moisture that should be in her living breath. The mirror remains dry. She wants to cry, but she cannot now that her tear ducts are dried-up with death. Dipping her finger, she takes water from the sink before her and pours it into her eyelid and watches it drip out and slide down her cheek. In the background, she hears Daniel's voice calling to her from the hallway for her forgiveness.

Outside the apartment building, the General and his rogue militia pull up in their army vehicles and open fire on all the dead people in the streets. He sees many of the zombies running into the doorway of Susan's building for protection. The General grabs a huge missile launcher from the back of his truck and fires it at them, taking down almost a third of the building with the blast.

In Susan's apartment the floor caves in, throwing her down into a bloody pile of rubble beneath her that breaks her fall. Tearing herself from the sharp spirals of concrete and iron, she sees both Daniel and the Preacher Man struggling to release themselves from the desert of shrapnel. The General's men enter the remains of the building with sharp cutting tools and baseball bats and start pummeling all the trapped dead people. Susan runs away and hides in the shadows, unable to find another way out of this place ...

As the General and his men are taking a well-deserved cigarette break at their vehicles, Susan comes stumbling out of the remains of the building stark-naked, and with a huge knife sticking out her abdomen; she yells to them that she is still alive and needs their help. They go running over and drag her back to the vehicle, unsure of whether or not to help her or fuck her. Before they have a chance to do anything to her, Susan pulls the knife out of herself and stabs the closest man in the eye, and then slices the one standing next to him. She grabs the guns from their holsters and opens fire on everyone around her wearing army fatigues.

The General grabs her from behind and slices her throat open, trying to pull her head off. Susan spins around and fires, blowing out his kneecaps. Another army truck comes charging by and just narrowly misses her. As she recovers her balance, they grab the screaming General on-board and start driving away. Susan picks up the nearby missile launcher and destroys the truck and everyone in it. She looks down and sees the thick red blood slowly oozing out of her throat with no heartbeat to pump it out faster. She spreads the sticky liquid onto her face and body as if covering herself up with something protective. Suddenly very calm, she turns and fires another missile into the remains of her apartment building, and watches as the rest of it quickly collapses and burns.

Susan gets into one of the now-empty, but weapons laden, army vehicle and drives away as quickly as possible as all the dead soldiers begin to rise again. Within a few blocks she turns a corner and nearly hits Mary and Grandma, her still-embryonic child wrapped in a blanket to hide it's undead origins. Mary is now blind and has a decorative porcelain mask strapped to the most damaged areas of her face. Susan screeches her vehicle to a halt and takes this opportunity to try and clear her head. Grandma rushes over and begs Susan to give her and the child a ride to a doctor. Susan helps Grandma and her infant into the vehicle, but pushes Mary away as Grandma protests. Against her better judgment, Susan agrees to drop them off at the nearest hospital as long as it looks safe and nobody tries to stop her.

Meanwhile, a group of scientists with a military escort finds Mary wandering along the open road; they question her about the pregnant woman she was seen staying with in the Motel holding area. She tells the group of scientists that she will assist them in anyway that she can if they will help her. They toss her into the back of their truck and drive off.

Later that night, Susan pulls her vehicle off to the side of the road and, using a military medical kit in the backseat, sews shut the slit in her neck and the gaping petals of Grandma's open-bellied flesh. As they sit together, knitting in the bright light of the full moon, they talk (and whiper) about their shattered lives and become friends. Grandma tells Susan about her about being raped by an Angel; the father of the child in her arms. Susan determines that this baby is far more important than either of them realize, suggesting that they get it to a hospital immediately. Their discussion ends with them deciding to name the embryo, it's sex as-yet-undetermined, "Tex." They get back into the vehicle and continue driving, looking for a quiet hospital.

Mary leads the scientists to the remains of Susan's apartment building, an apparent dead end until, from the ashes and debris, a three-legged hybridization of the Preacher Man and Susan's boyfriend Daniel, sutured together with wire and staples, rises and approaches them. The Preacher Dan introduces itself and delivers a most grandiose retelling of it's birth as a perfect creature created from two imperfect halves. Mary recognizes the voice of the "Preacher" half of the Preacher Dan and declares her allegiance to it. They toss the Preacher Dan into the back of the truck with Mary and drive off to the hospital.

At the hospital, Mary and the Preacher Dan are introduced to Dr. Louis Judd, who is is charge of the Resurrection Program at his facility. There are many questions to be solved concerning the issue of regaining death. Although the government has approved the construction of huge corporate-run oven facilities to fully incinerate the dead who can afford to be laid to rest, Dr. Judd does not personally approve of this answer. Death is for everyone, he argues, not just the rich. He shows Mary and the Preacher Dan all the suffering that has flowed out of the crowded rooms and onto the floors of his sterile corridors. But he promises to provide them with only the best he has to offer if they can help him and his men find Grandma and her child; or get them early on the list for incineration, if they prefer.

Dr. Judd manages to wrestle Mary from the possessive gaze of the Preacher Dan and escorts her into a high-security area so see she can meet the rest of his associates. The room he takes blind Mary into is a refrigerated laboratory with a series of tall glass cylinders at its center; floating in the amneotic fluid of each of these tubes is an as-yet-undeveloped embryo with various electrodes and probes attached to them. Every embryo-tube has it's own crude voice-box apparatus which allows each "child" to ask Mary a series of very articulately phrased questions concerning Grandma and the embryo she is now, literally, carrying. Mary, having not been told otherwise, believes she is part of a very-involved conference call as opposed to being in a roomful of dead babies. From her vague answers based on the short amount of time she actually handled the infant, they ascertain that this child is the missing link they so desperately need to complete their project.

Susan parks her vehicle behind the hospital and helps Grandma to the door of the emergency room; they are immediately surrounded by army security guards who escort them inside to the front of the waiting line. Susan is detained and locked in the same private room with Mary, while Grandma and Tex are brought to the office of Dr. Judd. After a couple of superficial questions, he takes the child from Grandma's loving arms without her consent and assigns armed guards to keep her restrained.

With her throat unhealed, Susan cannot speak, and with the ceramic mask covering what's left of her face, Mary and Susan do not recognize each other as they sit together in their little room. Using every means at their disposal, they try to communicate with each other and figure out what is going on. Mary tells Susan that she has already spoken to the people in charge and that all they want is Grandma and her child. Susan starts breaking stuff out of anger and frustration while Mary tries to calm her down, offerering to take her to see Dr. Judd and his associates. Susan calms down and nods her consent as Mary reads the answer off of her vaguely familiar face.

Pulling a long, sharp metal sliver embedded deep into her shoulder blade, Susan knocks on the door to their room; the guard outside knocks back, and Mary calls to him to enter and help her with something. When the guard enters, Susan throws him to the floor, handcuffs him, and uses the wire to clamp his mouth shut so he can't scream for help. They escape with Mary leading the way, counting her steps and the various twists and turns through crowded hallways and stairwells that will bring them to the office of Dr. Judd and his associates.

After working their way past various security guards, Susan and Mary find themselves standing in Dr. Judd's embryo chamber. At first, Susan tries to communicate with the babies by coaching questions through Mary, but the embryos tell Susan to simply think her questions since they are all telepathic. After a couple of blunt answers from the undeveloped infants, Mary realizes that the chairmen of the board are not the people she thought they were; horrified, she leaves the room, sobbing dryly to herself.

Susan continues her interrogation. The babies tell her that they have been born with all the knowledge of the universe trapped inside of their small minds; because they have never truly been born, an Angel of Forgetfulness was unable to press it's finger into their upper lip and leave the indent beneath their nose that draws all knowledge of the world from them. They have been suffering without voices, until Dr. Judd removed them from dead wombs and hooked them to speaking implements. They have been waiting for a ninth child among them to form a chorus of three times three, a divine number, to sing to the Angel of Death to come and wipe the Earth clean of those who have died and seek their peace.

Activity begins in the ninth amneotic tube as young Tex comes floating into it from below in a flurry of bubbles. Tex thanks Susan for helping bring him to the safety of Dr. Judd.

Dr. Judd enters the chamber and, furious at Susan and her breach of security, asks her to leave. The various embryos stop Dr. Judd from yelling at her, telling him that she is their invited guest to witness the beauty about to befall the planet. Dr. Judd apologizes to Susan, and begins his work. He hooks the signal that the embryos are generating into the worldwide internet and simultaneously broadcasts them into a huge radio telescope in the desert pointed straight-up at the sky.

Outside the hospital, the night sky suddenly lights up with the intensity of approaching daylight as a pillar of fire with wings comes roaring out of heaven and sweeps the Earth clean like an angry broom. Dead people burst into flames as their screams whip the hot air into a tornado of pain. The terrors of dying are beyond even what Dr. Judd imagined; horrified, he flees from his laboratory and disappears into the night.

In the embryo tubes, the babies begin to grow to their full-size as the tubes constrict and shape their bodies into large human worms struggling against the painful glass confines. Susan picks up a chair and smashes the twisted Tex out of his tube; he falls limply to the floor and, as Susan cradles his dying form, he whispers his final secrets into her ear. The Earth itself is being transformed into a new extension of Hell, and the last surviving humans are being swept off of it to a new planet, while those who must suffer for their sins will be redistributed along it's surface. The vengeful flame comes ripping through the room and clears away all the embryos, including Tex, leaving Susan sitting all alone as smoke rises from her singed form.

The door to the room opens and Dan sticks his head inside, calling to Susan as the smoke clears. Susan watches as Dan enters the room with three legs, and the Preacher Man's torso and head entering smilingly with him. Angry and defeated, Susan looks up and screams, but no sound comes from her tight throat as the air within her escapes through the trembling hole in her neck.

Mostra
internazionale
del film di
fantascienza
e del fantastico

MIGLIOR FILM INDIPENDENTE U.S.A.

al film
"SHATTER DEAD., di Scooter Mcrae

ROMA, 13-22 GIUGNO 1995

Silver Planco

FANTAFESTIVAL

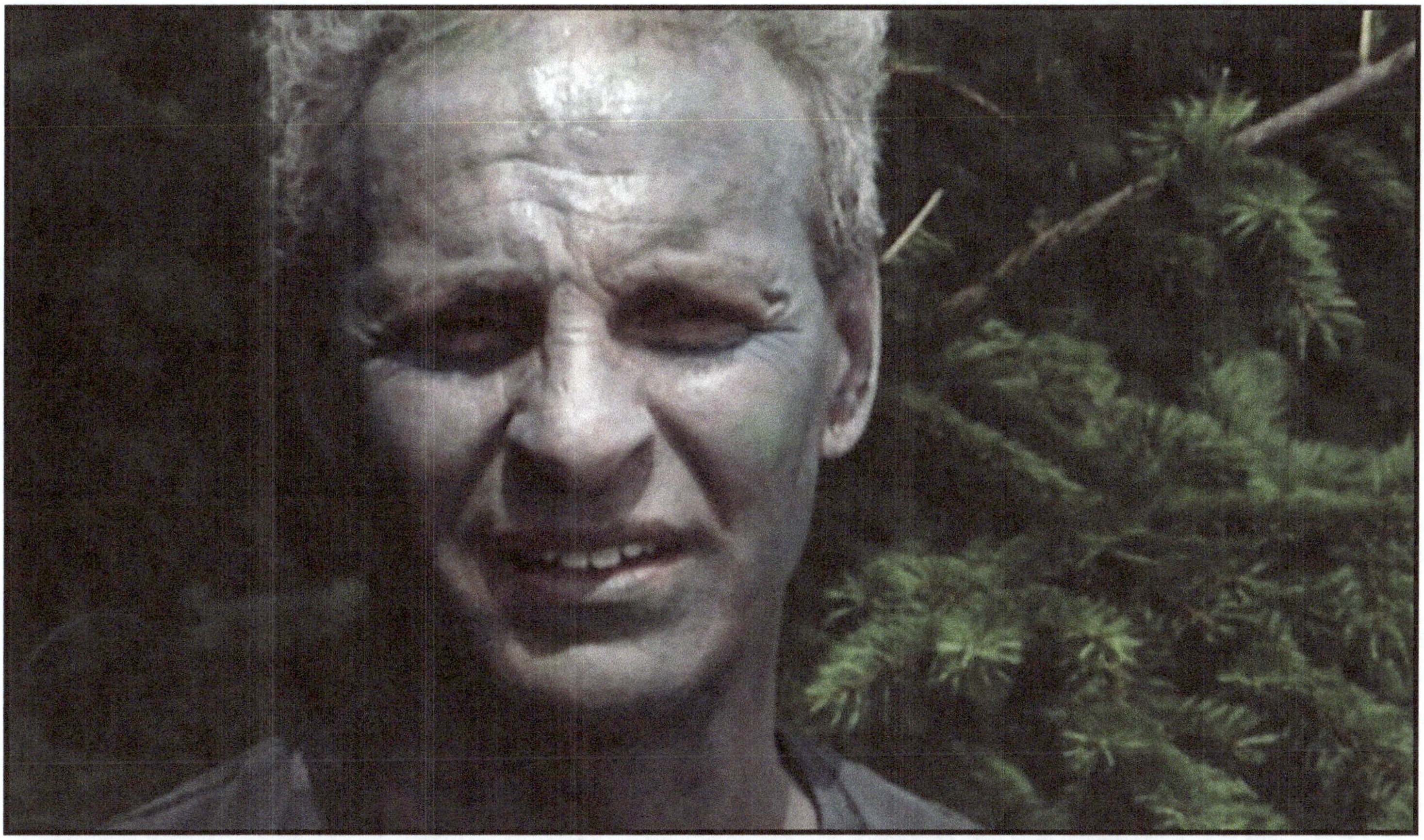

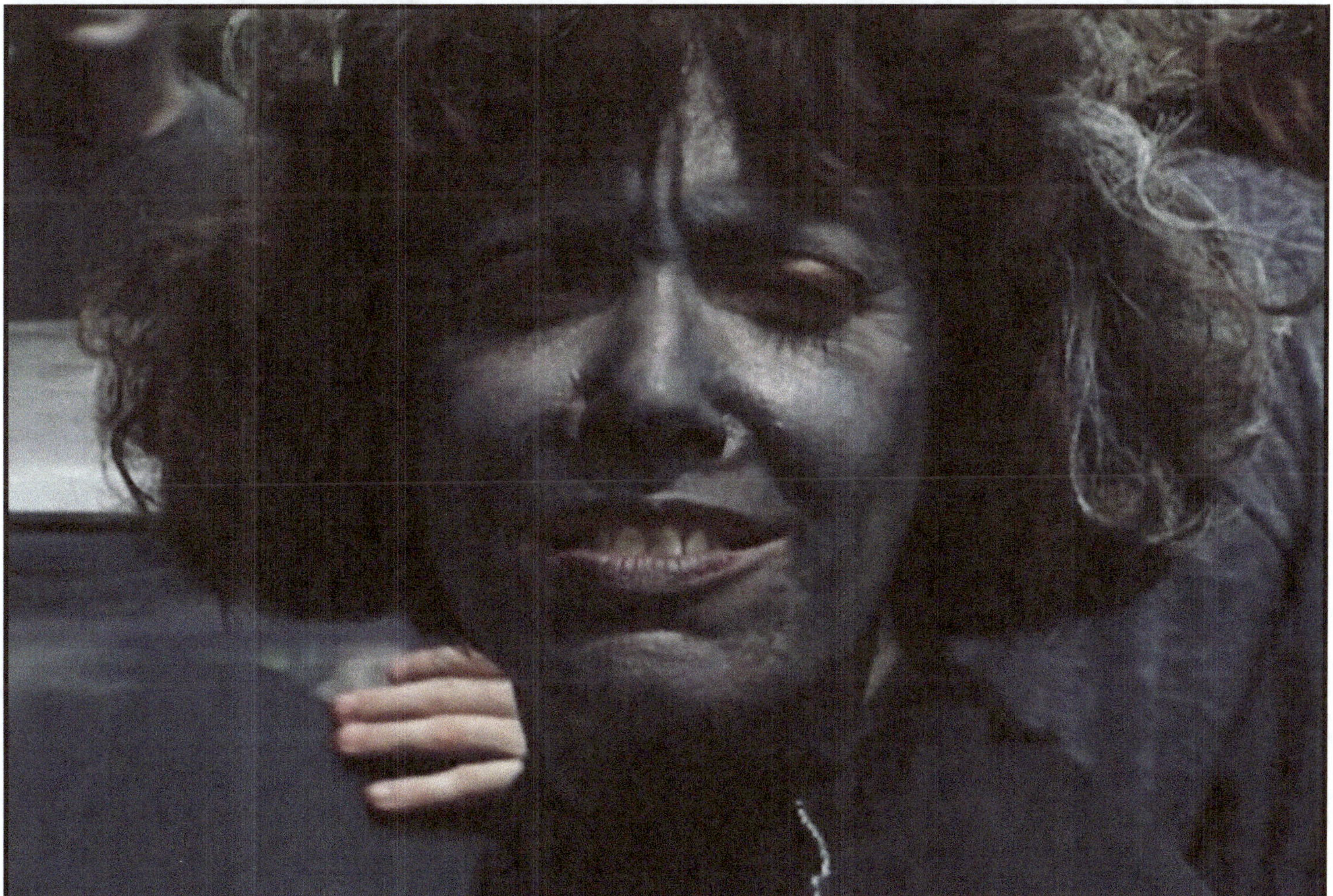

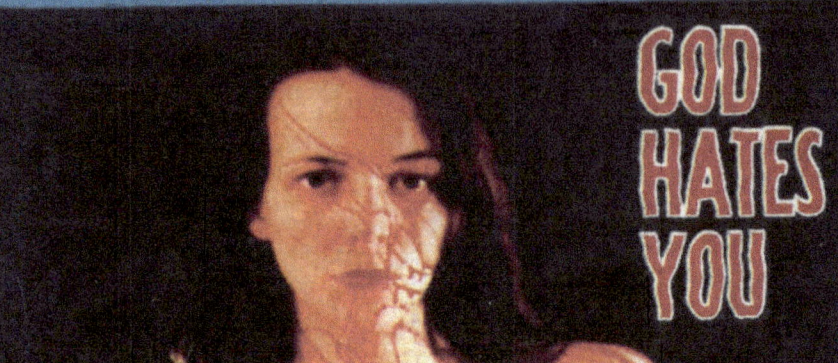

FRANK HENENLOTTER'S
SEXY SHOCKERS FROM THE
VIDEO UNDERGROUND

GOD HATES YOU

SHATTER DEAD

DIRECTED BY SCOOTER McCRAE
With Stark Raven, Flora Fauna, Larry 'smalls' Johnson

ADULTS ONLY!

SOMETHING WEIRD VIDEO ®

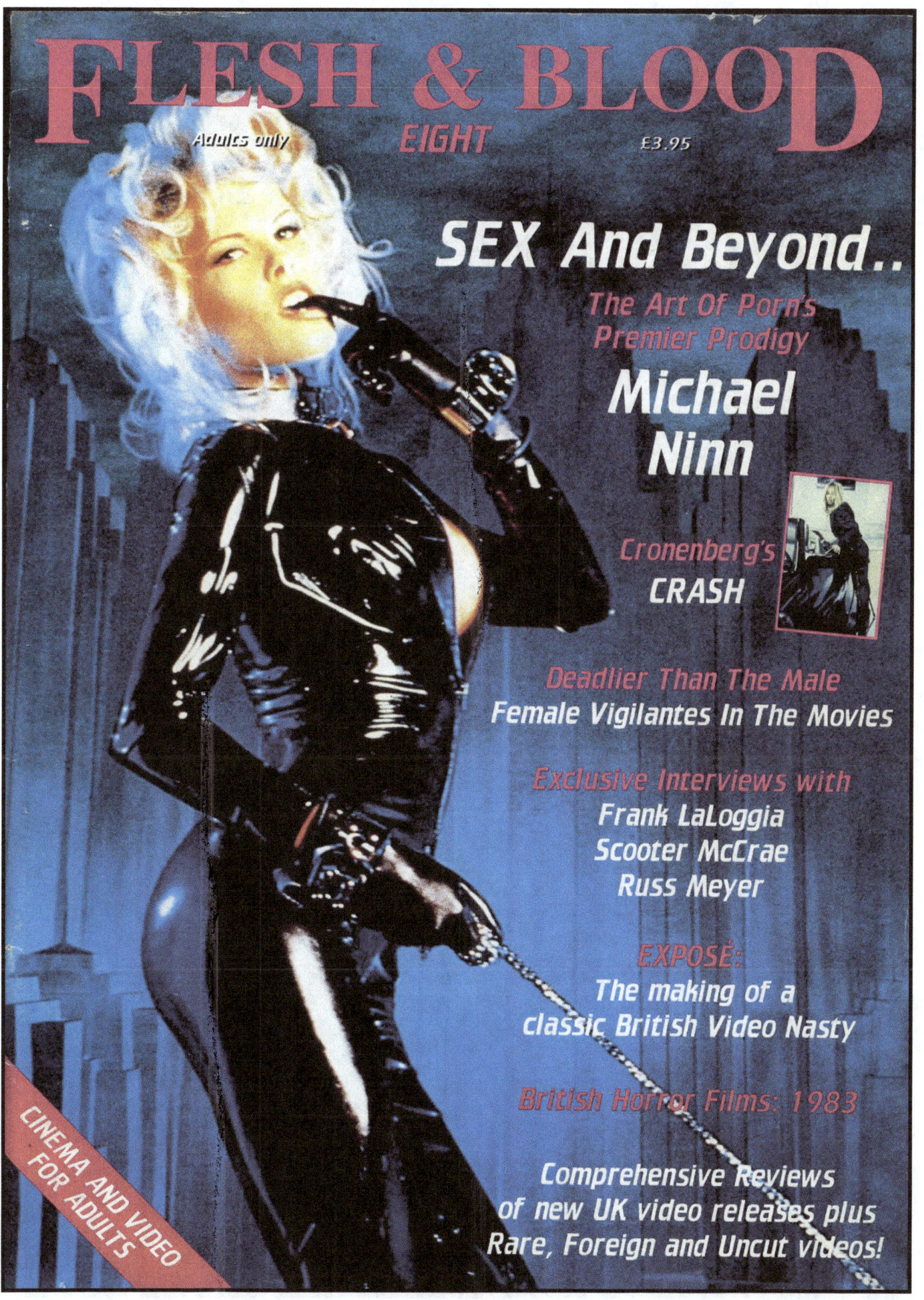

# FLESH & BLOOD

Adults only    EIGHT    £3.95

## SEX And Beyond..

The Art Of Porn's
Premier Prodigy

## Michael Ninn

Cronenberg's
**CRASH**

**Deadlier Than The Male**
Female Vigilantes In The Movies

*Exclusive Interviews with*
**Frank LaLoggia
Scooter McCrae
Russ Meyer**

*EXPOSÉ:*
The making of a
classic British Video Nasty

*British Horror Films: 1983*

Comprehensive Reviews
of new UK video releases plus
Rare, Foreign and Uncut videos!

CINEMA AND VIDEO
FOR ADULTS

113

# don't make God the villain

## Scooter McCrae Interviewed by Richard King

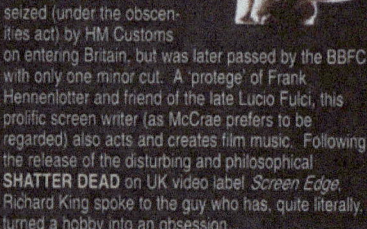

Scooter McCrae, dark genius or sick geek?... His award winning directorial debut **SHATTER DEAD** was seized (under the obscenities act) by HM Customs on entering Britain, but was later passed by the BBFC with only one minor cut. A 'protege' of Frank Hennenlotter and friend of the late Lucio Fulci, this prolific screen writer (as McCrae prefers to be regarded) also acts and creates film music. Following the release of the disturbing and philosophical **SHATTER DEAD** on UK video label *Screen Edge*, Richard King spoke to the guy who has, quite literally, turned a hobby into an obsession...

*Richard King: Most recent zombie outings have taken a scientific slant on the 'phenomena'... but in SHATTER DEAD, as in J.R. Bookwalter's more traditional zombie fest (or feast) you have taken the*

*religious path... To me it seems almost a natural progression, that is when science fails you turn to God... Was this a conscious move on your part?*

**Scooter McCrae:** I don't know if it's a question of us turning to God in a time of need, so much as an exploration of what happens when God abandons us. I'm an atheist, so the religious issues that are raised are not so much my own beliefs, but my understanding of a set of beliefs. I had a real fascination with Greek Mythology when I was growing up, and I see no valid difference between the ancient and modern ways of religion trying to find some way to explain all the fucked-up things that happen in the world from one moment to the next. I was actually quite religious myself for a number of years, but I just kind of woke up one morning realising that I was wasting more time trying to explain the mysteries of the world away instead of actually trying to explore them, and I think a lot of people fall into that trap. At least I see blind faith as a kind of brick wall; I don't want to offend anyone with strong religious beliefs as long as they don't interfere with my lifestyle. I've been there myself; it's just not for me anymore, and it never will be again.

The Bible has a long list of characters who have been appropriated for use in horror cinema, from Lilith to Golem. So much horror depends on one having or at least understanding the basics of faith; vampires and their reaction to crosses, how Frankenstein shouldn't have fucked with God etc. The Bible is filled with rules for you to follow, and many horror films are about breaking those rules and the punishment that comes down from above. In **SHATTER DEAD**; science hasn't failed at all; it has simply sat back and finally acknowledged the existence of God. As far as this project is concerned,

God is the one who broke the rules. Now what can we possibly do about that?

**RK:** *Something you have in common with Romero is the belief that women hold the only hope of survival, you each have strong yet vulnerable female leads (excepting of course the original NIGHT OF THE LIVING DEAD) who seem better equipped to survive in a hopeless situation. Is this something you believe in?*

**SM:** I don't think that female characters in any of my works to date are particularly strong. In fact, I don't think I realised just how bad things were in the modern horror film (and a lot of other genres) until I started getting so much attention over this issue that I don't think is anything special at all. I do think that in society, and especially in the horror film genre, we have gotten used to seeing women who are either ridiculously weak or who suddenly become absurd 'Rambo' figures when they're handed a gun and can suddenly hold their own with the 'big boys'. It's 1996 for crying out loud, and still I cannot believe the incredible amount of shit female performers have to put up with in this genre! I think it's gotten a whole lot worse now, actually, than it ever was when we look back at the stuff being made in the 1970s (especially in Europe, of course).

Special thanks goes to the Scream Queens here in the United States, who have done a marvellous amount of damage to the credibility of the modern horror film; they are an absolute embarrassment to anyone with even half a functioning brain. I don't know if any of this kind of shit gets exported to other parts of the world, but for your sakes I hope not. We have magazines and videos over here devoted to women who enjoy being famous for taking off their clothes and getting stabbed in the shower and other such stuff, which gives a bad name to the genre and the human race in general. I have much more respect for porn actors, who at least aren't

afraid to go all the way for their paychecks as opposed to these idiots who like to tease teenage geeks out of their parents hard earned dollars just to see them shake their tits.

If you're asking me if women adapt better than men to certain situations like the end of the world as we know it, for example, then I have to say yes. Who can blame them for wanting to see the fall of this idiotic patriarchal society in the hopes that something better will spring up? It takes much greater strength to adapt to a situation than to stand defiantly against it getting slapped in the face with your own spit while the wind laughs at you.

**RK:** *You also use full-frontal female nudity without titillation... a masterful stroke indeed... the shower scene is certainly a slap in the face... it actually made me feel!*

## DEATH & TAXES Introduction

I wrote and directed SHATTER DEAD when I was 26 years-old, back in 1992, and it wasn't until 2012 or thereabouts that I actively began thinking about revisiting the existential nightmare world I had created those many years earlier out of bits and bobs and whatever spare cash wasn't nailed down. Two decades between projects is a long time, especially between the tender age of idealistic mid-twenties boy and over-the-hump and done with all the bullshit of the modern world mid-forties boy-man.

I honestly do not remember what triggered the desire to write this screenplay in the first place. What I do remember is that I started working on it about the time that President Obama came into office, even though most of what I was reacting to initially was the time that President Bush Junior before him had spent ruining the country and the rest of the world.

(At least, until President Obama continued the reign of terror and ruination that President Bush had up-and-running, and added his smiling face to the awful policies, like wrapping a package full of arsenic in silken threads. New bottles for old wine, as I've heard Noam Chomsky say when referring to the national tragedy of the Clinton presidency. Which helped keep me inspired to keep on writing, so I can't complain too much, I guess.)

Revisiting previous projects or thoughts of sequelizing them almost never happens in my mind, so I do know that when my imagination wandered back into the SHATTER DEAD thematic minefield there must have been a reason. Undead people whose living souls are trapped in dead and rapidly decaying bodies is rich material to work with, especially as I suspect it's something all of us can relate to in our daily lives in one way or another.

DEATH & TAXES takes place concurrently to the events in the original SHATTER DEAD, but there are no recurring characters or events. SHATTER DEAD is a microcosmic story, whereas DEATH & TAXES is macrocosmic by comparison, showing what is happening on a much larger scale (or as large as I would allow what I believed to still be a very limited budget) as opposed to focusing on someone who is just trying to bring their groceries home to their boyfriend. In that sense, this script is my DAWN OF THE DEAD after the events of NIGHT OF THE LIVING DEAD, although I make no claims to my works being anywhere near the level of genius of George Romero's apocalyptic masterpieces.

SHATTER DEAD has lightly sprinkled in the background the reactions from the scientific community as commentary and addresses the religious ramifications in a more upfront manner without getting too deep into the theological weeds. DEATH & TAXES continues the conversation and goes much deeper into the cosmology, and while our main character this time (Ben Truman) is more proactively involved in the storytelling, he has no horse in either the ethical or religious ramifications; he's a scientist looking for answers without being judgmental about what he ends up discovering.

I wanted to talk about god, and faith and religion (which are two different things entirely) and about terrorism and the horrible people in charge of everything who make it all godawful the more they try to make it all better. Every day of our existence is often shaped for the worst by hopelessly amoral people who deserve nothing but our scorn but instead work for our votes (which we seem happy to give to them). It's an ugly fucking world where the illusion of choice is substituted for the actuality of any meaningful decision making.

The biggest trap to avoid when writing this kind of stuff is making sure you haven't gone off the deep end into pure dogmatic swill (much like this intro) instead of crafting credible human drama that also happens to explore important issues in-between the character cracks. It's always about interactions between imaginary people, not a treatise, although Aaron Sorkin's continuing career might lead one to believe otherwise.

I purposely wrote this to be a relatively low-budget project; something definitely under a million dollars, and possibly even doable for a quarter-million if done without star performers and keeping everything in the production trimmed close to the bone. I think being a bit rough around the edges would benefit the feeling of verisimilitude that the story demands. If nothing else—as written—it is not a movie that demands epic crowd scenes, major property damage or cameras mounted to cranes for sweeping overhead shots. It's small and intimate and speaks plainly. It's a story that proudly wears its heart on its sleeve.

I also wanted to take one more shot at coming up with some kind of explanation for what is turning people into the undead. This story expands upon some things that were suggested sotto voce in SHATTER DEAD, and here they become key issues—the most important of which is faith. This is a surprising meditation on what constitutes 'faith' and the core values of a belief system, especially as it relates to the notion of what zombies are and are not. I can see how what I came up with might not please zombie purists, but I do think that what I suggest with this script addresses the slow-beating heart rate of the undead in a way that points to something that goes beyond known science and takes faith to the next level. Faith, as we know it, has been so completely degraded by modern world consumerism as to be unrecognizable in the Biblical sense.

Faith is not a commodity to be bought, sold and traded.

I'm a big fan of Carl Theodor Dreyer, and if you've ever seen his film ORDET (which translates into English as THE WORD), then I think some of this will make a lot of sense. And if you haven't seen it, I cannot recommend it enough. Either way, the spiritual DNA of DEATH & TAXES can be traced back to ORDET and the dramatic arc it constructs and then deconstructs over the course of its running time. It is a compelling, heartbreaking and ultimately transcendent work of cinema that is second to none.

I try not to let my Atheism interfere with my admiration for the sincere beliefs of others.


**SPOILERS BEGIN HERE:**

Although I'm overall pleased with what I accomplished with this script, the one nut that I couldn't crack in the story was the conversion of our protagonist Ben into a terrorist by the end of everything he has been put through—which was something that attracted me to wanting to tell this story in the first place. That aspect of his character has been almost entirely removed from the 'final' draft in this book. In the initial conception, he would be reading the pamphlets he was finding all over the hospital, having additional heated conversations with his best friend Joe, and eventually even meet the author of those pamphlets at Ben's apartment after his attempt to put Mary down after her catastrophic burn incident.

Finding himself completely demoralized and at his lowest point, I was going to have Ben commit suicide so he could have most of the organs in his chest cavity removed and replaced with high-yield explosives, after which he would meet to shake hands with the President of the United States and blow up her, himself and the entire roomful of media reporters.

Which is pretty dark stuff.

During the writing process, I found I had just too much material to deal with in a script that I wanted to keep under 120 pages, and ideally wanted to have come in at no more than 105 pages (the current page count is 107 pages). And while I wrote many of the scenes mentioned above in earlier drafts, I was never fully satisfied with them and felt like they were also being rushed to make a point that felt forced. There was so much material already in play over the course of 107 pages that it was starting to feel like I needed closer to 150 pages to give the story I wanted to tell the justice it deserved. But as I'm not comfortable pitching projects that are over 90 minutes in length, I decided that making Ben and Mary's storyline the true heart of the matter was the better way to go. And in the end, I think I prefer the complete and total personal downer of an ending that the script goes quietly into the good night with.

The complete and total mental destruction of a single person can be more harrowing and land with greater impact than blowing up a roomful of people anyways.


**SPOILERS ARE NOW DONE.**

I hope that when you read this you'll see the humanity I tried to give at certain points to even the most odious of characters, especially the ones who are usually "the bad guys" in movies like these (ie: military and religious leaders, etc.). While there are a few people who do terrible things on both sides of the issues in the story, overall there isn't a single person who could be pointed to as being the antagonist. Everyone is just trying to get by in their own way and stay sane during insane circumstances, and some do much better than others trying to make it through—while a few others fail miserably. Just like in real life.

And besides—just like in the original SHATTER DEAD, the closest thing we have to a malignant hooligan 'bad guy' is god (especially the Old Testament bastard version that had to be rewritten into a more acceptable entity for the sequel).

I'd like to think that in the twenty-something years between these two scripts I've become a better writer with more meaningful insights to offer with the accumulation of years and experience along the way. But who knows? That will be up to you, dear reader, to decide. DEATH & TAXES is certainly meaner and leaner; no shower scenes, shotgun abortions or gun fucks to be had this time on the ride, although I do like to think that there are some images along the way to make a viewer feel uncomfortable or question why it is exactly that we get out of bed in the morning every day.

One amusing difference between the two screenplays is that over the course of time, the characters have gone from being jobless slackers to hard working people who have jobs and positions that are an integral part of their self-expression. I guess old age brought with it a concern for my characters to have a way to support themselves—which wasn't as big an issue for me in my mid-twenties. Perhaps it's something that is even reflected in the titles as SHATTER DEAD sounds horrific but could mean anything, whereas DEATH & TAXES is enough to make any adult over the age of 35 shudder at the precise terror being called out by its name. Is there anything more awful than having to deal with the soulless scumbags of the IRS?

I wish I could have made this movie, but it's not what the world is looking for now or any time soon, and I'm not getting any younger, so this seems like the best way to get people to experience this story that I'm happy with and proud of. Better that you should get a chance to read it this way than to never experience it at all. Thank you for your time and attention and lemme know what you think if our paths ever cross. It's a small world.

—Scooter McCrae

SHATTER DEAD: DEATH & TAXES

Written by

Scooter McCrae

INTERIOR HOSPITAL AUTOPSY ROOM - NIGHT

A montage of various recently used surgery implements being picked-up from the blood encrusted folded cloth draped over a rolling tray.

TECH CREDITS appear over various shots of the bloody instruments being washed clean by rubber-gloved hands in a silver industrial sink.  No faces are shown.

Small bits of flesh are flensed from the teeth of solid-steel mini-saws and torn human organs are unceremoniously dumped into the plastic liner within a metallic flip-top garbage can.

TECH CREDITS finish (sans title) and we begin to more clearly see the rest of the space.


INTERIOR HOSPITAL BASEMENT - EARLY MORNING

This room is in the basement of a hospital, all grey cinder block walls and no windows.  It is dark save for a single overhead light dangling over a female PATIENT who we see only in close-up at the moment.

The PATIENT is lying back in a chair similar to the kind one would find in a dentist office.  She looks completely calm and stares into the light as she brings up a cigarette, taking a deep drag from it and not exhaling for a long time. When she does exhale, the smoke does not come out of her mouth or nose, but from below screen.

As the camera pulls back from her face to reveal her body, we see that her chest is completely open and her organs exposed. The smoke comes snaking out of a hole at the top of her esophagus as her lungs pulsate.

Sitting across from her is BEN TRUMAN, a medical intern in his early 30's who is busy slicing away at her internal organs with a large metal scissor that cuts through muscle and bone with equal ease.

She appears to not be feeling any of it - if anything, BEN seems more concerned, even horrified by what he's doing than she is.

There is a particularly loud snapping sound as he gets his back into separating something that doesn't seem to want to be cleaved apart.

                         PATIENT
          That sounded pretty serious.

                         BEN
          Yeah.  You didn't feel it, did you?

                         PATIENT
          My ears felt it - sounded kind of
          unpleasant.

She takes another long cigarette drag and exhales through her
hole again, accidentally, in Ben's face as he's working on
separating her lungs.

                         PATIENT (CONT'D)
          Ooops.  Sorry, doc.  Didn't mean
          anything by that.

                         BEN
          No problem.

SNAP!  One of the lungs is now completely separated.

                         PATIENT
          Was that my lungs?

                         BEN
          One of them.

She sighs deeply with her remaining breath.  Her voice has
lost much more than the air power that one now-missing lung
had provided her with.

                         PATIENT
               Hey, howzabout you give me a minute
               to finish this before you separate
               the other one?

                         BEN
          Absolutely.

She inhales so deeply from the cigarette, with an exuberance
that indicates this could well be the very last inhalation of
smoke she will every experience, that her eyes widen with
emotion.

She holds it in for a very long time and looks longingly at
BEN as if they were sharing a moment bordering on sexual
intimacy.

And then she exhales.

                         PATIENT
          Our bodies are like cigarettes.
          The soul is the burning flame that
          consumes the tobacco body, and the
          filtered tip fills up with the
          residue that's everything we
          remember.

She sighs as BEN looks on, contemplatively.

                         PATIENT (CONT'D)
          Okay, last one.

She inhales for one last time, holding it in and letting her
eyes roll into the back of her head.  The pleasure passes
through her and then she unleashes the smoke.

Nodding to BEN, she indicates with her hand that he can go
ahead and cut away at the last connection between her and her
remaining lung as she places the remaining stub in a nearby
ashtray.

BEN reaches into the splayed cavity that is her chest and
with all the force he can muster, cuts the connected
cartilage pipe with his sharpened scissors with such force
that they both shake.

After the loud snapping sound, wisps of that final smoke seep
out of her organs and slowly spread into the air, obscuring
both of them from each other for a brief moment.

                         BEN
          Well, that's it.  Nothing in there
          is connected anymore.  Can you feel
          that?

She nods her head NO.

                         BEN (CONT'D)
          Do you feel anything at all?

Again, she nods her head: NO.

                         BEN (CONT'D)
          How about sleepy?  Faint?  Do you
          feel anything resembling an
          oncoming loss of consciousness,
          maybe light-headedness - a giddy
          sense of your soul rising out of
          your body maybe or some kind of
          final… finality… or, I don't know,
          death?

She continues nodding NO throughout his questions.

                         BEN (CONT'D)
               Well fuck me.  Another six hours
               wasted.

BEN sighs with frustration, tosses the surgical scissor to
the ground and stands up.  He rubs at his eyes and temple
with deep frustration.

                         BEN (CONT'D)
               Thank you for your time.

BEN walks over to an intercom next to the door to the room.
He taps it and leans next to it as he talks.

                         BEN (CONT'D)
               We're done down here in B49.  No
               new developments so you can send
               down a clean-up crew and stitch her
               back up. If anyone needs me, I'll
               be sleeping in the cafeteria.

BEN looks over at the PATIENT.  She looks very sad and mouths
the words I'M SORRY at him.

                         BEN (CONT'D)
               Not your fault at all, my dear.
               God just hates us.

BEN leans on the wall, exhausted, and looks up at the
security camera in the far corner of the room looking down at
him from above.

From the SECURITY CAMERA point-of-view, we get our first wide
look at the room with BEN standing defeatedly like a caught
naughty boy and his patient completely eviscerated.

                                        CUT TO BLACK:


TITLE FADES UP FROM BLACK AND THEN DOWN TO BLACK AGAIN:


INTERIOR HOSPITAL CAFETERIA - NIGHT

There is so much liquor sitting on the counter that this
place looks more like a bar than a hospital cafeteria --
save for the fact that people are standing around and
drinking while stained with blood.

A coffee machine and a pile of dried out donuts on a plate
are also amongst the choices offered.  These items are not as
popular.

BEN enters and pauses, looking at the TV hanging from a
ceiling support.  On-screen, the army is seen rounding up
citizens and moving them along.  Men, women and even some
children are being corralled into buildings by soldiers
brandishing weapons.

                    T.V. REPORTER (V.O.)
          …. These newly established
          internment camps on the outskirts
          of the city offer support for
          entire family units that have been
          affected by recent events.
          Unsupervised private housing of
          families containing more than one
          non-living member is no longer
          being tolerated in most larger East
          Coast cities by special
          presidential order…..

BEN goes to the counter as the TV continues droning in the
background and pours himself a double-shot of cheap scotch.
He sits down at a table across from another intern, JOE
STILLER, whose shirt and jacket are sprayed with blood.

                    JOE
          You hear that one, pally?  They're
          calling them internment camps.
          Didn't even try to come up with
          some kind of pretty name to soften
          the blow.  Hey, is that internment
          or being interred?

                    BEN
          Maybe the president will put her
          name up in lights on this one as
          well, eh?

They clink their cups together wanly and BEN gets his first
good look at JOE.

                    BEN (CONT'D)
          What the fuck happened?  Your
          patient explode?

                    JOE
          The lab jockeys got sloppy; didn't
          finish pre-bleeding my last one
          properly.  I had no idea until I
          started cutting, but by then, of
          course…

                    BEN
          I'm sure it was much more traumatic
          for the patient than for you.

                          JOE
               Eh, we both laughed.

Both men chuckle and look contemplatively at their respective
drinks.

                          BEN
               Coffee warm?

                          JOE
               It was before I poured in the
               Kahlua.

They raise their cups, toast each other and take a drink.

                          JOE (CONT'D)
               You should mix that with something
               else.

                          BEN
               I'm counting the peeled ceramic in
               the cup as the mixer.

                          JOE
               So be it.

They both take another sip of their drinks.

                          JOE (CONT'D)
               How many hours this shift?

                          BEN
               Fourteen.  I'm good for another six
               if I have to.

                          JOE
               Pussy.

BEN sighs and takes another sip of his drink.

                          JOE (CONT'D)
               Lose anyone today?

                          BEN
               Do I look like I lost anyone today?
               And you?

                          JOE
               Not even close after six solid
               hours of chopping away.

                          BEN
               How far did you get after all that?

                    JOE
          Every major organ separated from
          each other and most of the minor
          ones as well.  Dulled one blade and
          worked a second one damn near down
          to the handle.


                    BEN
          Did you leave everything in place
          or did you remove all of the pieces
          once you separated everything?


                    JOE
          Someone's feeling academic today.
          Severed everything but left it all
          floating inside the cavity like
          turtle soup, you know?  I already
          had enough viscera on me and wasn't
          in the mood to spend another hour
          putting it all back inside for the
          final stitch-up.


JOE reaches into his blood-stained pocket, pulls out a
cigarette and lights it.


                    JOE (CONT'D)
          Got a theory brewing behind those
          tired eyes?


                    BEN
          Why anything should make a
          difference at all at this point
          is totally beyond me.  The only
          theory I hold near-and-dear these
          days is to try every fucking thing
          possible.


JOE blows smoke towards BEN, who coughs and waves it away.


                    BEN (CONT'D)
          Christ, I just spent all day
          slaving over a chain-smoker and
          this is the thanks I get?


                    JOE
          Have some respect for the dead,
          willya'?


                    BEN
          The undead.


                    JOE
          The unliving.

As they are playfully debating the proper terminology in their exhausted state, GENERAL BRADFORD enters the room and catches the end of their conversation.

> GENERAL BRADFORD
> Bullshit, gentlemen - I don't want to hear you using that kind of idiotic horror movie slang to describe the people we're trying to help. They're casualties - that's the official term we're using around the front office and I'd prefer it if that were the language you used to describe these people as well.

Both BEN and JOE stand up to acknowledge the presence of the GENERAL.

> GENERAL BRADFORD (CONT'D)
> Sit down, please.

And the two men sit down again.

GENERAL BRADFORD takes the cigarette from JOE'S mouth after he sits down and puts it out in JOE'S cup of coffee.

> GENERAL BRADFORD (CONT'D)
> Why don't you go get yourself a fresh cup while I talk to Truman here?

> JOE
> Yes sir.

JOE gets up and leaves the table.

> GENERAL BRADFORD
> We've been keeping an eye on you and I just wanted to personally let you know that I'm very pleased with the way you treated your patient this morning. Allowing her to smoke and then deactivating her lungs last was a kind gesture. The way we like to see one human being treat another around here. Even under these circumstances.

> BEN
> Thank you, General.

GENERAL BRADFORD rises and gestures towards the door.

                    GENERAL BRADFORD
          C'mon, let's walk and talk.

                    BEN
          Yes sir.


INTERIOR HOSPITAL HALLWAY - NIGHT

The hallway is shockingly filthy and completely disorganized.
BEN and GENERAL BRADFORD walk towards the camera which
dollies along with them as they talk.

                    GENERAL BRADFORD
          How are the facilities holding up
          against the workload so far?

                    BEN
          Well, bluntly, the sanitary
          conditions here are horrifying - I
          think the only thing that keeps the
          rats from overrunning this place is
          the fact that most rodents die
          instantly from disease the moment
          they enter the grounds.  But under
          the circumstances and with the work
          we're doing here, I guess it's as
          good as we need things to be.  It's
          not like we need to be sterile when
          we're just butchering people.

                    GENERAL BRADFORD
          I don't want to hear you or anyone
          else describing the work we do here
          like that ever again.  You're a
          trained medical technician, NOT a
          butcher.

                    BEN
          General, with all due respect, I'm
          not even a doctor. I'm an intern
          who's been promoted to cutting
          people open until they die.  And
          since they're not dying anymore,
          I'm just slicing people open and
          letting them air out.  It's not
          exactly what I went to med school
          for.

                    GENERAL BRADFORD
          I can understand how confusing it
          must be for someone who's been
          trained to save lives.
                    (MORE)

                    GENERAL BRADFORD (CONT'D)
The whole world has gone topsy-
turvy and we're all trying to
figure out how to deanimate the
people we've sworn to protect until
now.

                    BEN
Yeah, god's got one hell of a sense
of humor that way.

                    GENERAL BRADFORD
I would have expected more science
and less religion out of you, of
all people.

                    BEN
You really think there's a simple
scientific explanation for when
people stop dying?

                    GENERAL BRADFORD
We have doctors and scientists from
all over the world working in top
facilities to generate an answer to
that question, and I can tell you
that progress is being made.

                    BEN
Well that's really a pretty
standard answer, isn't it?

GENERAL BRADFORD gives a sideways glance and BEN grimaces as
he realizes how out of line his response has been.  He nods
his head accordingly and respectfully.

                    BEN (CONT'D)
Sorry, sir.

                    GENERAL BRADFORD
I've spent my entire career making
life and death decisions based on
the findings that people much
smarter than me have come up with.
That's not about to stop now.

                    BEN
Hey, I'm a practical guy, but even
I have to draw the line between
where science ends and something
else entirely begins.  And I think
any good scientist would.

                    GENERAL BRADFORD
Helps keep you humble, does it?

                    BEN
          Yeah, maybe.

                    GENERAL BRADFORD
          Well save the humility for another
          time and place.  Keep up the good
          work you've been doing and you'll
          be up for a promotion on my
          recommendation, understand?

                    BEN
          Yes sir.

                    GENERAL BRADFORD
          Good.  How many hours have you been
          on duty today?

                    BEN
          Frankly sir, we don't measure the
          workday with anything as
          insignificant as hours anymore.  I
          have no idea if it's even day or
          night half the time, to be honest.

                    GENERAL BRADFORD
          That's not good, Truman.  The sun
          will be rising soon and I think
          it's time you go home and get some
          rest.  See your wife.  Practice
          making some babies.

                    BEN
          Thank you, sir.

GENERAL BRADFORD stops walking and BEN does likewise.

                    GENERAL BRADFORD
          One last thing, Truman.  I
          appreciate the honesty and
          forthrightness with which you
          addressed me as concerns your
          opinions about what's going on
          around here.  And I'll expect you
          to continue to do so in the future,
          but only when asked to do so.
          Just so we understand each other.
          And we do understand each other,
          don't we?

                    BEN
          Yes sir.

                    GENERAL BRADFORD
          Good.  Dismissed.

The GENERAL continues walking as BEN watches him leave.


EXTERIOR HOSPITAL - NIGHT

BEN and JOE are standing outside, behind the hospital near
the automatic sliding glass doors of the Emergency Entrance.
They are watching an emaciated dog walking along near the
fence perimeter as they share a mini weed pipe back-and-
forth.

                    JOE
          I had a dog like that when I was
          growing up.

                    BEN
          Oh yeah?  We had a cat that never
          left the house.

                    JOE
          Animals seem funny now, don't they?

                    BEN
          Yeah.  Well, they don't have any
          concept of their own death or
          dying.  They just live from day to
          day and don't worry about that
          kinda' stuff like we do.

                    JOE
          Lucky bastards.

                    BEN
          Uh-huh.

                    JOE
          It's not transmissible, you know?

                    BEN
          What's not transmissible?

                    JOE
          The disease.  Or whatever the fuck
          it is that's causing the problem.

                    BEN
          So I hear.

                    JOE
          When a dog dies, they DIE.  I can't
          believe I'm envious of a fucking
          dog.

                          BEN
          Don't be.  Living in ignorance of
          one's own mortality is overrated.

                          JOE
          Shit.  Sez you, old man.

                          BEN
          C'mon, being able to lick your own
          balls is overrated.

                          JOE
          We are obviously in disagreement on
          this issue.

A GUARD with an automatic rifle who has been lurking in the
background comes forward, raises and steadies his weapon, and
then aims it at the stray dog in the distance that JOE and
BEN are watching.

                          BEN
          We're looking for answers and
          they're looking for bones. The
          difference is what, exactly?

The GUARD pulls the trigger - BOOM - and scares both JOE and
BEN.

                          BEN (CONT'D)
          Huh?

The bullet hits the dog in the head and it collapses into a
dead heap.

                          JOE
          What the fuck?

                          GUARD
          No stray dogs.  They carry
          diseases.

                          BEN
          Oh yeah, that was necessary.

The three of them stand around looking at each other for a
moment.

                          GUARD
          Do either of you have permission to
          be out here?

BEN and JOE look at each other for a moment and then burst
out laughing.

                    BEN
          Uhm, okay.  Obviously it's time for
          me to go home.

                    JOE
          Shit.  Yeah, you go ahead and I'll
          get out of here myself as soon as I
          can.

JOE starts to go back inside the hospital but the GUARD stops
him and makes a gesture with his fingers.  JOE hands the
GUARD his still smoking pipe.

                    GUARD
          Liquor store in the cafeteria ain't
          enough for you clowns? You know
          this stuff isn't allowed on the
          premises.

BEN huffs and continues through the doors inside.  BEN walks
around the bend of the rear entrance until he's out of sight.

The GUARD puts the pipe in his mouth, takes a hearty toke and
leans against the wall.


EXTERIOR HOSPITAL - DAWN

The sun has not come up yet.  The sky is a dark, intensely
deep blue.

BEN comes out from behind the hospital.  There are TWO ARMED
GUARDS standing there who silently acknowledge him and let
him pass.

BEN walks through the hospital parking lot to a Guard Box
that watches over an open gate in the chain link fence that
surrounds the hospital.  There are more armed guards
scattered here protecting this entrance.

Beyond the open gate are about two dozen protesters with
signs and pamphlets who are against the undead experiments
going on in the facility.  The signs have graphic photos of
people who've been cut open and signs that read "Fuck the
pResident", etc.

BEN flashes his security pass at one of the GUARDS - his
nameplate identifies him as ROBERTSON.

                    ROBERTSON
          Do you need an escort to get
          through?

                    BEN
          I'm alright, thanks.  Same
          protesters, different day.

ROBERTSON doesn't find BEN'S comment amusing.

                    ROBERTSON
          We'll be keeping an eye out for you
          just in case.

                    BEN
          You must be a new guy.  It's all
          part of the colorful and harmless
          annoyance the locals provide.

As BEN passes through the gate, the protesters surround him -
letting him pass through, but keeping pace with him as he
tries to walk through them all as quickly as possible.

ROBERTSON watches closely, a look of annoyance on his face.

                    PROTESTER 1
          How'd it go today in there, Ben?
          Deanimate anybody you know?

                    BEN
          You know my name?  Hey, what's
          yours?

                    PROTESTER 1
          None of your business, army man.

                    BEN
          Sorry, just a civilian like you
          who's doing his job, jackass.
          Don't any of you have jobs or
          something else better to do?

                    PROTESTER 2
          One day it'll be YOU in there being
          cut open till you're deaimated.
          Whattdya' think of that?!

                    BEN
          If that's what it takes to get away
          from idiots like you, then so be
          it.

                    PROTESTER 3
          You're going against the will of
          god.  How does that make you
          feel?!?

                              BEN
                    Not bad at all.  Kinda' god-like
                    myself.

PROTESTOR 4 gets up in BEN's face, blocking him from walking
for a moment as he waves a large placard on a piece of wood
at BEN.

                         PROTESTER 4
                    You can make a difference - don't
                    deanimate!

BOOM!  The protest sign above BEN'S head explodes as gunfire
quickly decimates it before the sign is dropped to the
ground.

BEN turns around towards the hospital, as shocked and
frightened as any of the PROTESTORS, who are now scattering
quickly in every direction.

ROBERTSON lowers his rifle and makes eye contact with BEN.
He raises a bullhorn and yells into it.

                         ROBERTSON
                    Move along, people!

The soldier flashes BEN a thumbs-up and then turns to go back
to his station.

BEN is appalled and speechless.  He pats himself down to make
sure he hasn't been injured in some way.  In his jacket
pocket, he finds a pamphlet that someone in the crowd must
have shoved in there during the melee.

Itâ€™s a tri-folded sheet of paper covered in words on all of
its sides.  The cover fold simply states in large letters:
THE MANIFESTO OF THE NEW WORLD ORDER.

BEN crumples the paper, tosses it to the ground and quickly
walks away, still shaken.


EXTERIOR CITY STREET - DAWN

The sun is just starting to come up in the sky.

As BEN walks down the almost deserted street a loud gunshot
suddenly rings out.  He stops in his tracks and looks around
for cover.  Before he can move, another shot is fired.

Quickly, he moves into the shadow of a doorway and scrunches
himself up against the door.  Another shot is fired and
ricochets off a nearby wall at an angle that indicates he's
safe from being hit for now.

Across the street, BEN sees an OLD MAN shambling along, oblivious to the gunfire.

THE OLD MAN stops, looks up at the sky and starts yelling.

> OLD MAN
> Hey, what the hell is the matter
> with you?  Stop shooting at people,
> dammit!

BANG!  The sniper fires and hits the old man squarely in the head.  There is a gory explosion of blood and stuff and THE OLD MAN falls backwards onto the ground.

> BEN
> Fuuuuuck….

BEN pulls out his cellphone and dials 911.  A WOMAN answers.

> BEN (CONT'D)
> Hello?  911?

> WOMAN (V.O.)
> Yes, hello - this is emergency
> services.  What is the nature of
> your call?

> BEN
> I'm standing on the corner of
> Central and Acorn and there's some
> crazy sniper shooting at people.
> He just hit an old man who's lying
> in the street bleeding all over the
> place.

PAUSE.  No response from the WOMAN at the other end.

BEN watches as THE OLD MAN gets up and dusts himself off, wiping the blood off of his face, neck and shoulders.  THE OLD MAN looks up at the sky and yells to the sniper.

> OLD MAN
> I'm already dead, you fucking
> idiot!

Another shot rings out and hits the OLD MAN again, this time in the chest.

> BEN
> Hello?  Are you still there.

> WOMAN (V.O.)
> Yeah, I'm still here.  What else
> you got?

                    BEN
          Uhm, what else do I need?  There
          are people getting killed by some
          asshole with a gun.

                    WOMAN (V.O.)
          Sir, while I realize this is an
          urgent matter for you, I sincerely
          think that nobody is getting killed
          at the moment.  Is there a fire or
          some kind of other property damage
          being inflicted by this sniper?

BEN pulls the phone from his ear and lets his arm hang there
for a moment as he snorts the kind of laugh one reserves for
bitter defeat.  Exhaling, he talks to himself under his
breath.

                    BEN
          Ahhh, still living by the old
          rules, Benji.

He raises the phone back to his ear again and sighs.

                    BEN (CONT'D)
          No property damage, nope.
          Everything is otherwise under
          control.

                    WOMAN (V.O.)
          Sir, I'd like to help you out as I
          do know the area that you're
          talking about.  Have you considered
          taking an alternative route that
          would bypass this sniper?

                    BEN
          Never mind.  Thanks.

BEN quickly puts his phone away.  He calls out to the OLD MAN
now not too far away from him in the middle of the street.

                    BEN (CONT'D)
          HEY!  OLD MAN!

                    OLD MAN
          Yeah?  What?

                    BEN
          Come over here and get out of his
          line of sight!

                    OLD MAN
          Like it really matters?

THE OLD MAN shrugs and turns towards where the bullets are coming from.  He raises his hand and gives the sniper the middle-finger.

>                    OLD MAN (CONT'D)
>           Fuck you!  You're a lousy shot, you
>           little pisher.

THE OLD MAN walks towards BEN as shots continue to fire and ricochet off the ground around THE OLD MAN.

>                    OLD MAN (CONT'D)
>           Well lookit that.  Can't hit a
>           moving target for shit.

THE OLD MAN stops and stands before BEN.  Half his face is hanging open, but he continues talking as if nothing has happened.

>                    OLD MAN (CONT'D)
>           Okay, here I am.  Now what?

INTERIOR LENNY'S DINER - MORNING

The diner is half-full at best, mostly people passing through on the way to work and a couple of truck drivers grabbing a quick sit-down breakfast.

BEN enters first, holding the door open for THE OLD MAN and doing his best to try and block the badly damaged man from view of the other patrons drinking their morning coffee.

Once inside, BEN quickly ushers THE OLD MAN to a booth off to one side from the crowded area and all the way at the back of the diner and sits him down facing away from the rest of the customers.

BEN pushes THE OLD MAN all the way into the booth so he can sit on the same side of it with him.

>                    OLD MAN
>           Hey, not so pushy about it, please.

>                    BEN
>           C'mon, have a seat and pipe down.

BEN examines THE OLD MAN quickly, enough to see that the bullet that entered through the large, open gash in his face has cleanly exited out of the back of his head.

                    BEN (CONT'D)
          Excellent.  The bullet was expelled
          through the exit wound. I can just
          sew you up for now.

                    OLD MAN
          Shit.  I hate needles.  What's the
          point anyway?

                    BEN
          You wanna walk around with your
          face half open like a corned beef
          sandwich or you wanna pass for
          white a little bit better?

                    OLD MAN
          Okay, alright…..

BEN pulls a surgical sewing kit out of his pocket and unfolds
it on the table.

                    OLD MAN (CONT'D)
          Got a cigarette?

                    BEN
          I don't smoke.

BEN threads a surgical needle and tugs lightly at the thin
skin around the edges of the open wound of THE OLD MAN's
face, figuring out where to begin his stitching.

THE OLD MAN pulls a cigarette out of his own pocket and
lights it.

                    BEN (CONT'D)
          I can't seem to get away from
          smokers today.

                    OLD MAN
          I don't like giving them away.  I
          ain't got the cash and it's the
          only pleasure I've got left since I
          can't get drunk anymore.

                    BEN
          Really?  Alcohol doesn't have any
          effect on you?

                    OLD MAN
          Yep.  Ever since… well, you know.

                    BEN
          That's interesting.

                         OLD MAN
          Oh yeah?  Got dead people clogging
          up the bars near you?

                         BEN
          No.  I work at the hospital and
          we've been sedating our patients
          before we….

BEN begins the stitching process on the open wound.

                         OLD MAN
          Working on a cure, doc?

                         BEN
          Yeah, but there ain't no cure for
          love.

                         OLD MAN
          Well I can't pretend to speak for
          all the other folks like me out
          there, but I can tell you that
          since what happened to me no matter
          how much I drink it don't do a
          thing.

BEN gets lost in thought as THE OLD MAN takes a drag from his
cigarette.

                         BEN
          Still enjoy smoking, though.

                         OLD MAN
          I used to worry about getting
          cancer from these things. But the
          truth is, not worrying about it
          does take some of the fun out of
          smoking 'em.

THE OLD MAN takes a deeper drag off his cigarette and exhales
it thoughtfully.

                         OLD MAN (CONT'D)
          Death isn't what I expected it to
          be at all.

                         BEN
          Me neither.

THE OLD MAN cackles.

                         OLD MAN
          That's funny.  You're funny.

BEN stops stitching for a moment and looks THE OLD MAN in the
eye.

                         BEN
               What's so different than you
               expected?

                         OLD MAN
               Well, first of all, where was my
               bright light?  I got nothing like
               that at all.  I thought I'd feel
               the stepping over the threshold
               moment, you know what I mean?
               Crossing that dotted-line between
               life and death.  What do I get?
               Nuthin'.  So not only have I been
               cheated out of the rest of my life,
               but death didn't even give me the
               welcome-to-the-other-side
               handshake.

                         BEN
               And now?  What about how you feel
               now?

                         OLD MAN
               Well, my kids don't call me as
               often as they used to.

THE OLD MAN gives BEN a look and they both chuckle.  BEN goes
back to stitching.

                         BEN
               Sorry if that was too personal a
               question.

                         OLD MAN
               It's alright.  Nobody asks me
               questions anymore.  I've gotten
               used to being ignored.  I guess
               that makes me a wiseass sometimes.
               But you know what?  In my mind, the
               way I see things, and think about
               things - the way I experience
               things.  It's all barely changed at
               all.  I guess that's what makes
               being treated different all of a
               sudden by everybody so painful.

                         BEN
               Painful?  Like the pain you had
               while you were alive?

140

                              OLD MAN
                    You bet.  I may not feel the pain
                    here.

THE OLD MAN points to the wound that BEN is currently working
on repairing.

                              OLD MAN (CONT'D)
                    But I still feel it quite vividly
                    right up here.

THE OLD MAN points to the good side of what's left of his
head, indicating his mind.

From around the corner, THE WAITRESS finally approaches BEN
and THE OLD MAN, carrying menus and a pitcher of water.  She
slows her gait when she sees, from behind THE OLD MAN as BEN
continues sewing, exactly what's going on in her booth.

                              WAITRESS
                    No fucking way.  Not in my section,
                    dammit.

She slams down the menus and the water pitcher on the booth
directly across from theirs and gets right into BEN's face.

                              WAITRESS (CONT'D)
                    How dare you bring one of these
                    things in here! People are trying
                    to eat!  If the Department of
                    Health hears about this they'll
                    shut us down!

BEN says nothing but shoots her a look.

                              OLD MAN
                    Lady, I think that's his way of
                    telling you to fuck off.

She does not look at THE OLD MAN but continues yelling at BEN
as he continues to stitch THE OLD MAN's face.

                              WAITRESS
                    How dare you let this thing speak
                    to me like that!

                              BEN
                    Listen, if you've got a problem
                    with this, than send Lenny over.
                    He knows who I am and we go way
                    back, okay?

THE WAITRESS picks up her menus and water pitcher and stomps
away.

                    OLD MAN
          Hey, and bring me back a hot
          coffee, willya'? Cream and sugar on
          the side.

THE OLD MAN laughs.

                    BEN
          Careful.  You're gonna rip the
          stitches.


INTERIOR LENNY'S DINER KITCHEN - MORNING

THE WAITRESS comes storming into the kitchen and yells at
LENNY, who's flipping bacon and eggs on the grill.  LENNY is
a huge, burly man with a long white beard.

                    WAITRESS
          Lenny, there's some punk kid in the
          back booth embroidering a fucking
          homeless old corpse and telling me
          that you'll be okay with it.

                    LENNY
          Shit.  Anyone else back there with
          'em?

                    WAITRESS
          You think anyone wants to sit near
          that smell?

LENNY hands his cooking implements to the WAITRESS.

                    LENNY
          Take over.

He grabs a large bowel, one of the pitchers of water she just
put down and a large dish rag, and then storms right on past
her.


INTERIOR LENNY'S DINER BOOTH - MORNING

BEN is still sewing away as quickly as he can; he looks like
he's more than half-way through with connecting the right
half of THE OLD MAN's face with his left half when LENNY
comes around the corner, walks over and stands over them.

THE OLD MAN taps BEN nervously and points to LENNY, but BEN
ignores him and keeps his needle moving.

LENNY loudly puts down the large bowl on the table, tosses in
the rag and pours water over it till the bowl is half full.


142

                    LENNY
          You've got big brass ones, kid.
          Maybe even three or four of them.

                    BEN
          Thanks, Lenny.  I promise we won't
          be much longer.

LENNY sits down on the other side of the booth and watches
BEN stitch.

                    LENNY
          The shit I put up with.

                    OLD MAN
          We greatly appreciate your
          generosity.

LENNY just nods and waves his hand and accepts the comment
dismissively.

                    LENNY
          Yeah, well.  This kid's got a bad
          habit of helping people out even
          when it might cause trouble, right
          kid?

                    BEN
          Mmm-hmmm.

                    OLD MAN
          Pulled a thorn out of your paw, did
          he?

                    LENNY
          That's one way of saying it.

Without taking his eyes off what he's doing, BEN makes small
talk.

                    BEN
          How is your sister doing, Lenny?

LENNY bangs his knuckles on the table twice for good luck.

                    LENNY
          You know better than I do, kid.
          Now don't press your luck.  Finish
          up quick, wash up with this here
          towel so you're not covered with
          blood and then high-tail it out the
          back door before you cause too much
          trouble amongst my high-priced
          clientele.

                    BEN
          Gotchya.

THE OLD MAN talks to LENNY while BEN works.

                    OLD MAN
          I've been getting nothing but spit-
          on for weeks.  I didn't know there
          were any good people left.

                    LENNY
          Yeah, he's alright.  Don't give 'em
          a swelled head with that kinda'
          talk, though.

                    OLD MAN
          Is he married?  He seems so young.

                    LENNY
          He's got a beautiful old lady but
          he never brings her around anymore
          since he moved to the good side of
          town.

                    BEN
          Aww, c'mon, Lenny.  She's a
          vegetarian.  You don't even put
          lettuce on your burgers for
          chrissakes.

                    OLD MAN
          A nice fella like you, you should
          have kids.

                    LENNY
          Shit, Benji is still a kid himself,
          old man.  Give him some time.
          Though if I had your wife, I'd have
          had me a half-dozen critters by
          now.

BEN looks at LENNY and gives him a dry look.  He speaks
matter-of-factly without any emotion as he relates the
following:

                    BEN
          We can't have kids.  She can't have
          kids.

                    LENNY
          That's not fair, my friend.  You
          never told me that.

                    OLD MAN
          I'm very sorry as well …..

                    BEN
          It's a recent development.  I ain't
          been holding out on you, Lenny.

A moment of silence passes.  BEN waves them away and goes
back to concentrating on his stitching.

                    LENNY
          You really are made of tough stuff,
          kid.  We're gonna need lots more
          people like you to make it through
          these crazy times.  Everyone's gone
          stupid, it feels like.  Like
          they've forgotten that someday
          we're all gonna be dead or dying
          too. Where did the empathy go?  And
          where did all the hate come from?

                    OLD MAN
          I'm older than both of you so let
          me tell you, that hate you seem so
          mystified by - it's always been
          there.  Always just below the
          surface and coming up for air just
          when it's running out and choking
          for more. It's hard to breathe when
          politicians are always fanning the
          flames of hatred that keep us
          apart.

                    BEN
          Why don't you hippies keep it down
          so I can finish up these last
          couple of …..

Suddenly, on the wall behind LENNY, a small plate of apple
pie explodes against the wall, showering all three of them
with shards of broken glass and bits of food.

                    PATRON 1
          Go back to your dirt hole, zombie!

At the bend where the rest of the diner curves around and
away from the area BEN and the rest of them are sitting, a
couple of other DINER PATRONS are standing, looking
threateningly at THE OLD MAN.

                    PATRON 2
          Get that thing out of here.  I
          can't even bring my dog in here and
          you let THAT sit in a booth?

Furious, LENNY rises with intent.

                    LENNY
          Don't you be throwing my apple pie
          at me you cheap sonsabitches.  Now
          get back to your tables, finish
          your meal and pay up or just get
          the fuck out of here.

The DINER PATRONS stand there for a moment, unsure of what to
do next, and then back off.

                    BEN
          Sorry, Lenny.  Last couple of
          stitches.

LENNY places his hand on the BEN's shoulder.

                    LENNY
          Quick as you can, kid, and then the
          back door. Also, leave a nice tip
          for the waitress, willya'? She's
          gonna have to clean all this up
          now.

LENNY walks away towards the area where one or two PATRONS
are still loitering.  As he slowly approaches, they stand
their ground and give him a nasty look.

                    PATRON 1
          I'm gonna remember you, zombie
          loving piece of shit.  Nobody talks
          to me the way you did.

                    PATRON 2
          You best watch your back, asshole.

                    LENNY
          Get the fuck outta' my place you
          fucking scumbags.

The PATRONS do a slow-burn turn around and move towards the
front door.

                                        DISSOLVE TO:


INTERIOR APARTMENT BUILDING LOBBY - LATE MORNING

BEN enters the building balancing a bag of groceries and is
almost immediately met by the doorman, AVERY, who walks
alongside him towards the elevator with a large manila
envelope in his hand.

                    AVERY
          Good morning, Mr. Truman.

                    BEN
          Good morning, Avery.

                    AVERY
          Wow, you're not just getting home
          from work, are you?

                    BEN
          Indeed I am.  Today's been a rough
          week already.

                    AVERY
          That's incredible.  I do not envy
          you your hours, Mr. Truman.  I'm on
          my way home in a few minutes.

They reach the elevator and AVERY presses the button.  They
wait.

                    AVERY (CONT'D)
          By the way, I wanted to give you
          this to pass on to Mrs. Truman for
          me, if that's okay.

AVERY hands BEN the envelope.  BEN looks at it
uncomprehendingly with his free hand before sliding it into
the bag crooked on his other arm.

                    AVERY (CONT'D)
          It's my tax forms.  She was very
          gracious and said she'd be more
          than happy to do them for me again
          this year.

                    BEN
          Oh right.  Yeah, I've been so
          caught up with stuff I almost
          forgot about it.

                    AVERY
          She did such a great job last year.
          Saved me a lot of money.

                    BEN
          Yeah, not even the resurrection can
          hold back the April deadline, eh?

                    AVERY
          You said it, Mr. Truman.  Heck, not
          even sure we'll have the term
          'deadline" anymore, will we?

With a "ding", the elevator arrives and BEN laughs at that last thought.

                    BEN
          Well said, Avery.  Deadlines.
          Lifelines.  Got a whole lot of new
          language stuff to be worked out
          these days.

BEN steps into the elevator and sighs, grabbing an apple off the top of his bag and tossing it to Avery.  AVERY effortlessly catches the apple and gives a friendly bow to BEN as the elevator doors close.


INTERIOR APARTMENT BUILDING HALLWAY - LATE MORNING

The elevator doors slide open and BEN steps out into the hallway.  He proceeds quietly and slowly as he looks around to make sure nobody is watching as he walks towards the door to his apartment.


INTERIOR BEN'S APARTMENT - LATE MORNING

The apartment is dark when BEN swings open the door.  All the windows are closed, the blinds are down and the moist air is a thinly visible mist.

BEN tosses the thick envelope AVERY handed him onto the couch and then he places his bag of groceries on a table and begins immediately unpacking the goods.  The few food items on top, when removed, reveal a bag otherwise filled with cleansing agents and deodorants.

Pulling out a roll of duct tape, he seals the apartment door behind him, occasionally spraying the strands with some air freshener before tamping it all down with his flattened hand.

He sprays a bit more of the freshener around the room, waving his hands to spread it evenly in the air.

A woman's voice calls out to him from the other room.  It is his wife, MARY.

                    MARY (V.O.)
          Honey?

                    BEN
          Yeah, I'm home.

                    MARY (V.O.)
          I'm in the bedroom.

                         BEN
          Sure thing.  I'll be right there.

BEN picks up AVERY's envelope from the couch and heads
towards the bedroom.


INTERIOR BEDROOM - EARLY MORNING

MARY is lying in bed naked on her stomach, wearing only her
glasses and socks, surrounded by all sorts of tax forms,
charts and paperwork.  Pen in hand, she is finishing up some
long equation on a sheet of scrap paper as BEN gives her a
kiss on the forehead and sits on the edge of the bed -
displacing some of the stacked papers in the process.

                         MARY
          Careful, those are almost done.

BEN strokes the back of her leg and upper thigh as she
continues to work.

                         BEN
          You're a little bit stinky today.
          Did you wash up?

                         MARY
          Sorry, hon.  Got busy and forgot.

                         BEN
          No kidding.  Plus, you forgot to
          seal up the door the last time I
          went out.

                         MARY
          Shit.  I'm sorry.  I know that was
          a bad thing.

                         BEN
          Should have called from work to
          remind you.

BEN grabs a can of Lysol from the floor next to the bed and
does a quick, cursory spray of the room.

                         BEN (CONT'D)
          Howzabout taking a bath when you're
          done with that one?

                         MARY
          Sure thing.  I've just got to add
          up all this 1099 stuff before going
          forward, so it's a perfect time to
          take a break.

                    BEN
          I'll run it for you.

                    MARY
          Hmmm.  A nice hot bath?

                    BEN
          A lukewarm bath.

                    MARY
          With bubbles….?

                    BEN
          No bubbles today, babe.

BEN smacks MARY on the ass and rises towards the bathroom.

                    MARY
          Hey!  I can still feel that!

                    BEN
          Really?

She gives him a deadpan look.

                    MARY
          Don't be a jerk, baby.

BEN stops and turns back towards her.

                    BEN
          Oh, and before I forget, here's one
          from the doorman.

                    MARY
          Is that Avery's?

                    BEN
          Yep.

He tosses it onto the edge of the bed.

                    MARY
          I like him.  He's a nice guy and
          very helpful.

                    BEN
          Yeah, he seems alright to me.

BEN walks into the bathroom.

INTERIOR BATHROOM - LATE MORNING

MARY is sitting up in the tub as BEN washes her back with a
coarse rag to deep clean the pores.  Scented candles burn all
around the edge of the tub and the sink.

                    MARY
          I heard on the news this morning
          that some scientist in Utah is
          lobbying to have god added to the
          Periodic Table of the Elements.

BEN laughs derisively.

                    BEN
          Oh yeah, that's great.  That's a
          great idea.  Just what we need.

                    MARY
          Another rough day at work?

                    BEN
          Let's talk about something else,
          huh?  And lie back so I can scrub
          your feet.

She spins around, gives him a kiss and then tilts back in the
tub.

                    BEN (CONT'D)
          How many did you finish today?

                    MARY
          The Johnson's down the hall and the
          Epstein's on the third floor.  They
          were two of the more complicated
          forms so I just wanted to be done
          with them.

                    BEN
          See if you can't fit in the
          doorman's stuff sooner rather than
          later.  The less time he's giving
          us any special attention, the
          better.

                    MARY
          Okay.  I'll start on his this
          evening or early tomorrow.

                    BEN
          Tomorrow is perfect.  Thanks, hon.

INTERIOR BEDROOM - MIDDAY

The room is dark save for some dull ambient light sneaking
into the room from the spaces between the window blinds.  BEN
and MARY are lying in bed, intimately entwined, kissing and
stroking each other's bodies tenderly as they speak softly to
each other.

                    BEN
          Okay, so you wanna know how bad
          it's gotten at work?
          The other day we got a lecture -
          with a PowerPoint presentation, no
          less - on how some geek
          mathematician successfully
          incorporated the letter "G",
          representing "god", into his
          equations.  "G" to the nth power.
          Says it plugs into things quite
          nicely.

                    MARY
          The world did get strange last
          February, didn't it.

                    BEN
          Still, I don't like this mixing of
          god into my science. They're not
          the same thing.  Faith and proof
          got nothing to do with each other.
          Shit, faith is anti-proof.  I'm a
          doctor now and…..

                    MARY
          Almost a doctor.

                    BEN
          Yeah, almost.  But if I wanted to
          become a priest, I'd have studied
          for that instead.

                    MARY
          Is that the problem you're having
          at work?

                    BEN
          Kind of.  Everyone is just so
          tired, we've got protesters
          practically beating down our doors,
          military jack-knobs busting our
          chops for results and now religious
          loons trying to chop away at the
          last legs of validity science
          has left to offer.
                    (MORE)

152

                    BEN (CONT'D)
          So yeah, it's been an even worse
          week than usual lately.

                    MARY
          I'm sorry, babe.  You should get
          some sleep.

They kiss deeply and he strokes her face.

                    BEN
          Can I ask you about something?

                    MARY
          Always.

                    BEN
          Something uncomfortable.

                    MARY
          Uncomfortable for you or for me?

                    BEN
          Both of us, probably.

                    MARY
          Okay.  Sure.

                    BEN
          It's about your….. passing.

Pause.  They look into each other deeply and she nods her
head affirmatively.

                    BEN (CONT'D)
          I was talking to someone this
          morning in a situation similar to
          yours.  He told me that when he
          passed he didn't see any bright
          lights or feel any significant
          change at all.  And now, afterward,
          he still feels pretty much the same
          as he did before passing.  And so
          I've been wondering if it's the
          same way for you or not.

                    MARY
          Listen Benjamin, I don't wanna
          freak you out or anything, so I'll
          tell you if you really want to
          know.

                    BEN
          Yeah, I do.

                    MARY
          Last February, when this all
          started, I was so scared.  You
          remember all that confusion.
          Nobody knew what was happening or
          why.  Nobody trusted anyone,
          martial law and the funeral home
          raids …..

                    BEN
          When everyone thought it was a
          disease.  Zombie AIDS. Oh, I mean
          "ZAIDS".  For chrissakes, I hate
          all these stupid contractions.
          Those were some ugly fucking days.

                    MARY
          It's different now.  Not that we
          know so much better, I guess, but
          at least we're getting used to it
          now.  Accepting it.  But when I
          made my decision, it really did
          seem like the best thing to do at
          the time.  And I've never been so
          wrong about anything before.

                    BEN
          I wonder.  Maybe you weren't so
          damn wrong.

She takes his hand and kisses his knuckles as they continue
talking.

                    MARY
          That's sweet of you to say, but I
          know you're just saying it. You
          don't mean it.  You shouldn't mean
          it.

BEN turns her hand, still clutching his, around.  Now he
kisses her knuckles.

                    BEN
          Do you still feel anything?  Do you
          still feel this like you used to?

He kisses the back of her hand emphatically.

                    MARY
          I still feel everything.  It's all
          still working up here.

She points to her head.

                    MARY (CONT'D)
          Sometimes, even moreso.  Like right
          now, I can feel how much you still
          love me.  And I've never loved you
          more.

They kiss deeply and move in towards each other.

                                        FADE TO BLACK.


INTERIOR BED ROOM - EVENING

It's dark outside the windows and the room is lit by the
television as MARY sits on the unmade bed.  She takes turns
looking over at the TV and at BEN, who is visible in the
shower through the open bathroom door.

She's working on a tax form as she tries to ignore what's
being said on the TV by J.J. MUNROE, a talk show host with a
brusque manner and an agenda.

                    MUNROE
          Still developing in Kansas, the
          buckle of the Bible belt; undead
          man goes from gentle hombre to
          hungry zombie. What's the story
          there, folks?

MARY keeps her head down over her papers, but her eyes sneak
a peak at MUNROE.

                    MUNROE (CONT'D)
          Although not all the facts are in
          yet - and really, when are they
          ever when it comes to dealing with
          this new breed of zombies that are
          overrunning our country?  It
          appears that mild-mannered Harvey
          Newell went from being as law
          abiding and respectable as an
          undead American could be to a
          ravenous, flesh-craving basket case
          yesterday.

BEN finishes showering and turns off the water.  MARY turns
her attention back to her paperwork quickly while still
listening to the TV.

MUNROE (CONT'D)
Surprise, surprise - doctors and
scientists are naturally at a loss
to explain what happened, but
sources close to the incident have
been using the phrase "zombie
Alzheimer's" to describe the
condition of a man who went bone
simple, so to speak, and started
biting at the doctor who was
examining him in a contained space.

BEN is standing next to MARY now and continues toweling off.

BEN
Watching this shit?

MARY
It's background noise for when I'm
working.

MARY continues working and BEN sits down next to her on the
edge of the bed.  She leans into him and they both look up at
the TV.

MUNROE
Listen, who am I to judge, but it
seems to me that internment camps
serve a noble purpose, and that's
to separate the THEM from the US.
For our own safety.  Is this the
next step in the disease for our
undead loved ones?  "Zombie
Alzheimer's", which I'll call
"Zalzheimer's" for short is a
dangerous possibility, people of
America, and there's no reason we
should be putting ourselves or our
neighbors at risk by letting these
people run free.  We've got to stop
pretending that they're still just
like us and admit that at any
moment these….

CLICK.  BEN uses the remote to change the channel to another
interview program where a woman talks about her hysterical
pregnancy.  They are now illuminated by the steamy mist
provided by the bathroom light.

BEN
How you holding up?

156

                    MARY
          Have you had any cases like what
          he's talking about?

                    BEN
          Not a one.  I've read some academic
          journals that predicted something
          similar.  Atrophy of the nervous
          system and eventually degeneration
          of the cerebral cortex and logic
          systems.  Mindlessness, just like
          your standard issue cheap movie
          zombies.  No more personality, no
          more higher functions, just a
          walking, biting and eating machine.

                    MARY
          The president is lobbying congress
          for those camps.  I saw her press
          conference earlier today and she
          didn't sound much different than
          the stuff Munroe's spewing.

                    BEN
          What else would you expect?  This
          kind of rhetoric is what got
          Carlson elected in the first place.
          Someone that unqualified would have
          never gotten attention any other
          way.  It's a fucking joke.

MARY chuckles, but it's a dark reaction.

                    MARY
          How much longer do you really think
          we can keep this up?

                    BEN
          I don't know, but I say we keep on
          trying.

BEN folds down to his knees and kisses MARY's kneecap and
strokes her leg.

                    BEN (CONT'D)
          Didn't that used to be a tickle
          spot?

                    MARY
          Yeah, I guess so.

                    BEN
          Awww, I kinda miss that.

MARY laughs and playfully kicks BEN away from her.

> MARY
> Now look what you did!  You made me
> ticklish again.

BEN gives a faux maniacal laugh and speaks in a mock-evil
voice.

> BEN
> Suggestion is a very powerful
> thing, my dear!

The both laugh as BEN growls and goes for the knee again.

As they begin to wrestle and laugh the phone rings.

> BEN (CONT'D)
> Shit.  There's only one thing that
> could be.

BEN reaches for his cellphone on the night table next to the
bed and answers it.

> BEN (CONT'D)
> Yeah?  Wow.  Okay.  I'll be there
> as soon as I can.

BEN finishes the call and tosses it back down.

> MARY
> Back to work already?

> BEN
> Joe says for me to get my ass over
> there.  We've just been invaded by
> the clergy.

BEN gets up and starts gathering fresh clothes for himself.

> MARY
> What are you talking about?

BEN pulls on his clothes as he talks.

> BEN
> Chaplain services were suspended
> years ago at this facility due to
> lack of interest, but something's
> up now.  Nice of them to suddenly
> take an interest in us. I guess
> they see a whole new unending
> source of clientele they can entice
> into the fold.

                         MARY
          "Nobody expects the Spanish
          Inquisition..."

                         BEN
          Good one.

                         MARY
          Try to be polite to them, Benji.

                         BEN
          Sure thing, as long as they keep
          their clerical noses out of our
          scientific work.

MARY gathers up a bunch of papers she's been working on and
stuffs them into an envelope.

                         MARY
          Here's Avery's forms.  You can give
          them back to him on the way down.

                         BEN
          Damn, you are fast.

                         MARY
          It's practically an EZ form for
          him.  No 1099's, no kids to worry
          about.

BEN is fully dressed now.  He grabs the envelope and gives
MARY a quick kiss.

                         BEN
          See you eventually, hon.

                         MARY
          Be careful, fella.


INTERIOR LIVING ROOM - NIGHT

BEN goes charging through the room, stops at the front door
and undoes the locks, pulling the duct tape off from around
the door frame.

Before opening the door, BEN turns and goes back to the
kitchen table, grabs a can of Lysol and sprays the inside and
outside of the large manila envelope.

                         BEN
          Remember to seal up the door behind
          me.

                         MARY (V.O.)
          Okay.

BEN goes back to the door.  He looks out the peephole to make
sure the hallway is clear, and when he feels safe he quickly
swings open the door, flings himself out and pulls it closed
tightly behind him in a single, swift gesture.


INTERIOR APARTMENT BUILDING LOBBY - NIGHT

AVERY is sitting at his security desk on the telephone with a
building resident.

                         AVERY
               Yes, Mrs. Johnson, I understand
               that the smell is giving you a
               headache and I'll look into it.
               I'll make sure the cleaning crew
               isn't accidentally over-spraying
               their disinfectants in that
               section.

The elevator doors open and BEN steps out into the lobby
while AVERY is still talking.  BEN pauses at the desk, gives
AVERY a cursory smile and quietly hands him the envelope.

Before BEN can quickly walk away, AVERY holds up a finger and
BEN pauses.

                         AVERY (CONT'D)
               I'm going to have to briefly put
               you on hold for a moment, Mrs.
               Johnson.  Please hold on.

Click!  AVERY pushes in a button.

                         AVERY (CONT'D)
               Thank you so much, Mr. Truman.  And
               please thank your lovely wife for
               me as well - I feel like I never
               see her pass through here anymore.

                         BEN
               You're very welcome, Avery.  Gotta
               run but I'll tell her what you
               said.

BEN quickly heads towards the main doors of the building.

AVERY presses the button on his phone and gets back to his
conversation, at the same time taking a peek inside the
manila envelope.


160

                    AVERY
          I'm sorry Mrs. Johnson, please
          continue with what you were saying.

AVERY listens to her but also silently reacts sharply to the
smell of the paperwork in the envelope.  He pulls it out and
looks it over with a raised eyebrow.

                    AVERY (CONT'D)
          Sure, I know what you mean.  Kind
          of like that clean, hospital smell
          you get in the hallways, right?

AVERY flips through the pages, and then smells his fingers as
well.

                    AVERY (CONT'D)
          Yes, ma'am.  Well, I can tell you
          that our cleaning people usually
          have deoderent-based cleansers, and
          not the kind they use in hospitals,
          but I do know exactly the
          antiseptic smell that you're
          talking about.

AVERY slips his paperwork back into the envelope with a slow,
suspicious gesture.

                                        DISSOLVE TO:


EXTERIOR HOSPITAL - NIGHT

JOE is standing out front, smoking a cigarette as BEN
approaches the main entrance.

                    BEN
          Why you doing that out here?

                    JOE
          Not allowed to smoke inside
          anymore.  It's all going to hell,
          man.  The clergy are taking over.

                    BEN
          When did this start happening?

                    JOE
          Effective immediately upon their
          arrival.  First thing the fuckers
          did was remove the bar and clean
          out the coffee machine.
                    (MORE)

                    JOE (CONT'D)
Do you have any idea how much worse
the coffee is when that machine is
clean?

                    BEN
Alright, time to take some lumps.

                    JOE
Hold it.

JOE grabs BEN by the arm and stops him from leaving just yet.

                    JOE (CONT'D)
It hasn't hit the media yet, but
there's been two more biting
incidents.  One's an old man who
bit a family member who was giving
him home care and the other was a
small baby that was nursing and bit
the mothers breast nearly clean off
even without teeth.

                    BEN
Fuuuuuuuck.  A baby?

                    JOE
Stillborn but still moving.  Do you
blame the parents for trying?
Would you dump a kid or your wife
if it came down to it?

BEN stammers for a moment, unsure of what to say to that.

                    BEN
Uhm, I guess not.

                    JOE
Yeah, the last 12 hours have been
busy.

                    BEN
Any connection between the
incidents?

                    JOE
Well, both of the biters were
undead and both the bite-ees were
alive at the time they were bitten.
Any more info than that, you'll
need to ask the General.

                    BEN
Okay then.

162

                    JOE
          It's not looking good, man.  It
          seemed like things wer starting to
          taper off and I thought we'd get a
          handle on what's been going on, but
          this throws a whole new monkey's
          paw into the mix.

                    BEN
          Lots to think about.  I'm going in.

                    JOE
          Good luck, Benji.


INTERIOR HOSPITAL ENTRANCE - NIGHT

There is now a walk-through metal detector at the entrance in
addition to two armed security guards.

BEN walks through the detector and sets it off as the TWO
GUARDS, GUS and CHARLIE motion for him to stop.

                    BEN
          Hey there guys.

                    GUS
          Benji, General Bradford has been
          asking about you.

                    BEN
          Good, I need to talk to him.

                    CHARLIE
          Evening, Mr. Truman.

BEN continues walking, but CHARLIE blocks his path.

                    BEN
          Chuck, you're kidding me, right?

                    CHARLIE
          It's the procedure starting now.

                    GUS
          Sorry, Benji, but you know we don't
          make the rules.

                    BEN
          Yeah, yeah; I hear ya', Gus.

BEN empties his pockets into a tray.  Loose change, keys, ID.
Etc.

                    CHARLIE
          Don't forget your belt and
          cellphone.

BEN grunts his acknowledgement as he acquiesces.

                    BEN
          Okay, here we go again, fellas….

BEN walks through the metal detector and it goes off again.

BEN is nonplussed and GUS laughs.

                    GUS
          It's your wedding ring, Benji.

BEN looks at his hand and closes it into a fist.

                    BEN
          Listen guys, I'm not taking off my
          wedding ring for this, so you can
          frisk me if you want to or just let
          me through, but it's not coming off
          for this fucking machine.

CHARLIE moves towards BEN and GUS jumps in between them.

                    GUS
          No problem, I've got the wand I can
          wave you down instead.

GUS waves the metal detecting wand over BEN's entire body and
gets no sound.

                    CHARLIE
          Don't push us around, man.  We're
          doing our jobs, just like you are.
          You cut people open and we make
          this place a safe work environment
          even though you're knee deep in
          walking corpses.

                    GUS
          You see?  He's clean.  Benji's
          cool, Charlie.

                    BEN
          Thanks, Gus.

BEN gathers up all his personal belongings from the little
tray and quickly stuffs it all back into his pockets as he
walks away.

Rounding the corner, BEN checks his cellphone; the battery is nearly empty.

                    BEN (CONT'D)
          Shit.


INTERIOR NURSES STATION - NIGHT

NURSE FELTON is on duty and going through a stack of paperwork as BEN comes swinging in through the door. She doesn't even look up from what she's doing.

                    BEN
          Hey there.

                    NURSE
          General Bradford's been looking for
          you.

                    BEN
          You still have a phone charging
          station in here?

NURSE FELTON points as she responds.

                    NURSE
          Top drawer to your left.

BEN opens the drawer. Inside are a number of different chargers with various connecters. He fishes through the tangle of wires and discovers another MANIFESTO pamphlet at the bottom of the mess. He pulls it out, crumples it and tosses the paper into a nearby garbage can with an annoyed flourish.

BEN continues rummaging until he finds the charger tip that fits his device. He plugs it in and places the phone on a nearby counter where other phones are also charging.

                    BEN
          Pretty busy over here.

NURSE FELTON nods and goes back to her paperwork.

                    BEN (CONT'D)
          Thanks.

He spins and quickly exits.


INTERIOR GENERAL BRADFORD'S OFFICE - NIGHT

There's a knock at the door.

                    GENERAL BRADFORD
          Come on in, Truman - if that is
          finally you.

BEN opens the door and enters the room.  Three priests who
have been sitting rise and acknowledge his entrance with a
respectful half-bow.  They are FATHER TODD, FATHER BRANDT and
FATHER GANZ.

BEN gives them a small bow in return and then they sit down.

                    BEN
          Thank you.

GENERAL BRADFORD is sitting behind his desk looking less than
pleased.

                    GENERAL BRADFORD
          I'm all out of chairs at the
          moment, Mr. Truman, so I'll ask you
          to please stand.

                    BEN
          Yes sir.

                    GENERAL BRADFORD
          I want you to meet Father Todd,
          Father Brandt and Father Ganz, all
          of the order of St. Augustine.

FATHER TODD offers BEN a dismissive glance; he appears
impatient to get back to what was obviously a heated
discussion before BEN entered the room.

                    FATHER TODD
          Getting back to the point of this
          discussion before Mr. Truman
          arrived, we absolutely do not
          approve of your trying to outright
          kill people.

                    GENERAL BRADFORD
          And as I was saying just before Mr.
          Truman entered, we are not
          "killing" anybody, Father Todd, as
          our client base consists entirely
          of reanimated casualties.

                    FATHER TODD
          I object to your use of that term
          to describe people who are no
          longer living. "Reanimated" is
          vulgar and inaccurate slang.

GENERAL BRADFORD is polite, but firm.  Very firm.

> GENERAL BRADFORD
> Nonetheless, we refer to these
> people as "reanimated casualties"
> in our communiqués and we will
> continue to do so for the time
> being.

Breaking protocol, BEN jumps in with a comment.

> BEN
> I'd like to add that the process
> we've been trying to achieve
> is referred to as "deanimation",
> which I think is a correctly worded
> scientific attempt at an acceptable
> terminology.

FATHER TODD shoots BEN a look.  Nobody was speaking to him.

> FATHER TODD
> Gentlemen, I've got a couple
> thousand of years of church
> doctrine behind me, so I know
> politically correct bull chips when
> I smell them.  Don't try to flim-
> flam me or my associates with all
> this semantic nonsense.

BEN looks to GENERAL BRADFORD for permission to answer.

> GENERAL BRADFORD
> Don't be shy, Truman.  I've spoken
> my mind already and you have my
> permission to speak yours.

But FATHER TODD continues before BEN has a chance to respond.

> FATHER TODD
> Also, please keep in mind that when
> this medical facility was first
> given over to military control, we
> were in a state of confusion and
> panic.  That time has since passed
> and we'd like to get back to doing
> what this hospital was first built
> for - to help patients, not
> terrorize them.

                    BEN
          I don't know if you've watched any
          of the sessions we've recorded,
          Father Todd, and we do record every
          session for evaluation, but I can
          assure you that we create a humane
          and compassionate environment for
          our patients.

                    FATHER BRANDT
          I'd like to talk about what
          conditions now constitute the
          definition of "dead" in this
          facility.

GENERAL BRADFORD gestures to BEN.

                    GENERAL BRADFORD
          Then this is the man you will be
          able to answer all your questions
          on that subject.

                    BEN
          Well, that's a bit of a slippery
          slope these days.  Our patients are
          most certainly dead in the clinical
          sense. Body temperature is around
          72 degrees, give or take the
          ambient humidity in a room.  No
          peristaltic activity or involuntary
          muscular contractions.  Heartbeat
          and breathing are semi-conscious
          activities and slow to the point of
          almost non-existent, providing just
          enough oxygen for the ATP  flowing
          to keep the sarcoplasmic reticulum
          going - in fact, I'd say the only
          reason these people breathe or
          otherwise display any minimal motor
          functions is the self-defense of
          the entire muscular and lymphatic
          system fighting off atrophy.

                    FATHER TODD
          That last point sounds clearly like
          conjecture on your part.

                    BEN
          I didn't make it up.  It's an
          accepted point of discussion
          amongst everyone in the field.
          Obviously nobody knows for sure
          why, but it is an undeniable fact.
                    (MORE)

                    BEN (CONT'D)
The body has a muscle memory and it
continues to go through the basic
motions.  Not that any of our
patients will be running a marathon
any time soon.

                    FATHER BRANDT
So there's still something
resembling self-preservation at
work?

                    BEN
Involuntary self-preservation taken
to an extreme level, some are
saying.  The body is willing, so to
speak, even after the mind is
adverse to go on living.  Like a
car that drives the driver, the
mind of a person is trapped inside
a vehicle that won't stop moving.

                    FATHER BRANDT
The human soul suspended inside a
cage of moldering flesh.

                    FATHER TODD
A diabolical conceit, don't you
think Father Brandt?

                    FATHER BRANDT
Certainly discomforting in the
extreme.

GENERAL BRADFORD rises and clears his throat to get
everyone's attention; he does not like where this
conversation is heading.

                    GENERAL BRADFORD
Might I suggest a facilities tour?
It could help you to better process
our daily procedures with more
clarity.

                                        DISSOLVE TO:


INTERIOR BEN'S BUILDING HALLWAY - NIGHT

AVERY is walking down the hallway, sniffing his way along and
following an offensive smell with his nose leading the way.
He finds himself standing before the source of the smell, the
door with the name plaque "TRUMAN" right below the peephole.

With trepidation, AVERY looks up and down the hallway to make sure nobody is watching and then knocks on the door.

INTERIOR BEN'S APARTMENT BEDROOM - NIGHT

MARY hears the knock at the door; startled, she freezes and listens.  A moment later, there is another, slightly louder knock.  Whomever it is, they're not just going away.

She jumps up and grabs one of Ben's shirts from the open closet to cover her nakedness and then heads into the next room with quiet steps.

INTERIOR LIVING ROOM - NIGHT

MARY is buttoning up the shirt and approaches the door.  The knocking sound is urgent in its rapidity but not very loud.

                    MARY
          Who's there?

                    AVERY (V.O)
          Mrs. Truman, it's your doorman,
          Avery.

MARY looks completely surprised.  She slowly slides open the cover of the peephole and peers through it.  Yeah, there's AVERY on the other side, standing there all by himself, looking nervous and very uncomfortable.

                    AVERY (CONT'D)
          Please let me in.  I need to talk
          to you about something that's very
          important.

                    MARY
          I'm not dressed, Avery.

                    AVERY
          I'm sorry, ma'am.  I can wait here
          while you get dressed.

MARY is surprised by his forcefulness.

                    MARY
          Did my husband give you your tax
          forms?

                    AVERY
          Yes, he did.  Thank you very much
          for doing them so quickly for me.

                    MARY
          You're welcome.  Is there some kind
          of problem with them?

                    AVERY
          What?  Oh, goodness no, Mrs.
          Truman.  That's not what I'm here
          about at all.

                    MARY
          Excuse me for being so direct,
          Avery, but I'm really not in any
          shape to have any visitors at the
          moment.  If this could wait till
          the morning that would be so much
          better.


INTERIOR BEN'S BUILDING HALLWAY - NIGHT

AVERY sighs and shakes his head.  He's not sure what to do at
this point.

From down the hall, the door of a neighbor slowly opens a bit
- unbeknownst to AVERY, who does his best to continue talking
in a low, non-threatening manner.

                    AVERY
          Please open the door, Mrs. Truman.
          I'd like to talk about this to you
          without having to raise my voice
          like this.


INTERIOR LIVING ROOM - NIGHT

MARY grits her teeth and sighs loudly.  She unlocks the door
and, with the security chain in place, opens it up as little
as possible so they can just barely see each other.  They
both continue the conversation in hushed whispers.

                    AVERY
          Something has come up that I'm very
          concerned about and I really need
          to talk to you as soon as possible.

                    MARY
          Can you give me some idea of the
          nature of the problem?

                    AVERY
          Well, it involves complaints from
          your neighbors about the smell
          that's coming from your apartment.
                         (MORE)

> AVERY (CONT'D)
> I can smell it pretty strongly out
> here myself and can see why they
> would call to complain.

MARY sighs. This day has come much sooner than she'd hoped
or expected.

> MARY
> Yes, well, we've been doing a lot
> of cleaning lately and….

MARY stops. The air is thick with bullshit and even she
can't keep going with it.

> AVERY
> Ma'am, please.

> MARY
> Hold on.

MARY closes the door and undoes the chain, reopening it again
so they have a much better view of each others faces. As the
smell from the apartment hits him full-force, AVERY crinkles
his nose in disgust - which he tries his best to hide.

> AVERY
> I think you know why I need to see
> you right now. To see how you look.

> MARY
> Here I am, then. Do I not look
> okay or normal to you?

> AVERY
> You look fine, but something
> doesn't smell very good.

> MARY
> That's a bit impolite, Avery.

> AVERY
> I apologize, ma'am. I like my job
> very much. I've had it a long time
> and I'd like to keep it without
> going to jail. And if you're not
> what you appear to be, I can get in
> a lot of trouble.

> MARY
> I totally understand and don't want
> to get you in trouble.

You've always been good to us.

                         AVERY
              Same here, Mrs. Truman.

AVERY coughs loudly and chokes a little bit from the
intensity of the smell that's hitting him now that the door
is wide open.

                         AVERY (CONT'D)
              Wow, that's strong.

                         MARY
              Sorry about that.

                         AVERY
              Listen, I'm gonna go down to the
              lobby cuz there's nobody at the
              door, but I want you to clean
              yourself up and come downstairs so
              we can talk, okay?  I'm not an
              idiot and I think we both know
              what's going on here.  But I'm also
              not the kind of person who's gonna
              jump to conclusions without giving
              you a fair chance, okay?

                         MARY
              Okay.  Thanks, Avery.

                         AVERY
              I'll give you a half hour to clean-
              up, okay?

                         MARY
              Sure thing.

AVERY nods, turns and walks away.  MARY shuts the door and
falls to her knees, trying not to cry.

The door of the neighbor who's been watching all this slowly
and quietly closes as AVERY obliviously continues walking
away in the background.


INTERIOR HOSPITAL RECREATION ROOM -- NIGHT

GENERAL BRADFORD leads BEN and the THREE PRIESTS into a large
recreation room that's filled with patients who are sitting
on couches and makeshift cots.  Most are by themselves and
watching TV, but there are some families as well.  Children
are generally asleep, some people are knitting, etc.
Overall, it's a quiet bunch who are sitting around and
waiting for something.  Anything.

On the TV screen, we see PRESIDENT CARLSON talking at a press conference.

> PRESIDENT CARLSON (ONSCREEN)
> Our Middle East allies - who live
> amongst many of the holiest sites
> in the world - if I may be so bold,
> seem to firmly agree with my
> decision to round up and confine
> these so-called victims who have…

After a moment of listening intently, everyone loses interest in what she is saying.

CARL motions invitingly with a friendly hand gesture and walks towards BEN.

> CARL
> Hey there, doctor.

BEN does not recognize who's walking towards him

> BEN
> Hello?

CARL holds out his hand for BEN to shake, which he does while struggling to try and recognize him.

> CARL
> It's alright, doc, you don't know
> me yet.  I'm Carl and I'm all yours
> come this late evening.

> BEN
> Oh, great.  Okay.  Sorry, I just
> got in not long ago and got swept
> into this meeting before I had a
> chance to look at my schedule.

> CARL
> No worries, doc.  I've heard a lot
> of good things all about you and
> I'm looking forward to us making
> history together when you dim my
> lights for good.

CARL laughs.  His good spirits are infectious, causing BEN to smile back.

> BEN
> Well then, I'm glad to hear you say
> that.  I think you're the most
> enthusiastic patient I've yet
> encountered in the last 9 months.

                         CARL
          Yeah, that's just the way my momma
          raised me.  You gotta go towards
          dying with the same grace and
          enthusiasm as anything else in your
          life.  I'm tired of going against
          nature.  It just ain't right.

FATHER TODD asserts himself between BEN and CARL.

                         FATHER TODD
          You do know he's not actually a
          doctor, Carl?

                         CARL
          Yessir, just like I know you're not
          really my father either, "Father."

CARL pats BEN on the shoulder and walks away while flashing a
mocking smile at FATHER TODD.

                         FATHER BRANDT
          I'd like to see the basement,
          please.  The area we've heard
          people refer to as "the tombs".

                         BEN
          They don't normally like visitors.
          They don't like being stared at.

                         FATHER TODD
          I'm not familiar with what you mean
          by "the tombs", but I don't like
          the sound of it.

BEN motions for everyone to follow him over to the other side
of the RECREATION ROOM, away from where all the patients are
gathered and watching them.

                         BEN
          The Tombs is where the patients
          who've been opened up and are still
          functional are taken care of until
          they're transitioned to another
          facility.

                         FATHER GANZ
          Like an internment camp?

                         BEN
          Yes. And yeah, it also just so
          happens to be the basement of the
          facility.

                    FATHER BRANDT
          The lowest level of the inferno in
          this Hellish place.

                         BEN
          It wasn't an intentional symbolic
          choice, but one based on
          convenience.  Bluntly, these
          volunteer patients are more than
          happy to have a separate place to
          wait after the procedure.

                    FATHER TODD
          Take us there now.

BEN takes a deep breath and leads the way forward.


INTERIOR HOSPITAL BASEMENT - NIGHT

This is one large rectangular room with hospital beds lined
up in rows wherever they can fit, each one filled with a
silent patient tightly wrapped in gauze bandages to hold all
their various pieces together.  No life support machinery or
intravenous drips in this part of the hospital.  It is a
large, silent morgue where the bodies lie down and twitch
quietly every now and then.

The priests are dumbstruck by what they see.

                    FATHER BRANDT
          They look like mummies.

                         BEN
          The bandages are holding what's
          left of them together. It's the
          only practical way to keep them in
          one piece. We can't spare the
          manpower to sew everything back
          together after the procedure, and
          besides, once the skin reaches a
          certain point of decay the stitches
          just rip anyway.

                    FATHER TODD
          So all of these people are victims
          of the alleged "science" that goes
          on in this hospital?

                    BEN
          Actually, there are also patients
          who have been rendered casualties
          from severe burns, falls from high
          places or catastrophic car
          accidents and the like.  People who
          are still mentally animated but
          trapped in bodies destroyed beyond
          use.

                    FATHER TODD
          This is the single most appalling
          thing I have ever seen.

                    BEN
          It's a point we don't disagree on,
          Father Todd. Nobody is proud of
          what we've had to do down here.

FATHER TODD walks over to a wrapped patient who's bandaged
tightly from head to toe, leaving only their eyes exposed.

                    FATHER TODD
          No holes for the nose or mouth?

                    BEN
          No need to eat or breathe and
          incapable of speech. The bandages
          help keep the organs in place and
          maintain the shape of the head.
          They like to know where they are
          and what's happening, though.

The patient they are standing over stares wide-eyed at them
as bloody tears well-up and stream from the eyes.

                    FATHER TODD
          It's…. they're crying blood…?

                    BEN
          We should go now.  You're upsetting
          them.

FATHER TODD walks back over to the group.  He is silent and
grim.

                    BEN (CONT'D)
          Those weren't tears in the
          traditional sense, if that's what
          you were thinking.  Blood wells up
          sometimes when there hasn't been
          any movement for awhile.

                    FATHER BRANDT
This seems even worse than the
internment camps to me.

                    GENERAL BRADFORD
Most of these people are here by
choice.  They're volunteers.  And
one day, when a cure is found,
they'll be recognized as the
pioneers and heroes that they are.

GENERAL BRADFORD takes control of the moment and motions
everyone to follow him now.

                    GENERAL BRADFORD (CONT'D)
Attend to your duties, Truman -
we've used enough of your valuable
time.  The rest of you, back to my
office; we've got a lot to discuss.


INTERIOR APARTMENT BUILDING LOBBY - NIGHT

TWO POLICEMEN brandishing large automatic rifles enter the
lobby and walk over to AVERY, who is sitting at his station.

                    AVERY
How can I help you, officers?

                    POLICEMAN 1
We've gotten complaints about a
dangerously toxic odor emanating
from one of your units on the
seventh floor of the building.

                    AVERY
Yes, sir.  I have looked into it
personally earlier today and we're
working on getting the problem
under control.

                    POLICEMAN 1
Could you please take us up to the
source of the problem? There's
concern that the fumes might be
flammable.

                    POLICEMAN 2
Apartment 723.

                    AVERY
Hmm.  Okay then.

AVERY rises slowly, nervously. He does not want to take them upstairs.

                    AVERY (CONT'D)
              Perhaps you can just go up there
              yourselves? I really shouldn't
              leave the lobby unattended.

                    POLICEMAN 1
              Call up to the apartment and if
              there's someone there to meet us,
              we can do that. If not, we'll need
              you to open the unit for us.

                    POLICEMAN 2
              We have the tenant name as Mr.
              Benjamin Truman.

                    AVERY
              Of course, I know him and his wife
              quite well. They're wonderful
              people.

AVERY picks up the intercom phone and calls, terrified that MARY will answer it. But there is no answer.

The elevator door opens in the lobby, and MARY steps out of it. She freezes as she sees the POLICEMEN standing over AVERY.

AVERY turns to her with something resembling relief and panic.

                    AVERY (CONT'D)
              Ahhh, hello Barbara. Thank
              goodness you're here.

AVERY puts down the handle and pops out of his chair, moving quickly towards MARY, talking fast before giving her a chance to react.

                    AVERY (CONT'D)
              Barbara, these gentlemen are here
              to look into the problem with the
              odor coming from apartment 723, the
              Truman apartment. If you could
              please do me a favor and watch the
              lobby while I take them upstairs
              and let them in, I'd be very
              appreciative.

MARY is so frightened she cannot respond verbally. She simply shakes her head and moves out of everyone's way as they move towards the elevator directly behind her.

                    AVERY (CONT'D)
          Thank you so much, Barbara.  This
          won't take very long at all.  In
          fact, I'm sure we'll be right back
          down very quickly.

AVERY moves past MARY and steps into the elevator with
POLICEMAN 1.  POLICEMAN 2 stops and holds open the elevator
door with his hand.

                    POLICEMAN 2
          Wait a minute.

AVERY and MARY freeze.  AVERY responds with a croak.

                    AVERY
          Yes?

                    POLICEMAN 2
          Your keys.  You left them on the
          desk.

AVERY gasps and reacts emphatically.

                    AVERY
          Ahh!  Of course, very sorry about
          that, officers.

AVERY moves to his desk, grabs the keys that are on a large,
circular keychain, and dashes past MARY back into the
elevator, this time with both POLICEMEN on-board.

The doors to the elevator close.  MARY catches herself from
nearly falling over from fright and quickly moves to - and
then through - the lobby doors and out into the night with
nothing but the clothes on her back and the shoes on her
feet.


EXTERIOR APARTMENT BUILDING - NIGHT

MARY whips out her cellphone and speed dials BEN'S number.
She gets his voice mail and leaves a harried message as she
walks unsteadily.

                    MARY
          Hey There.  Big trouble at home.
          I'll explain later. Heading over to
          your friend Lenny's diner, so try
          to meet me there as soon as you
          can.  DO NOT go home.  Police came
          by.  It's not our home anymore.

She quickly dashes down the street and into the night.

EXTERIOR HOSPITAL - NIGHT

At the front gate, a SECURITY GUARD with a bullhorn is
clearing the protestors from the entrance gate.

> GUARD
> Please clear all personal property
> from the outer perimeter of the
> established hospital zone.  You
> will no longer be allowed to
> congregate within three-hundred
> feet of the main gate or any of the
> protective surrounding fence.
> Anyone who does so will be given a
> warning and then shot. There will
> not be a second warning given and
> there will be no exceptions to this
> procedure.

Although there are only a handful of protestors outside, they
are angry and loudly voice their objections to the SECURITY
GUARD, tossing bottles and garbage as they leave.


INTERIOR HOSPITAL CORRIDOR - NIGHT

BEN and JOE sit across from each other in the hospital
hallway, slumped in their chairs with exhaustion and
frustration.

> JOE
> This isn't what I signed up for,
> man.

> BEN
> And I thought it was bad before the
> holy triumvirate arrived.  Whew….!

> JOE
> I'm walking.  Seriously, I'm not
> gonna last the night.

JOE reaches into his pocket and pulls out a small flask that
he takes a drink from and then tosses to BEN.

> JOE (CONT'D)
> You know what's been bothering me
> since this whole thing began?

BEN takes a swig from the flask and tosses it back to JOE.

> BEN
> What's that?

                    JOE
          Why just us?  Animals still die.
          Insects still die. Why are we the
          only ones made to suffer like this?

JOE tosses the flask back to BEN, who takes a particularly
deep swig from it.  He's not done with it yet, though, and he
moves it around to punctuate his thoughts.

                    BEN
          I don't know.  Maybe we're the only
          creatures on the planet who are
          aware of our own mortality, I
          guess. Or maybe if there is a god,
          he's too distracted or stupid to
          have any idea what's going on down
          here anymore. Fuck should I know?

BEN takes another big swig from the flask.

                    JOE
          Hey, you keep that up and you're
          gonna kill that flask.

BEN laughs and tosses it back to JOE.

                    BEN
          Be nice to kill something these
          days.

JOE kicks back the flask into his mouth, finishing it.

                    JOE
          So you think that self-awareness
          has something to do with it?

                    BEN
          Awwww jeez, I don't know.  You
          asked a question, I'm just telling
          you what I think.  I don't have any
          grand theories about all this.

                    JOE
          Being self-aware is everything,
          man.  That's what a soul is,
          right?  We got souls and the
          insects and animals don't.  Right?

                    BEN
          Sure.  Like a placebo effect or
          hysterical pregnancies - something
          that only self-awareness could
          account for.
                    (MORE)

                         BEN (CONT'D)
                    Somatoform disorders is a whole
                    field of study, not that
                    I'm any expert on the subject.

                         JOE
                    Sure, you say Somatoe, I say
                    Somato…..

Both men laugh drunkenly at such a pitiful joke.

                         BEN
                    Shit, that's awful even for you,
                    pally.

JOE puts his empty flask away and pulls his chair towards
BEN, so they are now sitting quite close, face to face.

JOE leans into BEN and speaks in a low, serious whisper.
He's not acting drunk anymore.

                         JOE
                    Listen Benji, you're the closest
                    thing I've got to a friend in this
                    fucked-up world and I've got a
                    secret I need to share with you.

                         BEN
                    Well, this doesn't sound very good.
                    How worried should I be?

                         JOE
                    A little bit.  Yeah, definitely at
                    least a little bit.

                         BEN
                    So…… whatchya' got?

JOE waves his hand between their faces, like he's erasing
some kind of invisible dry erase board.  BEN remains playful,
feeling a bit loose from exhaustion and alcohol.

                         JOE
                    Look at me, Benji.  Look me right
                    in the eyes.

                         BEN
                    Okay, yeah.  I'm looking right at
                    you.  Right in the eyes.

                         JOE
                    What do you see, man?

                         BEN
                    You look a little bit drunk, maybe?

                    JOE
          No, that's definitely not it.  Not
          anymore.  I've taken my last drink
          of this stuff.  It doesn't have any
          effect on me anymore.

                    BEN
          You've given up drinking?  Shit,
          how could you leave me like this?
          I didn't even start drinking until
          I met you and all this crap started
          raining down on us.

From around the corner of the far end of the corridor a
SECURITY GUARD dripping with ammunition and toting automatic
weaponry steps into view.  He calls out to JOE and BEN.

                    GUARD
          Is one of you the intern Benjamin
          Truman?

                    BEN
          Yeah, that would be me.

                    GUARD
          The General wants you to report to
          him immediately.

                    BEN
          Gotchya.  I'll be right there.

BEN turns back to talk to JOE, but the SECURITY GUARD does
not move away.

                    BEN (CONT'D)
          I'm talking to a friend.  I said
          I'll be right there.

                    GUARD
          The General wants you to report to
          him immediately.

                    BEN
          Yeah, I've kinda' gathered that.

JOE stands up quickly and leans down into BEN's face, where
he talks quietly in a hushed whisper.

                    JOE
          Never mind, man.  You should come
          over to my place sometime soon so
          we can talk privately. This ain't
          the time or the place after all.
          Okay?

                              BEN
                    You got it, fella.

BEN rises and slowly walks down the hallway, away from JOE
and towards the SECURITY GUARD, stopping obnoxiously right in
front of his face.

                         BEN (CONT'D)
                    Okay, let's go then.

JOE watches them walk away and then drops his flask into a
nearby garbage can before he turns and walks away in the
opposite direction, normal and completely sober.


INTERIOR LENNY'S DINER - NIGHT

LENNY is closing the front door for the night and locking up.
A shadow streaks across his face from outside and he stops to
get a better look at what is moving outside.

Through the plate glass window right next to him, a brick
comes crashing into the diner as shattered glass flies
everywhere.

                             LENNY
                    Motherfuckers!

Another brick gets tossed - this one comes in through the
window of the door LENNY is standing in front of.  It hits
him in the head and knocks him to the floor.

LENNY is lying on the floor, bleeding, when the front door
gets kicked in.

PATRON 1 and PATRON 2 come charging into the diner, followed
by about a half-dozen other PROTESTORS.  They are carrying
bricks, baseball bats and even some Molotov cocktails that
are waiting to be lit and thrown.

                            PATRON 1
                    There he is - that zombie loving
                    scumbag I was telling you all
                    about.

PATRON 1 steps over LENNY, swings his baseball bat around and
slams it into LENNY'S leg, just above the knee.

LENNY cries out in agony while everyone looks down at him and
laughs.

PATRON 2 spits on LENNY and kicks him in the stomach.

                    PATRON 2
          Damn straight.  No way to treat the
          paying customers, right guys?

Everyone laughs again.

PROTESTOR 1 pulls out a gun and points it at LENNY'S head.

                    PATRON 1
          WHOA!  Don't pull the trigger on
          this nigger. I don't wanna kill
          him; I just want him to wish that
          he was dead by the time we're done
          with him.

PROTESTOR 1 pulls back his gun after a moment of thinking it
over.

One of the other PROTESTORS lights the wick and throws his
cocktail, smashing it against the wall near the booths where
BEN had been sitting earlier that day with THE OLD MAN,
unleashing a torrent of flame.

                    PATRON 2
          Only way to make sure it's been
          cleaned properly

is to burn it with fire, right?

Another Molotov gets tossed through the partition behind the
main counter and into the kitchen, where it explodes in a
ball of fire.

                    PATRON 1
          Okay, let's go.  Our work here is
          done.

Everyone hoots and hollers and steps outside, kicking LENNY
as they pass over his bleeding, still twitching body.


EXTERIOR CITY STREET - NIGHT

MARY is moving quickly down the dark street towards LENNY'S
DINER, which is just around the corner.  As the diner comes
into view, she sees the smoke and licks of flame emanating
from the broken establishment.

                    MARY
          Ohmigod.

And then she notices the PATRONS and PROTESTORS moving
purposefully towards her.

                    PATRON 1
          Hey lady!  Where do you think
          you're going?

MARY reacts immediately; turning around she starts running
back in the other direction.

The sound of a rifle firing pierces the silence.  The impact
of the bullet is dangerously close to MARY.  She stops dead
and looks back at her pursuers.

They are also stopped dead in their tracks, looking around
and trying to figure out where the shot came from.

                    PATRON 2
          There's a fucking sniper up there!

                    PATRON 1
          Shit!

MARY slowly backs away from the PATRONS and the PROTESTORS,
who remains frozen and looking up at the buildings, unsure of
where to run to next.

Another shot rings out - this one right near PROTESTOR 1.

                    PROTESTOR 1
          That came from over there.  Follow
          me!

PROTESTOR 1 runs forward - in the opposite direction of
LENNY'S DINER and crunches himself against a building
underneath a small awning that offers some protection.  The
rest of his gang quickly follow him.

MARY is terrified, standing out in the middle of the street
and unsure of which direction to run.

So she runs towards LENNY'S DINER.

She reaches the open door of the DINER but cannot run inside
as the fire has spread everywhere.

MARY sees LENNY on the floor crawling slowly towards her, an
inferno raging behind him.

                    LENNY
          Help…… me……..

A gun fires and the glass right near MARY'S head shatters.
She turns to look and sees that PROTESTOR 1 is now firing at
her as well from his much better vantage point.

                         PATRON 1
            You missed her, asshole!

                         PROTESTOR 1
            Fuck you, dude!

PROTESTOR 1 takes aim at her again.

                         MARY
            Oh god - I'm so sorry, Lenny…!

MARY spins and runs down the street away from PATRONS and
PROTESTORS.

A second and third shot rings out.  This time MARY gets hit
by a bullet and is thrown down onto the ground.

                         PATRON 1
            There you go!  Nice!

MARY struggles to right herself on the pavement and rises as
quickly as she can.  And then another bullet hits her, this
time in the throat, blowing out her trachea.

                         PATRON 2
            Fuck yeah!  She ain't gonna talk to
            anyone now, huh?

Shrieking in anger and disgust, the sound is just a roaring
hiss from MARY's throat.

As the sound of more bullets go whizzing nearby, MARY runs
away down an alley and into the darkness.

                         PATRON 1
            C'mon, we gotta nail this bitch
            before she turn us in to the
            fucking cops!

PATRONS and PROTESTORS chase after her as the sniper
continues to shoot at them.


INTERIOR GENERAL BRADFORD'S OFFICE - NIGHT

GENERAL BRADFORD is sitting at his desk and talking to BEN,
who is already seated and has obviously been there for a
little while.

                         GENERAL BRADFORD
            It's for your own protection,
            Truman.  The times they are a
            changin'.

                    BEN
We haven't had any biting incidents
here yet, sir. Maybe it's just
rumors and hype.

                    GENERAL BRADFORD
The media doesn't know the half of
what's been going down at the camps
and hospital facilities these last
couple of weeks.  There's lots more
biters been showing up on the radar
then have been reported.  It's not
even something we've wanted you and
your buddies to be privy to, but at
this point it's a matter of safety
in the workplace.

                    BEN
So what are the common denominators
between the reported incidents so
far?

                    GENERAL BRADFORD
Our lab jockeys say it had nothing
to do with how young or old the
biters were, but seems to be linked
directly to how long they had been
undead.

                    BEN
So those that were amongst the
first to die about nine months ago
have mostly been the perpetrators?

                    GENERAL BRADFORD
Not just mostly, but exclusively.

                    BEN
I heard something the other day
about a baby biting its mother….?

                    GENERAL BRADFORD
That so-called "newborn" was a nine
month old stillborn. The mother was
giving it her milk out of habit and
comfort, not because it was alive
and needed sustenance.  Media
hasn't gotten ahold of that story
yet, but when they do it's going to
make serious waves.

                    BEN
So you're suggesting that we
segregate the current patient
population?

                GENERAL BRADFORD
Yes, for our safety and theirs.
They don't just bite the living,
Truman.  They bite their own, too -
whoever is within reach.  They just
go mad and start grabbing and
biting.  They go mindless.  Not
mad, not crazy, not angry.
It's as if the last vestiges of
humanity have suddenly fallen
out of their bodies like a coin
down a slot, leaving pure instinct
and hunger in charge of the
remaining machinery. I've seen the
footage that has not been released
to the public, Benji, and it's
appalling.  The stuff of
nightmares.

                    BEN
We'll end up separating families
with the kind of arrangement you're
suggesting.  That's not going to be
good for morale.

                GENERAL BRADFORD
Ours or theirs, Truman?  We can't
worry about that kind of thing when
the safety of everyone - us and
them - is at stake.

                    BEN
I don't know what to say, General.
We've all been working so hard to
try and promote a sense of trust
between the staff and the patients.
It's really been a unique situation
during what has been nothing short
of an epidemic.  I don't know what
kind of reaction or cooperation
we're gonna receive.

                GENERAL BRADFORD
None of which is your concern.
It's mine.  You just keep on doing
what you do, and I'll make sure you
can continue to work with a sense
of security and as much safety as
possible under the circumstances.

GENERAL BRADFORD reaches into his drawer and pulls out a
cheap bottle of scotch and two paper cups.  He pours one cup
and offers it towards BEN.

                    BEN
          No thanks, General.  I'm already
          fueled up.  So any feedback from
          the three wise men this afternoon?

The GENERAL raises the cup towards BEN and then kicks it
back, emptying it.

                    GENERAL BRADFORD
          They're still in an observation
          stage.  Prepare for some additional
          pain-in-the-ass interactions in the
          hours and days and months ahead.

BEN shakes his head with exasperation.

                    BEN
          Months….

GENERAL BRADFORD crushes the cup and tosses it into the
trash.

                    GENERAL BRADFORD
          We'll begin the new security
          implementation over the course of
          the next week or so as troop
          reinforcements arrive and set-up a
          base of operations just outside of
          the facility.  For now, we're going
          to clear the perimeter of those
          jackass protestors before the night
          is out.  We don't need the
          distraction.

                    BEN
          Sorry to hear.  I was starting to
          make friends with some of those
          annoying assholes.

GENERAL BRADFORD reaches back into his drawer and pulls out a
pamphlet that he tosses on the desk in front of BEN.  It is
the MANIFESTO that BEN found in his pocket the previous day.

                    GENERAL BRADFORD
          Friends who gave you bullshit like
          this to read?

                    BEN
          I was making a joke, sir.

                    GENERAL BRADFORD
          Joke or not, we've been finding
          these damn things all over the
          place.  They've got at least
          someone or maybe even a few more
          people on the inside leaving
          manifestos in peoples jackets and
          desk drawers.  I don't like not
          knowing if we have traitors in our
          midst.

                    BEN
          Understandably.

BEN slumps back in his chair and rubs deeply at his eyes and
face as he sighs.

                    BEN (CONT'D)
          Fuck, I am just so exhausted beyond
          belief.

                    GENERAL BRADFORD
          Anything else on your mind, Truman?

BEN takes a deep breath as his hands shapes and creases his
face.

                    BEN
          No sir.

                    GENERAL BRADFORD
          Are you good to go or should I send
          you back home?

                    BEN
          I'm good.  I'm good.

                    GENERAL BRADFORD
          On the lighter side, I got my taxes
          done early this year. I hope you
          got them out of the way as well?
          One less thing to worry about.

                    BEN
          Yes sir.  My wife is a math whiz
          and took care of us.

                    GENERAL BRADFORD
          You're a lucky man with a good
          wife, Truman.

                    BEN
          Thank you, General.

EXTERIOR HOSPITAL - NIGHT

A group of about a half-dozen SOLDIERS equipped with high-powered weaponry are gathered around the side of the building, wearing night goggles and looking out onto the perimeter fence that surrounds the hospital.

                    SOLDIER 1
          There's some movement near the
          northern perimeter.

                    SOLDIER 2
          I see it.  Looks like a group
          approaching the fence.

                    SOLDIER 1
          One out in front, about a half
          dozen coming up from behind.

                    SOLDIER 2
          Protestors?

                    SOLDIER 1
          They're not carrying any signs.
          Looks like one may have a handgun.

The SOLDIERS disengage the safety's on their weapons and move forward.

As they draw closer, they can now clearly see MARY, who has blood all over her body from her bullet wounds, approaching the fence.

                    SOLDIER 1 (CONT'D)
          Yeah, it's a woman.  She's bleeding
          a lot.

                    SOLDIER 2
          Is she dead or alive?

                    SOLDIER 1
          Looks like a pretty serious throat
          hole.  Gotta be a zombie.

                    SOLDIER 2
          Shit.  Think she's a lover or a
          biter?

                    SOLDIER 1
          She looks coherent, but what does
          that mean?  No way I'm gonna find
          out the hard way.  A zombie's a
          zombie from now on.

                    SOLDIER 2
          What about the rest of them?

MARY is at the fence now, her fingers curled around the edges
of the chain links for support.

                    SOLDIER 1
          Looks like she's gonna try to make
          the climb over. Not on my fucking
          watch.

SOLDIER 1 stops, raises his weapon and fires at her - hitting
MARY in the kneecaps, bringing her down fast and flat to the
grass.  She hisses loudly as her mouth yawns open to unleash
a scream.

                    SOLDIER 1 (CONT'D)
          Check this shit out.  She can't
          talk, man.  I'll bet she can't
          scream, either.

                    SOLDIER 2
          Dude, what the hell are you
          thinking?

The PATRONS and the PROTESTORS come to a full stop and watch
with terror as MARY writhes on the grass by the fence.

                    PATRON 1
          Great fucking shot!

                    PROTESTOR 1
          It wasn't me!

They all freeze and look at each other.

And one by one, each PATRON and PROTESTOR watches as the
precision bullets of the SOLDIERS on the other side of the
fence start to tear all of them to ribbons.

Eventually, those who don't run away fast enough fall down,
twitch a little bit and then lie still, groaning in agony.

SOLDIER 1 lowers his weapon and pulls out a flask from a leg
pocket.  He takes a swig and offers a drink to SOLDIER 2, who
furtively waves it away.

                    SOLDIER 1
          Look, if you don't have the guts to
          have a little bit of fun with these
          fucking zombies, then go back to
          the tent with the rest of the
          pussies.

                    SOLDIER 2
What if they ask me where you are?

                    SOLDIER 1
Tell 'em I'm over here fucking some
dead bitch through the chain link
fence.

                    SOLDIER 2
You're a total asshole, man.

                    SOLDIER 1
Look at her and tell me you
wouldn't fuck her.

                    SOLDIER 2
I don't stick it to cold slits,
asshole.

                    SOLDIER 1
Fine, fuck it.  No sense of humor
at all.

SOLDIER 1 pours the remainder of his flask onto MARY.  He
then pulls out a match, lights it and tosses it onto her
prone form.  MARY bursts into flames and kicks and screams in
pain.

                    SOLDIER 2
What the fuck is wrong with you,
man?

                    SOLDIER 1
Just cremating another dead bitch,
soldier.

SOLDIER 1 laughs as MARY continues to roll around and burn in
the grass.

A moment later, three other SOLDIERS appear from the
darkness.

                    SOLDIER 3
What the fuck is happening here?

                    SOLDIER 1
She was trying to climb the fence
and break the perimeter. We got to
her just before she made it over
the top.

                    SOLDIER 3
          Holy shit, somebody get a carcass
          wagon out here with a fire
          extinguisher.  She could set one of
          the trees on fire and we'll all be
          in trouble.

                    SOLDIER 1
          Yep, the general likes his trees.

SOLDIERS 1 and 3 whoop it up as SOLDIER 2, appalled, cries
into his portable radio.

                    SOLDIER 2
          We need an ambulance by the south
          gate ASAP!  I've got a casualty in
          flames rolling around here!

SOLDIERS 1 and 3 continue laughing and walk away into the
darkness.


INTERIOR NURSES STATION - LATE NIGHT

NURSE FELTON is still on duty and still has a huge stack of
papers in front of her.

BEN enters and goes to grab his now fully charged phone and
puts away the charger.

                    NURSE
          I think I heard your phone ring
          earlier.

BEN is too wrapped up in his own mind to have really heard
what she said.  His tone is intense and he is single-minded
in purpose as he speaks.

                    BEN
          I've got a patient being worked up
          for our session in the next couple
          of hours.  I'd like to make some
          changes in the standard
          preparations.

                    NURSE
          Like what?

                    BEN
          For starters, I don't want him to
          be anaesthetized.

                    NURSE
          I'm sorry?

                    BEN
          No local.  No nothing.  I want him
          injected with a saline solution,
          but he's not to be told that this
          isn't his anesthesia.  If this is
          too difficult to understand, please
          tell me so and I'll have someone
          else do it.

                    NURSE
          There's no need to be rude about
          it.

                    BEN
          This is not a matter of politeness,
          Nurse.  I need to know that you can
          do this without drawing suspicion.
          Can you do this thing?

NURSE FELTON thinks for a moment.  She is obviously NOT
pleased with the request, but she is considering it
nonetheless.

                    NURSE
          Does General Bradford know about
          this?

Without missing a beat, BEN lies through his teeth.

                    BEN
          These are direct orders from him.

                    NURSE
          Then okay.  I can do that.

                    BEN
          Thank you, Nurse.  My patient,
          Carl, should be passing through
          here in the next half hour to be
          drained and given his shots.  I'll
          be prepping my station if you need
          me for anything.

BEN turns to leave but stops suddenly at the door.

                    BEN (CONT'D)
          Oh, and one other thing.  Do we
          have any aspirin lying around?

NURSE FELTON points to a cabinet near the door.

                    NURSE
          In that cabinet on the middle
          shelf.

                        BEN
           Thanks.

BEN reaches into the cabinet and pulls out a beat-up bottle
of aspirin that looks about 30 years old.  He opens it up and
pops one of the large pills into his hand.  On the counter is
a box of tissues; he grabs one and wraps the aspirin in it
and tosses the wadded up paper into his pocket.

He puts the bottle back away, closes the cabinet and exits
the room.


INTERIOR WASHING STATION - LATE NIGHT

BEN washes up, removes his watch and cell phone and lays them
on top of a clean shirt that he has off to one side.

Before turning off the cell phone, he checks it and sees a
call from MARY.

Before he can listen to the calls, the door to the room opens
and NURSE FELTON sticks her head inside.

                        NURSE
           Carl is here; ready and waiting.

                        BEN
           Okay, I'm coming.  Thanks.

BEN tosses his phone into his back pocket.  He'll deal with
his calls later.


INTERIOR HOSPITAL AUTOPSY ROOM - LATE NIGHT

Tonight's undead patient, CARL, is lying back on the
operating table with his arms safely strapped into place as
BEN rolls over his tiny cart of surgical implements.

                        BEN
           How you feelin' tonight, Carl?

                        CARL
           Little nervous.  Kinda' anxious.
           Hopeful. but….

CARL moves his arms around in the restraining straps a little
bit.

                        CARL (CONT'D)
           Nobody mentioned anything about
           these.

                    BEN
          Hmm.  Yeah, about that…

                    CARL
          It's not like I came here to hurt
          you or anything.

                    BEN
          My first time with them, too, Carl.
          I don't like them either but it's
          the new rule now ever since the
          Kansas incident the other day with
          the biter. If it were up to me, I'd
          say….

The door to the room opens and FATHER TODD enters.  He walks
over to CARL and pulls out some holy water and his bible.

                    FATHER TODD
          Bless you, son.  In the name of…..

                    CARL
          Whoa!  Hold it.  Definitely nobody
          told me anything about this shit.
          What's he doing here?

                    FATHER TODD
          I'm here to help you on your
          journey.

CARL turns to BEN and looks at him emphatically.

                    CARL
          No fucking way, doc.  Get him outta
          here.

BEN looks at FATHER TODD and shrugs.

                    BEN
          You heard the man, Father.

FATHER TODD leans into CARL's face, attempting to project
warmth but failing miserably.

                    FATHER TODD
          Carl, I'm not here to hurt you, I'm
          here to help you.

                    CARL
          Help me how?  You aren't a doctor,
          are you?

                    FATHER TODD
          No, just a priest.

                    CARL
          Well, as I don't believe in your
          god, I don't see how there's any
          good you'll be doing for me.  So if
          you would please leave it would
          give me great comfort to not see
          you here.

                    FATHER TODD
          Carl, how could you be lying here
          in your current condition, an
          example of the existence of god,
          and deny that truth to yourself?

                    CARL
          Bullshit.  I want a doctor looking
          over me, not a priest. I ain't
          buying your rapture nonsense.
          There's a scientific reason for
          what's happening and I want this
          guy, this doctor… I mean, intern….
          What's your name again?

                    BEN
          Ben.

                    CARL
          Yeah, I want Ben here working on me
          without any of your caucasian
          Voodoo rituals.

FATHER TODD is beginning to lose his patience.

                    FATHER TODD
          Carl, you are strapped to this
          table because you are seeking a
          cure to the malady you are
          suffering from that leaves you
          trapped somewhere between the land
          of the living and the land of the
          dead, correct?

                    CARL
          Yeah.

FATHER TODD'S tone becomes more cold and calculated.

                    FATHER TODD
          You should then be aware, Carl,
          that there are about at least two
          hundred other people in this
          hospital alone who desire the same
          thing - a cessation of being
          trapped between two worlds.
                    (MORE)

                    FATHER TODD (CONT'D)
          A respite from the numbing desire
          to finally be released from the
          land of the living to enter the
          afterlife where they truly belong.
          Perhaps this is not the wording
          you'd choose to use, but I think we
          agree on the basic premise; you'd
          like to finally pass on, wouldn't
          you?

                    CARL
          Sure.

                    FATHER TODD
          Well then, you're simply going to
          have to accept the protocol. Or we
          can just remove you from the
          operating table and find a half-
          dozen other people who'd be more
          than happy to take your place right
          now, no questions asked.  And maybe
          we'll get back to you sometime
          before the end of the year if
          you're lucky.  Of course, the way
          things seem to be working, it looks
          like the number of dead and dying
          people probably won't be tapering
          off anytime soon.

CARL sighs angrily and shakes his head.

                    CARL
          I hate you self-righteous
          motherfuckers.  I always have.
          Go ahead and say your shit out
          loud, priest, but don't get in the
          way of what my doctor needs to do
          to get me where I wanna go.

BEN moves towards FATHER TODD, practically stepping into his
face.  BEN is angry and talks in a low, hissing voice to the
priest.

                    BEN
          A good soft touch goes a long way
          around here. By what right have you
          taken over this facility?

                    FATHER TODD
          This is our hospital, intern.  You
          and your superior officer have
          merely been borrowing it from us
          for the last couple of months, but
          now we're taking it back and there
          are going to be plenty of changes
          you'll have to get used to as we
          move forward. Do you understand me?

                    BEN
          Are you telling me you have greater
          authority than the General from now
          on in how I do my job?

                    FATHER TODD
          We can discuss that later - after I
          see exactly what it is that you do
          in the first place.

FATHER TODD steps away from CARL and lets BEN freely move
towards his patient again.  BEN ignores the priest and turns
his attention back to CARL.

                    BEN
          Okay, so you were prepped
          beforehand, correct?  They gave you
          your shots and cleaned you up?

                    CARL
          Yeah, I'm clean and ready to get
          cut-up.

BEN picks up a scalpel from his cart and brings it up to
CARL's stomach flesh to begin making his incision.

                    FATHER TODD
          Hold it.  I want you to talk me
          through this, intern.

BEN is frustrated.  He is getting really tired of being
called "intern".

                    BEN
          For starters, Father Todd, you can
          call me by my name or simply don't
          address me at all. I don't like
          your tone of voice when you address
          me as "intern".

                    FATHER TODD
          And you watch your tone with me.
          You do realize this is all being
          recorded, don't you?

202

                    BEN
Very well aware.  And my tone
stands as-is.  Please note that I
have enough respect to refer to you
as "Father".

                    FATHER TODD
Fine.  Now explain to me what
you're doing.

                    BEN
The patient has been prepped.  He
was dosed with anesthetics to numb
all the areas we'll be working in
and then he had most of his blood
drained.

                    FATHER TODD
Why's that?

                    BEN
Even though he's technically
deceased, the heart continues
to beat slowly, about one-sixth the
normal rate.  More out of habit
than any practical need.  Kind of
like the heart is daydreaming, so
to speak.  Average heart rate is
sixty beats per minute.  Undead
beating is about 10 or 15 per
minute.

                    FATHER TODD
So draining the blood does what?

                    BEN
It makes for less of a mess to
clean up.  That's about it.

                    FATHER TODD
That kind of heart rate you
describe isn't really death. It
sounds more like a comatose state.

                    BEN
The street term making the popular
rounds is "zoma" instead of "coma".
Getting a little sick and tired of
people putting a "Z" in front of
their words; howzabout you?

FATHER TODD thinks for a moment and then understands.

                    BEN (CONT'D)
          So, may I begin?

                    FATHER TODD
          Just a moment.

FATHER TODD closes his bible and kisses it before saying a
prayer over CARL.

                    FATHER TODD (CONT'D)
          God the father, have mercy on Carl.
          God the son, have mercy on Carl.
          God the holy spirit, grant Carl
          peace. Bless Carl, your loving
          child, as he enters surgery so
          that, no matter what happens, he is
          secure in your love.

FATHER TODD crosses CARL with his small bottle of holy water
and then motions to BEN.

                    FATHER TODD (CONT'D)
          He's yours now.

                    BEN
          Thank you.

BEN pushes the scalpel into CARL's chest and begins slicing
open his entire chest cavity.  As the air escapes from the
incision, CARL sighs deeply and moans.

                    BEN (CONT'D)
          Are you feeling that?

                    CARL
          I thought I did for a moment, but
          now I don't think so.

                    BEN
          Okay.  Good.

The smell of the inside of the body hits FATHER TODD and he
reacts with a phlegmy cough, covering his mouth.

                    BEN (CONT'D)
          Give it a minute, Father.  You'll
          get used to it.

CARL gives a light, derisive laugh.  This annoys FATHER TODD,
whose tone is now sharp and direct.

                    FATHER TODD
          What's the next step?  Explain it.

                         BEN
          All major organs are disconnected
          from each other. We attempt to
          deactivate each organ individually
          through a process in which we
          inject high levels of toxic
          solution into each of the separated
          tissues.  For this session, we'll
          be attempting our highest level of
          toxicity yet.

                         FATHER TODD
          And how has that level been
          determined?

                         BEN
          We're now going as high as we can
          go without outright melting the
          organs and turning our patient into
          a pile of toxic jelly.  We're
          trying to deanimate our patients,
          not create putrescent slabs of goo.

FATHER TODD looks directly at CARL.

                         FATHER TODD
          Were you aware that what he just
          described would be happening to
          you?

                         CARL
          I am now.

Pause.  CARL laughs.

                         CARL (CONT'D)
          Oh Hell yeah, priest.  That's what
          I signed on for.  I'd rather do
          this of my own free will and
          hopefully be done with it then be
          stuck mouldering in some internment
          camp until they decide one day to
          do this to us with or without our
          permission.  And don't think that
          day ain't coming sometime soon.

FATHER TODD points to Ben,

                         FATHER TODD
          Which makes you a simple murderer.

And then FATHER TODD addresses CARL

                    FATHER TODD (CONT'D)
          And you a fancy case of suicide.

                    BEN
          I prefer enabler.

                    CARL
          Hah!  That's a good one, kid.
          Yeah, and I'm enabled. Thanks to
          him.

FATHER TODD opens up his bible and begins to say a prayer
over BEN as he continues working on CARL.

                    FATHER TODD
          I pray that god gives you the
          ability to recognize what you are
          doing and prevent you from killing
          anyone else.

                    BEN
          Amen, brutha'.  If only people were
          dying…

FATHER TODD turns and begins to bless CARL.  BEN and CARL
exchange glances as all this is going on.  Neither of them is
entertained by this.

                    FATHER TODD
          The sixth commandment invokes us
          not to murder, and that includes
          self-murder.  But in thy divine
          mercy, we beg thy forgiveness,
          especially for Carl, who has been
          so confounded by the pressures of
          life…..

                    CARL
          Life was never a problem for me.
          THIS is a problem for me.

CARL gestures to his open chest as BEN continues to slice his
way through all his vital organs.

                    FATHER TODD
          …. Been so confounded by the
          pressures of life that they felt
          that there was no way to continue.

                    CARL
          How old is that fuckin' prayer
          anyway?
                         (MORE)

206

                    CARL (CONT'D)
          Shit, you better start rewriting
          this stuff cuz that kinda' crap
          ain't gonna  cut it anymore in this
          crazy new world.

FATHER TODD pauses and exhales loudly as he works up his
energy again.

                    FATHER TODD
          We beseech thee, that they be
          forgiven their terrible sin and
          accepted into your divine
          providence.

FATHER TODD finishes and slams the bible shut loudly.

                    FATHER TODD (CONT'D)
          I'll be over here if you need me.

The priest sits down on a chair near the door.

                    CARL
          Hey Father?

FATHER TODD perks up a little bit.

                    CARL (CONT'D)
          Howazbout you run along and get me
          a Coke or something?

CARL laughs and, despite his best efforts not to, BEN laughs
as well.

Furious, FATHER TODD rises and exits the room.

                    CARL (CONT'D)
          Good riddance, asshole.

                                        DISSOLVE TO:


SAME ROOM LATER THAT EVENING

CARL is lying back with his entire chest opened up and all
the organs disconnected from one another.

BEN puts down his cutting tool and, exhausted, wheels up a
chair and sits down to wipe the sweat from his brow.

                    CARL
          Too bad that priest ain't here to
          see this now.
                         (MORE)

                    CARL (CONT'D)
          You've got me opened up into a
          classic sacred heart position.
          I'll bet he'd have loved that.

                    BEN
          He's probably upstairs watching all
          this on the monitor.

BEN motions to the camera in the ceiling.

                    CARL
          I didn't get you in any trouble,
          did I?

                    BEN
          No more than I'm usually in.  I'll
          be alright.

BEN sighs deeply and stands up again and leans in close to
CARL.  BEN looks over his shoulder to make sure his back is
to the camera that is recording them and he whispers.

                    BEN (CONT'D)
          Hey Carl, listen.  I wanna try
          something with you. Are you up for
          a little experiment?

                    CARL
          That's what I'm here for, isn't it?

                    BEN
          Yeah, that's true.  Look, you came
          here hoping for me to find a way
          for you to finally pass on, right?

CARL nods his head affirmatively as BEN screws up his courage
to the sticking place.

                    BEN (CONT'D)
          Well, not too long ago, one of the
          doctors slipped me an experimental
          drug that nobody else is in on yet.
          It's strong stuff and there's a 95
          percent chance that it'll work,
          unlike anything else that's been
          accomplished here.  So I want to
          be absolutely clear with you and
          tell you that if you take this
          medication you more than likely be
          dead within a minute of ingesting
          it.  That's how strong this
          medication is.

CARL exhales in disbelief.

                    CARL
          Whew!  That sounds incredible.

                    BEN
          It is.  Which is why I don't want
          to give it to you unless you tell
          me for certain that this is what
          you want.  To die.  Right now. You
          can't have any doubts whatsoever
          about this.

                    CARL
          Shit, man.  If you had this pill
          all along, why did you have to gut
          me like this?

                    BEN
          Procedure, Carl.  Also, I was
          testing for something else before I
          could figure out if you were the
          right candidate for this special
          pill.

CARL practically has the closest thing to tears in his eyes
that an undead person can have.

                    CARL
          Look at me, man, all pried open
          like a fucking lobster; you've even
          got my pinchers held shut with
          these damn restraints.  I'm more
          ready to die right now than I've
          ever been and I'm looking forward
          to it.

                    BEN
          Then look me in the eyes and say it
          to me.  Tell me how much you want
          to finally, really die.

                    CARL
          Doc, there is nothing in the world
          I want more right now than to
          finally be rid of this life and
          this fucked-up world I'm stuck in.
          I have never wanted anything more
          in my entire life than to finally
          be dead.  DEAD.  Buried, gone and
          forgotten forever dead.

                    BEN
          Okay then, Carl.  Let's do this.

BEN turns away from CARL, reaches into his pocket and pulls
out the aspirin that's contained in a wadded-up tissue.

                    BEN (CONT'D)
          One more thing, though.  If this
          doesn't work, you can't tell
          anybody we tried it.  Agreed?

                    CARL
          You have my word of honor, Doc.

Turning around, BEN faces CARL and holds up the "miracle
pill."

                    BEN
          Here it is then.

                    CARL
          I'm ready, man.  Let's do this.

                    BEN
          Okay.

BEN leans over CARL and puts the aspirin in his wide-open
mouth.

CARL swallows the pill quickly, violently, and then grits his
teeth in anticipation of finality.

BEN watches in both fascination and disbelief.  The idea he's
had is just so crazy.  Will something come of it?  And if so,
will it be something he can work with?

CARL's head goes back limply.  His breathing becomes labored
and his eyes begin to creep under his heavy lids and into the
back of his head.

                    CARL
          Thank you, doctor……

CARL is now dead.  REAL dead.

And BEN is flabbergasted.

                    BEN
          Holy fucking shit.

BEN looks down at CARL's open chest cavity and sees the
undigested aspirin sliding down the foamy, open trachea and
coming to rest - perfectly undigested in the middle of a sea
of sliced guts.

Still in a state of shock, BEN looks up at the clock on wall and then turns around to face the video camera on the other side of the room and walks towards it.  He stops and talks into it and we see his image on a monitor somewhere as the following is recorded for posterity.

                    BEN (CONT'D)
          Please let it be noted that for the
          first time in nine months we are
          recording a known, willful and
          final passing-on of a patient in
          this hospital at exactly 2:17am on
          April the 11th. Recorded by
          Benjamin Truman, residing intern.
          Drinks are on me tonight.

                                        FADE TO BLACK.

                                        FADE UP FROM
                                             BLACK.


GENERAL BRADFORD'S OFFICE - LATE NIGHT

BEN is exhausted and slumped over in a chair before GENERAL BRADFORD, who is sitting contemplatively behind his desk.

FATHER TODD is pacing around the room; annoyed, anxious and full of an energy that is lacking in everyone else in the room.

                    GENERAL BRADFORD
          I've spoken to the security detail
          and the footage of your session has
          been removed and erased from the
          database. I don't want some jackass
          posting it to youtube in the next
          half hour for all the world to see.

                    BEN
          Yes sir.

                    GENERAL BRADFORD
          I've got mixed feelings about all
          of this, as I'm sure you're aware.
          You may have started something
          truly extraordinary here this
          evening, but I do not like
          secretive way you went about it.

                    BEN
          Understandably so, sir.

                    GENERAL BRADFORD
          Do you mind telling me exactly what
          led to this behavior on your part,
          Mr. Truman?

                    BEN
          Hard to say exactly, sir.  I was
          very tired.  Desperation, maybe?
          I was thinking about a lot of
          things while I was exhausted, and a
          few crazy ideas came to me and I
          just decided on the spur of the
          moment to try it out since nothing
          else seems to have been working up
          until now.

                    GENERAL BRADFORD
          It was certainly a bold move on
          your part.

                    FATHER TODD
          And a successful one as well.

FATHER TODD has swooped in between them now, although neither
of them acknowledges his presence.

                    GENERAL BRADFORD
          Was this experiment something you
          discussed with any of your medical
          drinking buddies beforehand?

                    BEN
          No sir.

                    GENERAL BRADFORD
          I'd like to start by reviewing some
          of the issues we're going to have
          to face in the next couple of hours
          if word of this gets leaked to the
          general public.

                    FATHER TODD
          "IF?"  Don't you mean, "WHEN?"

Again, his comment is ignored.

                    BEN
          I'm figuring your biggest concern
          is an investigation into what drug
          was used and how did we develop it
          in secret?

                    GENERAL BRADFORD
That's as good a start as any.  I
think there's gonna be a lot of
disappointment in the
pharmaceutical community when the
second autopsy reveals that a cheap
bottle of aspirin is at the heart
of all of this.

                    BEN
But that's not all you're worried
about, is it?

                    GENERAL BRADFORD
No.  I'm concerned about the social
implications.  How are the maniacs
gonna take this kind of power into
their own hands now that they'll
have this kind of power?  I'm also
not at all pleased that you broke
rank and didn't come to me first,
as this is exactly the kind of
procedural crap we should have been
discussing before you went ahead
and attempted something like this.

                    FATHER TODD
I think both of you are more
concerned about how faith trumps
science and the military at the end
of the day on this issue.

For the first time, GENERAL BRADFORD turns his angry gaze
upon FATHER TODD.

                    GENERAL BRADFORD
Sir, might I inquire as to what the
hell you're suggesting?

                    FATHER TODD
Well then, using your own logic, it
sounds like the process should be
explained to the public as an act
of faith.  A kind of affirmation,
if you will.

                    BEN
I don't understand what you're
saying.

                    FATHER TODD
I'm saying that your people are no
longer necessary to handle this
problem.
                    (MORE)

                    FATHER TODD (CONT'D)
It should obviously be turned over
to the clergy for further
rumination and application.

                    GENERAL BRADFORD
Because?

                    FATHER TODD
I think at this point we'll all
agree that there's no medical
aspect involved in helping these
people achieve their passing.  It's
the power of suggestion that is
giving them their release, and this
power is directly related to faith.
What just happened in that room
could just as easily have been
performed in a church with much
more dignity and none of the
butchery.

                    GENERAL BRADFORD
It's only been tested once so far.
We don't even know if it'll work
again.

                    BEN
I think it will.  I mean, the
person it worked on wasn't even a
believer - he was a pretty defiant
atheist and still the suggestion
I placed in his mind worked.

                    GENERAL BRADFORD
Are you saying this is some form of
hypnosis, Truman?

                    BEN
I don't know.  Is living death a
form of self-hypnosis? It's not my
area of expertise.

                    FATHER TODD
Faith is not the cheap magic trick
you're describing and we're not
about to lose our five thousand
year franchise nurturing a belief
in a higher power to a bunch of
self-doubting amateurs like
yourselves.

                    BEN
          Back in the O.R., you called our
          methodology "suicide", which is
          against you beliefs.  Why are you
          okay with this method now?

                    FATHER TODD
          What you have developed here is an
          extension of free will, in my mind
          and under these circumstances,
          and that is something I can
          advocate towards - although with
          some trepidation.

A moment of silence as FATHER TODD finally takes a seat.

                    GENERAL BRADFORD
          We'll be examining and keeping a
          close watch on Patient X for the
          next couple of days.

                    BEN
          "Patient X?"  You mean Carl?

                    GENERAL BRADFORD
          You know us military folk, Truman.
          We love to give everything and
          everyone a code name.

                    FATHER TODD
          I think next time you should try it
          with a communion wafer.

BEN chortles with disbelief and rises from his chair to exit.

                    BEN
          Okay, I've got one more session to
          go for the evening and then I'm
          homeward bound.

                    GENERAL BRADFORD
          Were you thinking about testing out
          your new method again?

                    BEN
          With your permission, yes.

                    GENERAL BRADFORD
          Then the answer is NO for now.  I
          know you're anxious to take this to
          the next level, Truman; so am I.
          But let's all sleep on this and
          regroup in a few hours after we see
          how Patient X is doing, okay?

                    BEN
          Begging your pardon, sir, but I'm
          not sure I understand this
          trepidation on your part?

                    GENERAL BRADFORD
          We're in freefall at the moment,
          Truman.  Yes, this looks like a
          major breakthrough, but it comes at
          just around the same time we're
          starting to see this disease - this
          whatever- it-is - devolve into its
          next level, which is mindlessness
          and biting.  Do we know for sure
          he's really dead?  Maybe he's just
          moments away from sitting up, empty
          minded and hungry for flesh.  I do
          not want to take any unwarranted
          risks.  Can you blame me for that?

BEN looks to the floor and taps his foot impatiently, rolling
his eyes but keeping his annoyance under control.

                    BEN
          Sure.  Okay.  I understand.

                    GENERAL BRADFORD
          Thank you, Truman.

BEN turns and exits the room.  After a brief moment of
silence, FATHER TODD turns towards GENERAL BRADFORD.

                    FATHER TODD
          Incredible.  Only someone with no
          faith in the Lord and all his
          subjects in this living world would
          choose to delay the revelation of
          something akin to a miracle that
          will elevate all of us.  I do not
          understand you at all, General.

                    GENERAL BRADFORD
          Nine months of the living hell
          we've just experienced is enough to
          squeeze any and all faith out of a
          man with his eyes open to the true
          nature of the world, Father. I'm
          sure I'm not the only one who feels
          that way.

                    FATHER TODD
          If nine months of exposure to
          constant miracles is what blinds a
          man to the existence of god, then
          I'm happy to not have your
          coarsened point of view, General.
          Good day.

FATHER TODD storms out of the room and slams the door.


INTERIOR HOSPITAL BASEMENT HALLWAY - NIGHT

A stern looking man with a clipboard, HARRY, is making notes
as the elevator doors open and BEN appears and walks towards
him.  Another intern, CRAIG, is sitting in a chair half
asleep from exhaustion.

                    HARRY
          You're late.

                    BEN
          Sorry.  Meeting with the General.

HARRY motions to CRAIG, who begins to rise when gestured to
do so.

                    HARRY
          Okay, intern, on your feet and
          we'll figure out your dance card
          for the evening.

HARRY reaches into his pocket and pulls out a coin.

                    HARRY (CONT'D)
          Truman, it's your turn to call it.
          Heads you get Joan of Arc, tails
          you get the pregnant one.

                    BEN
          Jeezus, what a choice.  Sure, flip
          it.

HARRY tosses the coin.  It lands in his hand and he clenches
his fist.

                    HARRY
          And?

                    BEN
          Heads.

HARRY opens up his hand for both men to see.  BEN reacts with
no emotion in his voice.

                    BEN (CONT'D)
          Hooray.

                    CRAIG
          Shit.

                    HARRY
          Room B64 for you, Truman.  Your
          Jane Doe is fresh and crispy from
          being set on fire barely a few
          hours ago. No photo ID survived,
          other singed personal belongings
          are in the tray.  She's in terrible
          shape and probably in a lot of
          mental anguish.  Good luck with
          getting her ready for The Tombs.

                    BEN
          Thanks.

BEN walks away to his room and HARRY continues to talk to the
CRAIG.

                    HARRY
          Okay, that leaves the pregnant one
          for you.  We're treating this one
          delicately as the woman had an
          aneurysm while attempting to get an
          abortion, so….


INTERIOR ROOM AUTOPSY ROOM - NIGHT

BEN enters the room and is shocked by the burnt and broken
body stretched out on the slab before him.

                    BEN
          Oh maaaaan…..!

BEN covers his mouth as he takes in the details of the burnt
body; hairless, shriveled skin at the joints, barely any
details left in the face except for the piercingly wide-open
look of the tortured eyes.  There is still smoke coming off
of it as it attempts to shift position.

                    BEN (CONT'D)
          What the fuck happened to you?

BEN picks up a chart on the table near a medicine cabinet and
scans it.

                    BEN (CONT'D)
          Right outside the facility they did
          this shit to you?
                         (MORE)

                    BEN (CONT'D)
          I've gotten to know some of those
          protesters.  We've traded insults
          as we walk on by.  Shit, maybe the
          General is right about these new
          security measures.

He tosses the chart back down.  The body moans with pain as
it tries to move.

                    BEN (CONT'D)
          Don't move.  You're only gonna
          cause yourself more pain.

BEN sits for a moment and puts his head in his hands.

Trying to regain his composure, something shiny embedded in
MARY'S blackened flesh captures BEN'S eye.  He picks up a
small forceps, inserts it into the remnants of MARY'S neck
and he pulls out a bullet.

                    BEN (CONT'D)
          Whew.  I am no forensics expert,
          but this is probably a 9mm short --
          like a handgun bullet.  Must have
          blown out your larynx and hurt like
          a sonofabitch.

BEN drops the bullet into a nearby silver tray and notices
something else of interest.

                    BEN (CONT'D)
          And what have we here…..?

Using the forceps again, he pulls another bullet out of the
charred mass just above one of MARY'S kneecaps.

                    BEN (CONT'D)
          Different caliber entirely?  Jeez,
          how many people were taking shots
          at you?

BEN holds the bullet up to the light to get a better look at
it.

                    BEN (CONT'D)
          Hmmm.  Looks like something one of
          the military monkeys around here
          would be using.

BEN places this bullet in the same tray as the other one -
the size differential between them is immediately noticeable.

                    BEN (CONT'D)
          But if you were already wounded,
          why the fuck

would they go shooting you in the leg like that?

BEN tosses down the forceps, frustrated now, and rubs at his
eyes crankily.

                    BEN (CONT'D)
          I just don't think I can do this
          anymore.  I mean, for chirssakes,
          what the fuck is going on in the
          world that someone has to suffer
          like this?

BEN breathes deeply and rises.  He walks over to a cabinet
and opens it up, looking through it for whatever he can find.
In addition to the usual supplies there is a half-full bottle
of cheap whisky.  He pulls it out, opens it up and takes a
jolt.

                    BEN (CONT'D)
          Look at you.  How could so-called
          human beings do this to someone,
          dead or alive?  I couldn't imagine
          doing this to my worst enemy.
          Imprisoning someone in the cremated
          Hell of their own destroyed body is
          a crime I can't even design a
          punishment for.

He coughs as the crappy alcohol hits his throat.

                    BEN (CONT'D)
          I'm sorry; I don't normally do this
          kind of thing during a session, but
          I have to tell you that you have
          totally rattled me.  I'm gonna do
          my best to help you, but please
          just bear with me for a minute
          while I get my sanity back.

Still rifling through the drawers, he finally finds a bottle
of aspirin.  He opens it and slides out a pill into his hand.

                    BEN (CONT'D)
          Because this is all pretty insane,
          isn't it?

No answer.  Just the sound of MARY's painfully labored
breathing on the soundtrack.

                    BEN (CONT'D)
          I shouldn't even be here.  I should
          be home with my wife.  I should be
          asleep next to her.  Shit. Sleep.
          That's what I really need.

MARY struggles to make her broken body function.  With much
shaking and agony, she raises her hand towards BEN, but can
barely move at all.  BEN sees the gesture and tries to get
his act together.

                    BEN (CONT'D)
          Okay, enough of me and my problems.
          Look at you lying here in agony.
          Let me help you go away from this
          shitty place and go somewhere
          painless and quiet.

BEN pulls out the aspirin with a flourish and brings his face
close to hers.

                    BEN (CONT'D)
          This pill is an experimental drug
          that has been tested successfully
          on a number of subjects.  Once
          ingested, it will allow you to
          finally pass away in peace.
          Although I normally ask a patient
          permission to administer the drug,
          in this case I'm going to assume
          you'll want this to help
          immediately end the pain and
          suffering you must be experiencing.

MARY uses her last remaining bits of strength to very lightly
shake her head back-and-forth into something barely
resembling a "yes".

BEN reaches down uses a finger to slide open a corner of her
crinkled mouth and slide the pill inside.

                    BEN (CONT'D)
          You probably can't swallow it in
          the condition you're in, so just
          let it dissolve in your mouth.  It
          may take a little bit longer that
          way, but the final effect will be
          the same.

MARY's eyes begin to flutter as the pill slowly dissolves in
her mouth and the last grip of life begins to flow out of her
body.

                         BEN (CONT'D)
               Atta girl.  There you go.  Let all
               that pain slide away and you'll go
               to a much better place.

Summoning the remainder of her will, MARY raises her hand and
reaches for one of BEN's.  Surprised at this show of
strength, BEN reaches out and takes her horrifically
malformed hand and claps it.

                         BEN (CONT'D)
               Don't worry, you've got nothing to
               be afraid of anymore.

Tears begin to flow from MARY's eyes down her blackened
cheeks, her tear ducts still functioning.

                         BEN (CONT'D)
               Hey, watch out; I'm a married man.
               If my wife finds out I've been
               holding hands with one of my
               patients, I'll never hear the end
               of it.

BEN looks down at her hand more closely, a shiny object
amidst the charcoal skin.

                         BEN (CONT'D)
               Is that a ring you're wearing?  You
               also married? God, I've really got
               to give Mary a call after this…

BEN watches the life fading out of MARY'S eyes on the table
below him.  She is dying.

                         BEN (CONT'D)
               That's it.  Let yourself go to that
               quiet place.  You're almost there.

MARY closes what's left of her eyelids and dies.

BEN turns towards the surveillance camera on the other side
of the room and looks at his watch.

                         BEN (CONT'D)
               Time of death is 4:17am.  Thank
               goodness this new procedure seems
               to work even on the most
               grotesquely mutilated patient.  I
               don't think I'd be able to live
               with myself if it didn't.

Emotionally exhausted, BEN pulls out his cell phone and dials
a number as he walks towards the door.

In the tray of personal belongings, MARY's cell phone rings.

BEN does not react to the ringing in the room at first.  It's only after a few chirps that he turns his attention towards the sound of the phone behind him.

He looks at the cracked screen of the charred and ringing cellphone at the top of the pile of personal belongings as a picture of him and MARY mugging for the camera pops-up on it.

BEN stumbles towards MARY in disbelief and takes her hand. He looks at the ring on her finger more closely, and then brings up his hand to place it next to hers.  The etched design on it is a perfect match for the ring he's wearing.


SEEN FROM THE POV OF THE VIDEO SURVEILLANCE CAMERA:

In a complete state of shock, BEN turns away from MARY and moves towards the door. Opening the door, BEN exits the room and closes it behind him


INTERIOR HOSPITAL BASEMENT - NIGHT

GENERAL BRADFORD is standing in the hallway, leaning against a wall and waiting for BEN as he brokenly exits his workroom.

                    GENERAL BRADFORD
          I'm sorry to bother you at this
          hour, Truman, but I wanted to make
          you aware of something I couldn't
          talk to you about in front of that
          damned priest.

BEN, like a zombie, turns to look at the GENERAL but does not speak.

                    GENERAL BRADFORD (CONT'D)
          It was NOT my decision to go silent
          running on what happened here the
          other night.  I think what you did
          was incredible and the leap of
          logic you made was truly
          commendable.  You may very well
          have turned everything that's going
          on right now upside down in the
          best possible way.

BEN continues to listen without making a sound or facial expression.

> GENERAL BRADFORD (CONT'D)
> The orders that are now
> constricting me come directly from
> Washington, D.C., and there's
> nothing I can do about it.  I know
> what you did and what you want to
> do are right, Truman, but it's all
> beyond my control now and I'm no
> longer in charge of what goes on
> here, but I don't want Father
> Thomas to know that.  A lot of
> people don't like to hear phrases
> like "I was only following orders"
> anymore.

BEN nods slowly and quietly, pretending that he understands
any of this.

> GENERAL BRADFORD (CONT'D)
> Also, starting tomorrow, we need to
> prep this place to proactively
> protect us from potential biters.
> Down here in the Tombs, away from
> it all, we'll be setting up
> stations to remove the teeth of
> anyone who has been dead since this
> whole thing started.  Security
> needs to be tightened before we
> receive a visit from the commander-
> in chief - but you didn't hear that
> from me, Truman.

The GENERAL warmly pats BEN on the shoulder for emphasis.

> GENERAL BRADFORD (CONT'D)
> I'm sure I don't have to tell you
> why we'll be hosting such a visit,
> Truman, but I will suggest that you
> go home and get some sleep, stat.
> Meeting you will be at the top of
> the President's to-do list.

BEN nods indifferently in agreement.

> GENERAL BRADFORD (CONT'D)
> Not that I voted for her.  In fact,
> I don't know anyone who voted for
> her.  But maybe it's better not to
> question these kind of things.

GENERAL BRADFORD turns, walks down the hallway in the
opposite direction and disappears around the corner as his
footsteps echo along the corridors.

BEN slides down onto a bench that allows him to view most of
the entirety of The Tombs and all the occupied but quiet beds
that run its length.  A tear rolls down one cheek but he
quickly wipes it away.  He struggles to keep his eyes open,
but eventually they wither shut, his jaw slackens and he
blacks out into something resembling sleep.

                                        FADE TO BLACK.

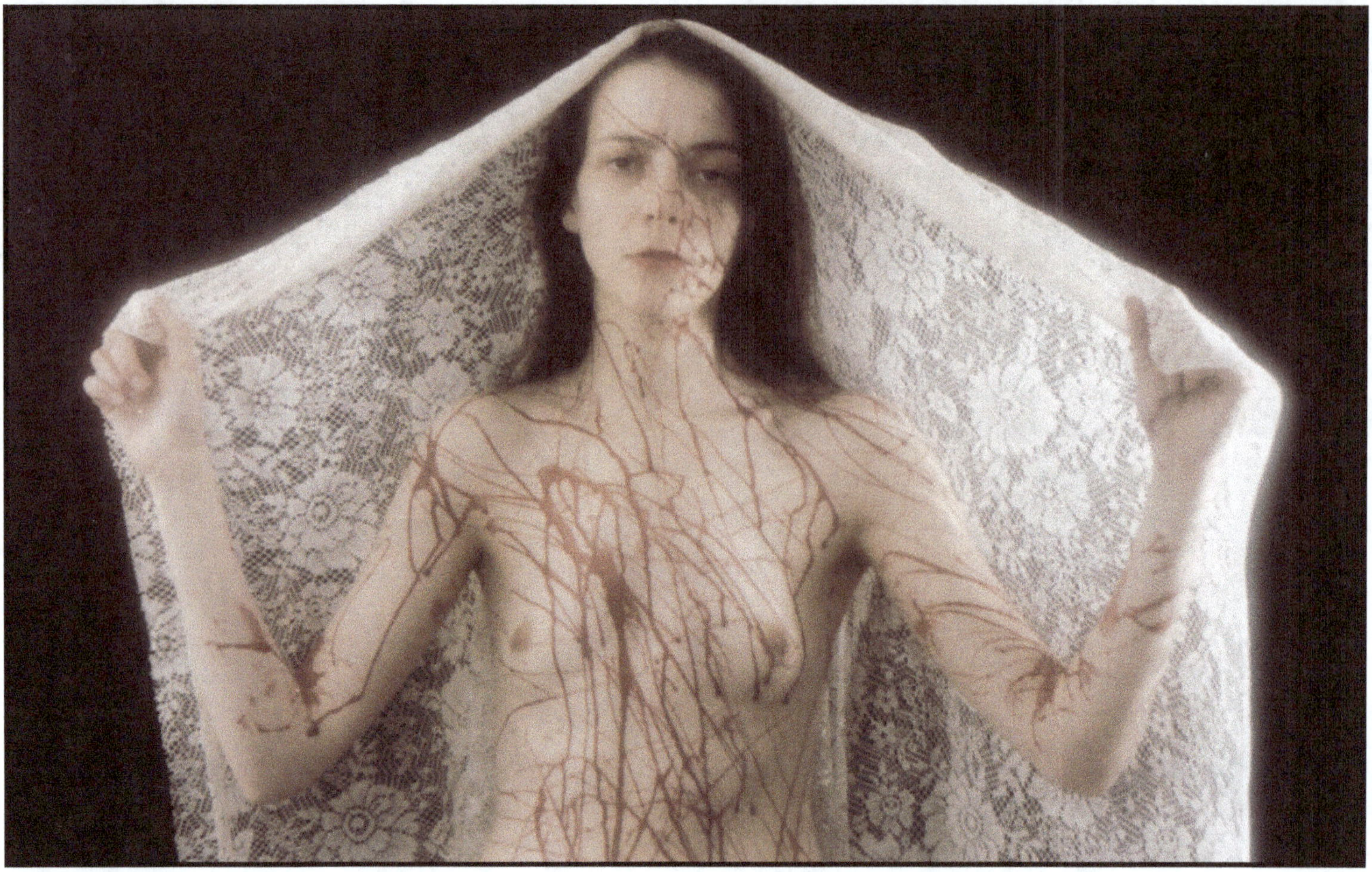

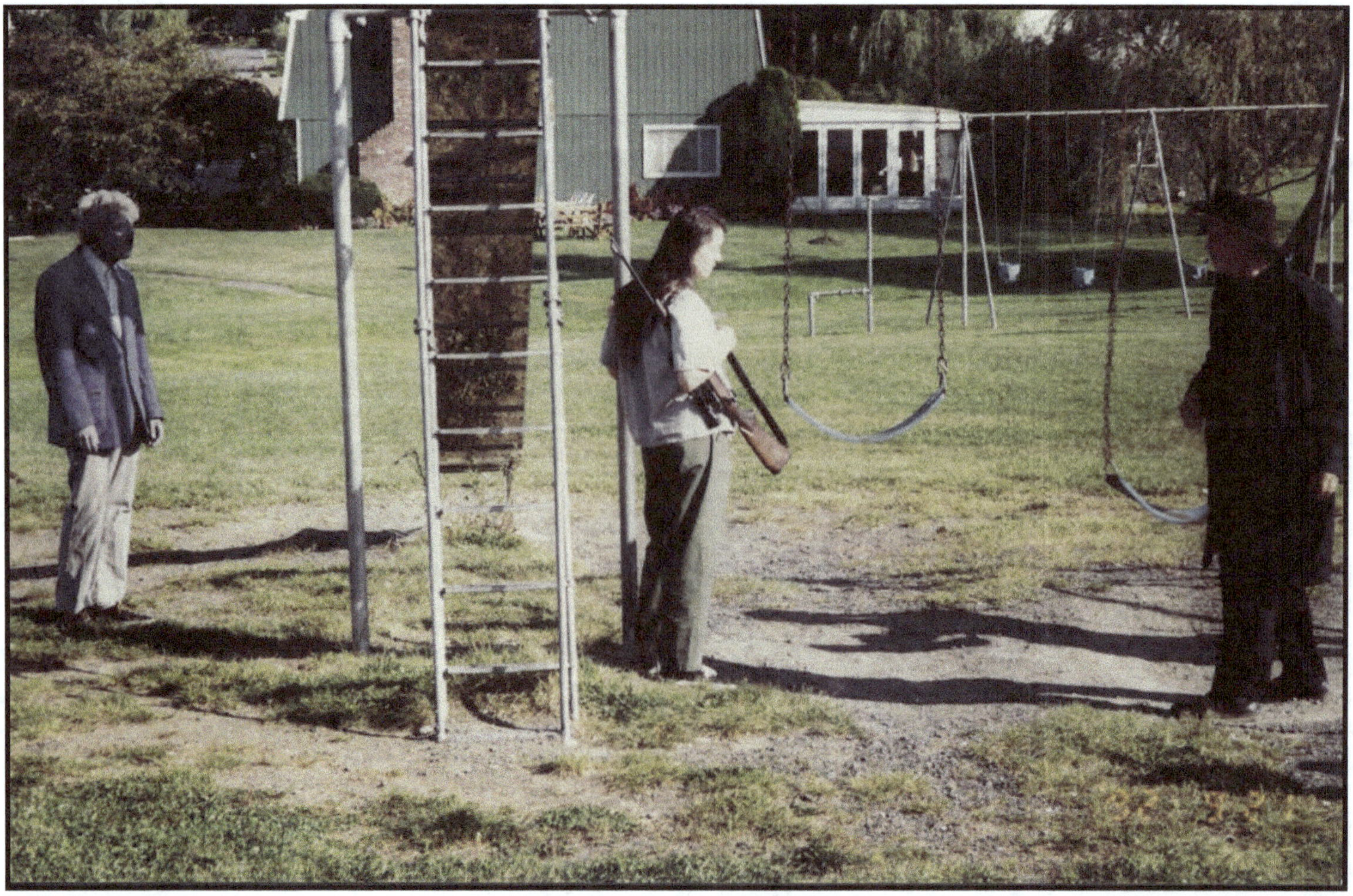

SHATTER DEAD
USA 1994

directed by Scooter McCrae

duration 84 mins

English language
Colour

GOD HATES YOU!
Winner of Award for
Best Independent Production
Fantafestival 1995

SCREEN EDGE

SCREEN EDGE

THERE'S NO MORE ROOM IN HEAVEN EITHER!

So begins SHATTER DEAD. God has abandoned the earth and the angels are playing a huge sick joke on mankind. Death is no longer an option. There is a new class system and if you're dead you're at the bottom of the pile. But things are changing... for a start there are more dead than living and the new order of the dead want a better deal.

Susan is trapped, she's alone. All she wants is to get home to her lover. She's got to eat, there's evil around and she's alone. Her brutal odyssey leads her from skid row for the dead to the eerie sanctuary of Grandma's 'safe house'. Here she survives a bloody battle with crazed gun-toting vigilantes. However the disciples of the quasi religious leader known as 'The Preacher Man' are never far behind.

But nothing could have prepared Susan for the shocking revelation awaiting her return home. This is never going to be over! This is only the beginning... of forever!

Scooter McCrae's award winning slant on the zombie genre breaks new ground in horror film making. SHATTER DEAD is certainly not for the faint hearted... neither is it for the faint headed! Gruelling, gory and very intelligent!

SHATTER DEAD

a Scooter McCrae film

"The most original zombie film since Romero raised the dead!"
Fangoria.

18
SUITABLE ONLY FOR PERSONS OF 18 YEARS AND OVER
NOT TO BE SUPPLIED TO ANY PERSON BELOW THAT AGE

Screen Edge
PO Box 30
Lytham St.Annes
FY8 1RL
England

18

18

EDGE 12

nothing like hollywood

5 013929 740129

228

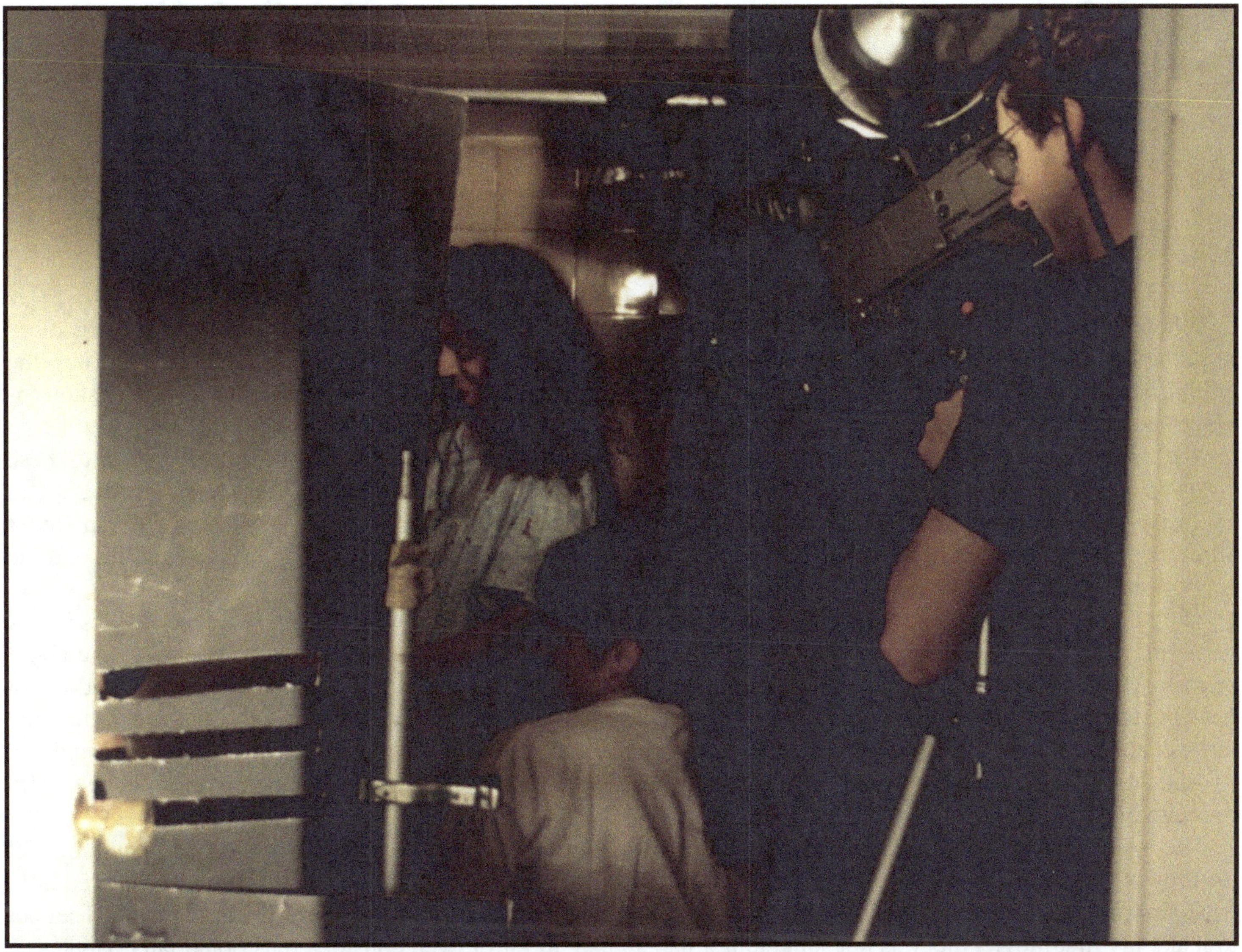

## THE CENSORSHIP OF SHATTER DEAD
[Originally appeared in *Exploitation Nation* #7, 2018]

When you're a low-budget moviemaker putting together your first project, there's almost nothing more important than securing publicity and attention for your baby once it's finally completed and released into the wild. Back in 1994, when my first feature—SHATTER DEAD—was taking its first steps into the SOV (shot-on-video) marketplace, I was lucky enough to secure an article in Fangoria magazine that eventually led to it being picked-up by Tempe Video. From there, it made the rounds in all the usual suspect periodicals dedicated to these kinds of movies in the United States; Film Threat, Alternative Cinema and Draculina (for which I even shot an exclusive set of nude photos of lead actress Stark Raven to sweeten the deal). If you're old enough to remember all of these titles, than you'll probably also have a touch of nostalgia for that golden age of SOV movies and the support they were given in these publications.

The relative success of SHATTER DEAD within this tiny genre—along with the overall good notices it was garnering amongst the kinder reviewers—put it on the radar of overseas distributors who contacted me about releasing the title in their part of the world. I'm happy to say that Japan, Germany and the United Kingdom all gave me the opportunity to sign a contract for legitimate availability in their region (remember—this is before the internet appeared to bootleg and disseminate titles for free to everybody an hour after they were pressed to a disc).

And the only place that had censorship problems that needed to be dealt with before my movie could be legally presented in their country was the United Kingdom.

This was an interesting dilemma for me back in 1996. I do not in any way advocate censorship of anything, yet the only way my movie could now be seen on the other side of the world was for me to let go of my beloved little backyard project and allow it be neutered in the hands of uncaring strangers. I can honestly say that when I set out to make my first movie, this was not something I had signed up for or even considered as potentially happening after the fact.

Still young enough to consider myself an artist but also not stupid enough to think of my premiere flick as anything other than a commodity that might eventually lead to further work (well, so much for that.... ), I didn't make too much fuss about it being butchered in the U. K. —as long as I didn't have to pay for it. Richard King, who was then in charge of releasing company Video Edge, was a lovely guy who would take care of the whole process of re-editing and submitting the cut to the BBFC, so it was no slice off my financial nose. Richard was already a pro when it came to dealing with these particular censors after a far more involved re-edit of Michael DiPaolo's feature TRANSGRESSION removed seven minutes from its running time before it was eligible for release via his company.

As an interesting aside, when I first sat down to write this piece I was also in the process of cleaning up my apartment and happened to stumble across the initial letter I received from Mr. King on the subject of releasing SHATTER DEAD in August of 1995 (in case you think YOU save everything!). Funnily enough, I also found the SECOND letter he sent to me two months later in October as it appears I did not respond to his first missive. Is it possible back then that I knew what I'd be in for if they tried to release my movie over there?Or was I just some jackass?Hard to remember that far back, so I'll give myself the benefit of the doubt and proof of history in choosing the former over the latter. Richard also informed me in the second letter (complete with a bunch of excellent press clippings for the Screen Edge label attached) that he was capable of watching NTSC tapes, just in case that was what was holding me back from bothering to respond to him. Which, come to think of it, might have also been a valid concern on my part in not immediately responding.

(Hard to believe nowadays that we had incompatible video formats from one country to the next back-in-the-day that prevented casual viewing of overseas content, but this is one technical advance in our modern age that I heartily approve of—although the introduction of region encoding of digital media is a hateful thing. )

So I sent Richard King a VHS copy of SHATTER DEAD through the mail sometime in October. And not long after that, he received a Notice of Seizure of Indecent and Obscene Material from H. M. Customs and Excise Mount Pleasant Department in London—in other words, they confiscated the tape I sent him after opening up the padded envelope and WATCHING IT before deciding whether or not it should get passed along to the intended recipient. Can you believe that this was standard operating procedure in an English speaking country that we have an intimate relationship with in the mid-1990's on planet Earth? Because it fucking was, pally, and don't let your grandkids forget that.

Despite phone calls and a written appeal, Richard not only could not retrieve the tape from the customs office, they would not even allow him to watch it in their very same offices that they themselves had watched the tape. At this point he just wanted to view the tape to see if it was at all worth pursuing the idea of trying to release it in the U. K. in the first place. One of the 'friendlier' officials at the place who had deigned to even speak to him on the subject passionately assured him that it was certainly not worth all the effort to watch or release SHATTER DEAD on their side of the pond.

Under normal circumstances, that would have been the end of that, but Richard pursued his contact, Loris Curci, at the Fantafestival in Italy (where SHATTER DEAD had played and won the award for Best Independent Film from the U. S. a few months earlier in June of 1995) and got him to send along another VHS copy of the movie that somehow made it under the radar of government officials and safely reached its intended destination. Richard finally had a chance to watch the movie for himself and found that he liked it quite a bit and now very much wanted it to be a part of the Screen Edge lineup. And with a couple of minor edits, the movie was released with a BBFC 18 rating certificate.

Let me take a moment to make clear what was and what was not censored in SHATTER DEAD when it was unleashed in the U. K. What was not objectionable: a pregnant woman getting shot in the stomach that blew out her unborn baby, a zombie repeatedly getting its head bashed in with a rifle stock and a woman getting her face crushed with the butt of a handgun (amongst all sorts of other explicit gun inflicted damage). Here's what was considered over-the-top objectionable: a sex scene between two characters who were involved in a relationship in which a gun was used as a replacement penis as the boyfriend could not achieve an erection since he was now undead. To be completely clear, the scene did involve a couple of shots of explicit (and unsimulated) vaginal penetration with a gun, although this footage was part of a series of visual dissolves to help make it a bit less 'pornographic' and a bit more 'arty. ' Needless to say, the BBFC did not find that this made the images any more artful in the least.

(By chance, I happened to end up in England a few years after all this ridiculousness had faded away, so I finally got to meet Richard in-person over a long lunch and he showed me the re-edited scene from my movie which I was never able to watch at home since he sent me a PAL videotape and all I could play at home back then was NTSC stuff—and I was very pleased to see that the brief amount of snipped footage did no damage whatsoever to the original intent or the overall impact. And for that, I consider myself a very lucky person, indeed. )

At this particular juncture in video history, when the only way to see many movies by cult directors had to be ordered as VHS bootleg tapes from outlets like Video Search of Miami and Midnight Video (amongst many others), I was used to the idea that there were often multiple cuts of a single movie released in various parts of the world that might have differing footage or entirely different edits altogether due to subject matter, local ordinances, etc. , so it was kind of fun at first to be joining the league of edited gentlemen. In some ways, I wore the distinction as a badge of honor, as I remembered the wise words of dear friend and SHATTER DEAD cinematographer Matt Howe: "picket lines equal ticket lines!" He saw this development as a bit of controversy that could help boost sales of the tape in Europe, and I was cool with that.

Admittedly, what I did not expect is that SHATTER DEAD— and its director, yours truly—would come to be denounced by name on the floor of British Parliament during the height of the Video Nasties scare. Monty Python fucking nailed it: NOBODY expects the Spanish Inquisition!

Splashed across Page 8 of the Sunday Sport in all-caps on November 10th, 1996, was just the kind of headline I could never afford to have purchased on my own: FURY AS CENSORS PASS BLOODIEST VIDEO EVER!

Yep, that's their exclamation point at the end, not mine. These words displayed, of course, amidst a selection of salacious stills from the movie to drive home the visceral wretchedness of it all. The lower third of this page is dedicated to explicit phone sex adverts because that's okay and my movie is just garbage. It's a SHOCK NEWS EXCLUSIVE that begat a nearly half-page showdown of text on the vices and virtues of censorship between Tory MP Nigel Evans and Video World magazine editor Allan Bryce. Do you need me to tell you that the tape got a nice sales boost starting November 11th?

All that being said, I have no idea if it's just me having gotten older or just the general condition of the world we're living in these days, but whatever "charm" I might have felt at the time this was all happening has been supplanted by a kind of low-level dismay at the world we left behind as opposed to the one we now openly embrace. Nowadays, it seems so quaint that postal police used to open up packages and watch the tapes we were sending to one another, compared to the modern invitation we send out to our various technologies on a daily basis to come and invade our privacy through our internet activities and cellphones and televisions that listen to what we're saying when we think they have been turned off and rendered mute. We've invited the censors to abandon the points of entry at our countries borders and enter our homes instead. The strangulation of our assumption of privacy has come to roost in our bedrooms, kitchens and living rooms and we've welcomed the invasion with open arms and exposed necks. Electronic Dracula crosses the threshold and drools with delight as we crane our collective heads to one side and sigh with abandon.

# YOU THE JURY

## Is there too much violence on our screens?

PRIME Minister John Major this week launched a new initiative over video "nasties." Ministers condemned the decision to give 18 certificates to chilling movies like Natural Born Killers and documentaries such as Executions. They have also ordered censors to explain how they plan to cut down on video violence. But, in the week when the BLOODIEST and most HORRIFIC film yet goes on OPEN SALE in Britain we ask IS there too much violence on our screens? We've brought in two experts to give their views, but the final vote is down to YOU.

**YES** says Nigel Evans, Tory MP for Ribble Valley.

**NO** says Allan Bryce, editor of Video World.

I WELCOME all moves from the Government to clamp down on gratuitous scenes of sex and violence on our screens and I believe there should be even more research into the link between violent movies and real-life crimes.

While I am not calling for all films to be turned into The Sound Of Music, there is a need for film-makers to take a far greater responsibilty for what they produce.

I appreciate that action movies make good box-office and that producers are in the business to make money but they should be accountable for the results of their films .

I find it very disturbing that films like Shatter Dead, which feature notorious scenes like "The Shotgun Abortion" have even been made let alone given a certificate by the British Board of Film Classification.

By doing this they are basically giving the green light to violence and saying there is no link between films and copy-cat killings.

How anybody can watch films like this, where intestines fly across the room and a woman is forced to abort her living dead child through a shotgun hole in her belly is beyond me.

I do not want to be seen as dictating to people what they should or shouldn't watch but how can this sort of material be allowed to get through the net when it is so over the top and gratuitous.

I am not convinced that in today's society people can distinguish between fact and fiction.

### Research

And as long as films containing violence and sex are screened there is always the chance somebody will come out of the cinema and try to recreate what they have just seen.

The truth is that there is a market for such films and as long as film-makers keep producing such movies people will always get their hands on them.

I think the BBFC should be tightened up to prevent certain films getting through and also greater research into just how close serious crimes are to scenes from films.

I appreciate that people will always get their hands on explicit or violent material through other forms of media but we should not be making it an easier for them.

The responsibilty lies with film-makers who should be working closer with the BBFC to ensure we strike the right balance.

IN a society where there is a growing level of social problems, I find it amazing the Government can point the finger of blame on films and video which contain scenes of violence and sex.

They seem to think that if they dictate what we can and cannot watch on films and videos then the world will become a better place.

This is absolute rubbish and another example of the Government trying to pass the blame and make out films are responsible for the problems that exist today.

We are constantly exposed to violent scenes in the papers, on the news and in everyday life so it is foolish to say it is all down to what people see in films.

They are living in the Victorian age, if they think that by dictating what we watch, there will be less crime on our streets.

We are living in the 90s where every possible sort of material is available if you want it.

The introduction of the Internet is just one form of powerful media which makes it possible to get whatever you want.

I believe the Government is making a stance now because it wants to be seen as doing something positive which goes down well with voters.

Instead of addressing the real problems of unemployment, drugs and violent crime they are saying: "People who watch violent films like Natural Born Killers will go out and blow somebody's head off."

This is nonsense and largely the fault of the media who blame every violent crime on one film or another.

### Foolish

We are all being treated like kids when we should have a right to watch what we want. Although I am not encouraging youngsters to watch porn or violence, the fact is you cannot deny an adult audience of what it wants.

I find it amazing that a handful of elderly members on the British Board of Film Classification can tell us what we watch simply on what they enjoy watching.

Young people will get access to what they want, no matter how strictly we censor films. And for every person trying to cut a film there'll be another five producing a more violent or pornographic movie.

There is no proof that violent films lead to copy-cat killings or sex films lead to violent rapes and it is foolish and disturbing to think the Government see this as the root of the problems.

> **LAST week we asked: Do soccer star louts deserve your cash? This is how you voted...**
> **YES:55** **NO:1,723**

## WHO'S RIGHT? REGISTER YOUR VOTE ON OUR PHONE LINES
## YES: 0990 118873 NO: 0990 118874

(It costs no more than 10p to register your vote at any time)

233

# AFTERWORD
## By Mike Watt

The book you're holding in your hand, the one you presumably just finished reading, is the tale of a miracle willed into existence. But then again, all movies are and indie movies even moreso. Movies are the recreation of reality, and that's expensive. And difficult. And cannot be achieved in a vacuum. Indie filmmakers rely on scores of other people catching their dreams and assisting in the construction. Nobody ever built a skyscraper single-handedly. Neither, too, has an indie feature been done by a single person. Indie movies are an odd combination of hope and insanity writ large. Thus: any movie completed is a miracle.

In the late '90s, Amy Lynn Best and I had just seen our first short, Tenants, land international distribution through what was then Salt City Video—Ron Bonk's outfit before he changed the name to Sub Rosa—on a collection entitled The Night Basement. Ron was a filmmaker (The Vicious Sweet) and distributor and through him we met a host of folks who had pulled off multiple miracles. On one particular Chiller Theater afternoon, he introduced us to Michael Gingold, editor of Fangoria Magazine who also had a short on The Night Basement. He then introduced us to a filmmaker I'd already admired: Scooter McCrae. We had just watched Shatter Dead for the first time (thanks in no small part to an incredible video store in Pittsburgh called Incredibly Strange Video, run by a mensch named Bruce Lentz).

Shatter Dead gutted me. It was a zombie movie at a time when only indies were beating the zombie drum. Hollywood hadn't yet rebooted Romero's Dawn of the Dead yet. And yet, Shatter Dead was a very different type of thing. It had a philosophy, for one thing. It wasn't about flesh-eating hordes savaging gun-toting citizens. It was about how our society treats the "cast-offs." The dead folk in Shatter Dead were our invisibles—the homeless, particularly those left homeless in the wake of Reagan's AIDS crisis. Our society is cruel to the strong; the weak are utterly disposable. And in Shatter Dead, which delighted this recovering Catholic, everything was God's fault. God was a petty, off-screen tyrant who hated his creation. Which is how I grew to see the Christian God. So the subversive in me loved Shatter Dead.

It was clear McCrae had no money for the film—neither did we, nor Ron, nor anyone in our orbit, but we had our sights set on the miracles. See? Miracles come from work and will. God had nothing to do with it. (The Film Gods on the other hand, demanded fealty, or else it'd snow on your only outdoor shoot in the middle of June...)

Meeting Scooter that day cemented a friendship that has lasted decades. In 2005, Scooter and Happy Cloud Pictures collaborated for the score on our "vampire" movie, A Feast of Flesh. Scooter also scored our most powerful miracle to date, Razor Days. In return, we promoted his features, including his incredible cyber-punk atrocity exhibition, Sixteen Tongues, which does for the future what Shatter Dead did for the present, with the message that humans, if left to their own devices, will revert to cannibalism rather than co-exist peacefully. It's a grim message, but I've yet to hear an argument that it's wrong.

We have dozens of Scooter McCrae stories: from the time he took us to a deli that was closing for the season while we were eating, to the time legendary writer Harlan Ellison berated him over the course of four hours at the World Horror Convention, calling him a "carbuncle" in appreciation for getting him out of an unpleasant conversation.

(Scooter told the very best non-PC joke I've ever heard, one that I will not share here, but if you hit me up out in the drunken wild, I will repeat it in hushed tones.)

But getting back to the point, having the opportunity to read a screenplay and witness its evolution, with notes from the creator, and to further bear witness to the hopes of returning to this bleak world, in proposed sequels and aborted follow-ups, it's difficult to put into words how rare this is. Not to blow my own horn, but I wish something like this had existed when we were shooting our first film because it's a nice way of saying: You're not crazy and you're not alone.

Remember, most indies setting out to make a movie have no idea what's going to happen to it when it's finished. It's not like Netflix and Amazon come to us. Hell, those two outfits don't even want indies around much any more. Where once you could get both Shatter Dead and 16T (or A Feast of Flesh, or ...) through

Netflix in their happy red envelopes. Now, streaming is king and '90s SOV...

Well, I wanted to say that the SOV era is over and forgotten, but it ain't, is it? Vinegar Syndrome is leading the charge in restoring a lot of '90s indie fare on their "Saturn's Core" line, and Shatter Dead was one of the first. (Thanks much to Ross Snyder and Bill Hellfire!) It landed on blu-ray in November, 2021, and it's gorgeous. It's almost too gorgeous for such an eye-level philosophical horror featuring a graphic gun-fucking. But the blu-ray is saying, in its own way, that this movie is culturally significant. It's like the beginning of the indie Criterion Collection and I hope it lasts forever.

This is a dense-enough tome that filmmakers and film scholars should be able to return to it time and again and find something new, some nuance missed on initial glance. I know I have and continued to throughout the editing process.

It's a thing to behold, history. Film or otherwise. History tells us who we were. Art tells us who we are. Shatter Dead tells us whose fault it is.

— Mike Watt, 2021

*L-R: Mike Watt, Susan Miller, Amy Lynn Best, Alex Kuciw, Scooter McCrae. 2019*

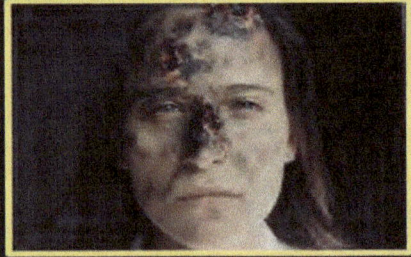  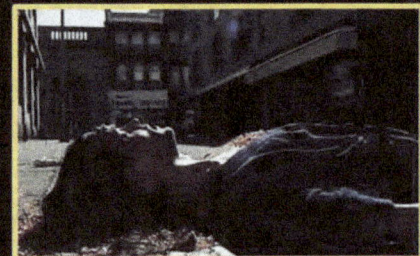

www.ingramcontent.com/pod-product-compliance
Lightning Source LLC
Chambersburg PA
CBHW080957020726
47505CB00009B/2242